Teenage Psychic on Campus

by

Pamela Woods-Jackson

Teenage Psychic on Campus

Cover Art by *Tina Lynn Stout*

The Wild Rose Press, Inc.
PO Box 708
Adams Basin, NY 14410-0708
Visit us at www.thewildrosepress.com

Publishing History
First Fantasy Rose Edition, 2017
Print ISBN 978-1-5092-1435-8
Digital ISBN 978-1-5092-1436-5

Published in the United States of America

The attractive older woman Gary had been talking to reached over and hugged Gary's shoulders. Just as I was thinking how creepy it was for a woman her age to be so friendly with a guy in his teens, one of those mini-flicks went through my mind. I relaxed a little. "Is this your mom, Gary?"

"Brenda Riddell," she said as she turned to me with a smile that lit up her face.

Despite Annabeth and Sean's efforts, I wasn't the least interested in Gary, but I liked his mother immediately.

Gary ran his fingers through his dripping bangs. "Come on, Mom, I gotta hit the shower."

Brenda nodded but stopped to speak to some other adults as Gary playfully punched Sean in the arm. "Thanks for the ride, Sean. And for bringing"—he glanced at me with either disdain or indifference, I couldn't tell which—"friends." With that, he gave Sean the universal fist to ear signal for "call me" and turned to leave.

But then he stopped mid-stride. I watched in amazement as Gary stared at a tree, then put his hands on his hips and spoke to…the tree? Huh?

I grabbed Annabeth's arm and pulled her back. "What's that guy doing?"

Annabeth followed my gaze and saw the same thing I did, but seemed a lot less concerned. She shrugged. "Rehearsing?"

Rehearsing? After the play? That made no sense.

Dedication

To Nancy,
family friend and psychic medium,
who encouraged me to continue writing about Caryn

Chapter 1

I picked up my ringing phone off the bedside table without bothering to check the caller ID. One of the things I've always been able to do is predict phone calls, a "parlor trick" as Mom calls it. I was just five years old when I told her Dad was on the phone and she said the phone hadn't rung. And then it did, and of course it was him. But there are times when I really should check to see who's on the line. Like now.

"Hey, Caryn. How are ya?"

My heart skipped a beat, my pulse started to race, and I got butterflies on top of butterflies in my stomach. "Uh, oh, hi, Quince," I gulped, hoping he couldn't hear the nervousness in my voice.

"I just wanted to say 'hey,'" he said. "I thought maybe we could…"

Meet up somewhere? Have a date? Get back together? I was freaking out, barely able to catch my breath.

"…be friends, you know? You busy this afternoon?"

Good news, bad news I guess. He said the dreaded F word—friends—but the fact that he wanted to get together with me after all these months was encouraging. "Um, well, I have some clients, but…"

Suddenly the tone of Quince's voice changed. "Yeah, right. Never mind. Have a nice summer." And he hung up.

Tears sprang to my eyes as I plunged into the pits of despair, a place where I'd spent a lot of time lately. Before I could collect myself, my phone rang again. "Hi Annabeth!" I sang out, trying to sound chipper.

"Hey, Caryn." Annabeth paused. "What's wrong?" It's like she's the psychic.

I couldn't answer. All that came out was a squeak and a sniffle.

Annabeth let out a sigh. "You wanna talk about it?"

"Um, well…" I tapped my foot on the floor.

Annabeth knew I'd been in a funk for months. I may be psychic, but my skills don't extend to my own life, so I was as blindsided as any other girl would have been when my boyfriend dumped me. Nothing says Merry Christmas like the guy you care about showing up on social media with his arm around a gorgeous girl at some holiday frat party.

Annabeth kept telling me I needed to snap out of it, but it wasn't so easy getting over that kind of hurt. And it hurt a lot. So I couldn't tell her that Quince called and messed with my head again or she might strangle him.

"Uh, Caryn? You there? Did I catch you at work or something?" Annabeth asked.

"No, I'm still at home." I shoved aside some t-shirts that needed to go downstairs to the laundry and sat down on my unmade bed. Before heading to work I needed to clean up my bedroom, but as I glanced around at the untidiness, I was still proud of the DIY decorating job I did. My stepdad was a good sport when he gave up his home office. I painted the formerly gray walls a pale green, picked out a coverlet with peace signs all over it, and hung more peace signs on the built-in white bookshelves that doubled as a headboard.

George's house was the nicest place I'd ever lived. Back when I was a new transfer at Rosslyn High, my mom was struggling financially, what with opening her New Age Bookstore in eclectic Rosslyn Village in Indianapolis and trying to keep it afloat. My bio dad contributed when he could, but he's a struggling actor, so Mom and I lived in a small apartment close to both the store and my school, and cut corners every way possible. Then one day a pharmacist named George Desmond came into the store. He kept coming back and coming back, and I was pretty sure he wasn't there to buy books. One thing led to another, one date led to another, and finally he proposed to my mom! They got married a few months later and we moved into his house in Rosslyn Village.

With more financial stability than we'd ever known, Mom was finally able to afford to buy both of us cell phones and laptops. Uncle Omar, who's sort of my spirit guide, was duly impressed. He rubbed his hands together in excitement when I stood behind the check-out counter at Mom's store and booted up my new computer for the first time.

"Let's get us some Twitter followers!" he exclaimed.

Of course, no one but me heard him, so I got a few weird looks from store customers when I burst out laughing. My mother's half-brother may be long dead, but his sense of humor didn't die with him.

Annabeth was getting impatient on the other end of the line, waiting for me to answer. "Caryn?"

"Yeah, I'm here."

"Girlfriend, you need to lighten up! And I know just how to change your mood. You up for some fun?"

Annabeth Walton has been a great friend to me, not only these last few months after the breakup with Quince, but before that when I was the new kid in town. It was kinda weird how we met, because she went to a private school up in the ritzy suburb of Belford while I attended an urban school in Indianapolis. Who knew a preppy girl like Annabeth could be so into the paranormal?

I stretched out on the bed. "What did you have in mind? I do have to work today, you know. I've got back-to-back readings set up." The very same readings that so unnerved Quince that he hung up on me.

"But it's summer break, Caryn," she said with a hint of whine in her voice. "And then you'll be off to Texas to visit your dads and won't be back till it's time to start college. We need to make the most of our time before you go."

"Mom's got the time slots all booked at the store and I can't disappoint my clients. Besides, I need the money."

"Why do you need the money?" Annabeth asked. "You've got three dads pitching in to finance your college education!"

Some kids I know barely have one parent, so I was lucky to have four—Mom, George, my bio dad Guy McNamara, and his partner Michael Ferguson. They all get along great, too. Dad and Michael even flew to Indianapolis for Mom's wedding, and Dad walked her down the aisle! All four of them are contributing to my college expenses, and I also scored some scholarship money to study journalism. But I was still gonna need spending money. Besides, being psychic is who I am, a gift I was born with. Giving readings made me feel like I was helping people.

"I get done with my clients around six," I told Annabeth. "So what did you have in mind?"

Annabeth giggled. "How 'bout some Shakespeare in the Park?"

I could visualize the whole setting, and not just in my imagination. I could see what I knew to be the real thing in my head: the outdoor gazebo-turned-stage, decorated with what was supposed to be a forest setting. I saw audience members sitting on blankets or lawn chairs, and then I got a quick "hit" of Annabeth's boyfriend Sean Paxton shaking hands with one of the actors. "This Sean's idea?"

Annabeth sighed. You'd think she'd give up trying to sneak things past me. "Yeah, okay, his best friend Gary is playing Puck. Mid—"

"Midsummer Night's Dream," I finished for her. When she groaned, I said, "Oh, come on, we read that play in English class junior year."

"Well," Annabeth sniffed, "Gary's cute. And it's been months since you and Quince…"

Now it was my turn to groan. Loudly. "Oh, please, Annabeth. No more fixups." In the months since Quince and I broke up, Annabeth had been relentlessly trying to find me a new Mr. Right. But the guys always seemed to fall into one of two categories: the ones who got creeped out thinking I was reading their minds, which I wasn't because I can't, or the ones who wanted an impromptu reading and then headed off to find the girl I told them they'd soon be meeting. So no thanks, I was done with dating. Besides, talking briefly today with the former love of my life was like breaking open a wound that had just barely scabbed over.

"Too late," she sang out. "I'll pick you up at seven." And she hung up before I could object.

"Gary's interesting," said a disembodied voice.

I still jumped sometimes when Uncle Omar popped in unannounced. "I've asked you not to do that." I turned around to see my dead uncle, looking solid like he always did, standing in the corner of my bedroom leaning against the wall, his biceps bulging out of the army fatigue t-shirt he was wearing when he died. His dog tags caught the light flowing in through my bedroom window. Too bad he died so young, because he was a handsome guy, what with that blond hair and those soulful eyes.

Uncle Omar shrugged. "If you'd keep your antennae up I wouldn't surprise you."

I rolled my eyes. Being tuned in twenty-four/seven would never allow me any peace and quiet. I crossed my arms and glared back at him. "What about Gary?"

"You'll see." And just like that, he vanished into the ether.

Today I was scheduled to read a new client who called the store and talked to my mom. He asked a lot of questions about me, about the whole process, but she assured him that I was the best.

The client was right on time. Mom greeted him and then walked him back to me in the storeroom where I have a table with my grandmother's white lace tablecloth, two chairs and a low-wattage lamp. Since it was Saturday, he was dressed casually in khakis and a navy golf shirt with the Polo logo prominently displayed. Professional, well-educated, I told myself.

"Hi," I said, reaching over to shake his hand. "I'm Caryn."

"I'll just leave you to it," Mom said.

Once we were alone the client looked me over. "Uh, nice to meet you," he mumbled.

"And you are…?"

He blushed. "Oh, sorry. Ned."

I smiled, hoping to put him at ease. "I guess you were expecting someone more…"

"…mature?" he offered.

I shrugged. "Yeah." I looked him in the eye. "I'm eighteen in a couple of weeks, and off to college in the fall if that helps." Apparently it didn't, judging by the expression on his face. "I may be young," I reassured him, "but I've been a psychic medium all my life."

Ned's eyes widened. "You're a medium? I thought you were, uh, that is, I hoped to find out, I mean, just ask about…" His eyes darted around the space like he was looking for a crystal ball or something.

Ned was one of those clients that needed clarification about what I do before I could help him. And let's face it, there was a lot of misinformation floating around in cyber-space, not to mention all the skeptics who made fun of people like me. "A person can be psychic and not be a medium," I explained, "and there are mediums who aren't psychic, but I'm both. So one way or another I hope I can help you sort out your questions. If that's what you still want."

"Well, I'm here, so…" His voice trailed off.

"How did you hear about me?" I motioned to the chair opposite me, and after giving the cane seating some serious study, he sat down on the edge. I don't know how he didn't fall out.

"One of my law partners. Harvey Walton?"

Okay, I got it. This guy worked with Annabeth's dad. I guess she must have convinced her father that I was the real deal if he was recommending me to people.

Still, Ned looked dubious. He sighed and ran his fingers through his thick, blond hair. "Harvey said you might be able to tell me…"

I held up my hand. "I don't want to know anymore, if you don't mind. It skews my readings."

He shrugged.

I closed my eyes to concentrate. When I opened them, a lovely woman was standing behind Ned. She appeared to be in her seventies, stylishly dressed in a lavender silk suit, her graying hair framing her face in a short bob, and a huge diamond ring on her left hand. Unfortunately, she was holding a lit cigarette, causing me to flinch and fan away the invisible smoke.

"Did a family member recently pass? I'm hearing the name Olivia?"

Ned's eyes got wide. "My grandmother. She died about a year ago."

"From lung cancer, right?"

Ned seemed stunned. "How did you know?"

"She's here." I watched as Ned did a visual search of the room. "I see symbols and smell things other people can't."

"Now that we've settled that," Olivia said with a frown as she tossed the cigarette into the ether, "get him to talk about his son."

"Olivia says you have a son," I told him. Ned nodded as he eyed me suspiciously. Now sometimes I get information like a little mini-movie in my head, but this time I felt like someone had sucker-punched me.

Bad news: Ned and his son were estranged. More than estranged. "You don't really know each other."

"That's got to change," Olivia said.

Ned put both feet on the floor, hands knotted in fists on the table, and looked me square in the eye. "No, we don't, but…"

"Your grandmother is very concerned about that." I closed my eyes again to visualize more of the story. "You and your son's mom were in high school, right? And your parents didn't approve."

Olivia shook her head, sadness in her voice. "I insisted his parents end that relationship, but now…"

"You're right, they didn't approve." Ned ran his fingers through his hair again, messing it up. His eyes wandered off and he gazed up at the ceiling, like he was reliving the whole scenario, and it wasn't a happy one from the expression on his face. "She and I were from different schools, completely different backgrounds. I met her at a movie theatre that summer. She was only fifteen. I was seventeen and headed to Harvard in the fall. When I found out about her condition, my parents told me to make it go away." He refocused his attention on me. "Sorry. Lawyer talk."

I nodded in response to Olivia's pleas and told Ned what I was hearing. "Your grandmother is very sorry now that she didn't support you, but she says it isn't too late." Then the rest of the story slammed into my head. I saw Ned giving the girl a wad of money and telling her to get an abortion. She was broken-hearted, pocketed the money, and hadn't spoken to him since.

Ohmigod. What a nightmare. I didn't know what to say.

Ned looked miserable, his face all contorted like he

was fighting back anger, tears, frustration, or maybe all of those emotions. "I didn't even know she'd had the baby until I graduated law school and moved back from Boston. By then he was already in school. I wanted a relationship with him, but his mom wouldn't return my phone calls. Still won't. Now my son hates me."

"My great-grandson is just angry," Olivia said as she faded out.

"Your grandmother is stepping back," I told him, "so let me..." I silently asked for help from Uncle Omar. My answer came in the form of his voice in my head.

"Tell him to keep trying, even if the kid acts like a jerk."

"Don't give up on your son," I told Ned, filtering out my uncle's commentary. "He's had years to build resentment, but deep down he wants a father." Then something else, a vague feeling or hint of a future event flashed into my head, but it was fleeting, like waking up from a dream and not being able to remember it. "I don't know why I'm getting this, but there's something coming up related to another relationship you had. But I can't quite see the outcome."

Ned seemed puzzled. "Okay..." He shook his head, stood up, pulled some cash out of his wallet and handed it to me. "Thanks for your help, Caryn."

When he was gone, I asked Uncle Omar, "Why couldn't I see the rest of Ned's future?"

I could hear my uncle laughing. "Not psychic about yourself, remember?"

I scrunched up my face. "Please don't tell me I'm going to meet Ned's son. He sounds like a royal pain."

More laughing, then silence. Great. I'm about to

meet the jerk.

****

"Where are you going?" Mom asked me, checking out my outfit.

I wasn't quite sure how to dress for a hot June evening of sitting in a park on a blanket. Since I was going with Annabeth and hoped to not be too much of a fifth wheel on her date with Sean, I went for understated New Age-y. Not only am I really into all that stuff like what's in Mom's shop, which had now been renamed Bethany's New Age after she bought out her business partner Sybil, I've always loved browsing the consignment store across the street. I went over this afternoon after my last client left—a twenty-something who wanted to know when she'd meet her soul mate—and picked up this vintage outfit. It was a dark blue maxi peasant skirt, which I paired with a blue and orange striped t-shirt. Then on impulse I bought a crochet handbag that was on sale.

"Annabeth's picking me up." I glanced at the digital clock on the kitchen stove. "Five minutes ago, actually. We're going up to Belford for Shakespeare in the Park. You and George got any plans?" I stifled a giggle at the metaphorical image that floated across my brain: Mom in the ocean, standing on a sofa as if it were a surfboard.

Mom kinda pointed at her black capri-length leggings with an oversized white t-shirt, an apron that read Kiss the Cook, and flip flops. Before she got married she used to have to work six days a week, but after our financial situation improved, she was able to hire help in the store and take Saturdays off.

The stove timer dinged. "My plans include keeping

this crab meat tetrazzini warm till George gets back from his golf game." Mom stuffed her hands into potholders and opened the oven door. "And then planting myself on the couch for the rest of the evening." She gently set the casserole dish on top of the stove.

Yeah, so I'd already picked up on the couch surfing. "And maybe watch that Michael Bublé special on TV, right?"

Mom smiled. "How was that client today? The nervous guy?"

"Interesting. And he tipped well." I displayed my new handbag.

"Can you share?" Mom's face lit up, making her look younger than her forty-five years. A few little lines were starting to appear around her eyes, and there were flecks of gray in her short brown hair, but she still had the figure and energy of a woman half her age. I was pretty sure it was her youthfulness that George found attractive when he came into our store that cold November day three years ago. And Mom thought George, with his tall athletic build and head full of white hair, was "hot." Her word, not mine.

"I have to respect the client's privacy, but I can tell you he didn't ask the usual questions about his love life." Just then I heard a car honk outside. "Annabeth's here. I'll see you later." I gave her a quick kiss on the cheek and headed to the front door.

"It's good to see you so happy!" Mom called after me.

I guess she was as tired of seeing me depressed about my breakup with Quince as I was tired of being depressed. Maybe Annabeth was right. A night out with friends would do me good. After all, it was late June, we were high school graduates, and only had two months left before we started college.

"Hi, Annabeth." She had the car windows rolled down because it was a nice evening. I jumped in the passenger side and fastened my seatbelt.

Annabeth readjusted her rear view mirrors and slowly pulled out of the driveway onto the busy street. "Sorry I'm late. What's with the traffic in this neighborhood?"

I shrugged. "People have to get home from work." George's house—now our house—was in a neighborhood a few blocks from a private university and close to, but not in, an area of Tudor-style homes built in the 1920s and priced close to a million dollars. Our house was big, but nowhere near that price range. It was more what you'd call upper middle class. The exterior was gray brick, the big picture window in the living room looked out onto the busy street, and the house had what Mom called curb appeal—big trees, flowers and plants lining the front walk, and a well-manicured lawn.

"Where's Sean?" I asked Annabeth.

"Sean's going to meet us there," she said. "He's giving Gary a ride."

"Oh, okay. Gary doesn't drive, right?"

Annabeth took her eyes off the road to glance at me in the passenger seat. "How did you…?" Then she burst out laughing. "Never mind."

For some reason I can't get a clear picture of this Gary guy in my head. But I did see—and by "see" I mean the psychic hit that ran through my mind like a mini-byte on steroids—a generic guy with an overstuffed backpack strolling across a college campus. I figured that symbolically meant he didn't have a car.

Annabeth shoved in a Taylor Swift CD, and for the rest of the way up to her hometown we sang loudly off key and laughed a lot.

Once we got to the large open-air park in Belford, the hunt was on for a parking space in the small lot. After several passes, Annabeth finally found one about to become available. She put her signal on and endured honks and glares from cars behind us, but it took forever for the family to load their kids and gear into the car, start the engine, and back out. Annabeth tapped impatiently on the steering wheel. "While we're young!" she muttered. Once they were out, she zipped into the spot and popped the trunk to pull out two lawn chairs, each in its own carrying bag. She shifted hers onto her shoulder, handed me mine, beeped the car locked and off we went.

This Shakespeare performance was being held in a big city park with walking trails all around and through, a fountain in the middle of a paved square, and a large white gazebo, which sat regally in the lawn. The stage was set exactly as I'd seen it in my vision, with fake greenery and Styrofoam boulders to create a forest, spotlights strategically placed in the roof, and a curtain in the back for actors to enter and exit.

We both scouted out the grassy seating area surrounding the gazebo. I guess we were late, because the place was already crowded and all the good spots near the stage were taken.

Annabeth sent a quick text to Sean. She sighed with relief when his answer pinged right back. "He says he's got us a spot saved." She shaded her eyes and did a quick search. "There!" She pointed off to the right, where Sean was waving both arms at us.

Sean had managed to get a great spot near the front. I guess that's what comes of giving a ride to an actor with a six-thirty call time. As soon as we got close enough, Sean pulled Annabeth into a big hug followed by a mushy kiss.

"Get a room, you two," I grumbled.

Sean let loose of Annabeth and winked at me. "Good to see you too, Caryn." He chivalrously relieved us of our chairs and set them up on either side of his.

Just in time, because an unseen announcer came on the PA to announce the start of the play. It included the usual admonishments to not snap photos of the actors during the performance, turn off cell phones, and of course no smoking. Ewww.

It was eight o'clock, which in late June meant broad daylight, so the few spotlights on the stage merely created ambience. Four actors, three men and a woman, entered from behind the backdrop, and the play began. Luckily the actors were miked up, because the audience was still noisy, powering down cell phones, shushing restless kids, or gathering picnic trash. The girl playing Helena was particularly hard to understand, since she was delivering Shakespearean dialog with a thick Middle Eastern accent. But overall the actors weren't bad.

Act One ended and they went right into Act Two with no break, opening with Puck speaking to a Fairy. A very tall, handsome, slender guy with slicked-back blond hair appeared onstage, dressed in what looked like bike shorts covered in plastic leaves, his shirtless chest adorned with something like a Hawaiian lei. For some reason, he looked familiar, even though I knew we'd never met.

"How now, spirit? Whither wander you?"

Well, I didn't have any trouble hearing this actor. His presence onstage was commanding, as was his delivery of the complicated Shakespearean dialog. He almost didn't need a mic. "Is that Sean's friend?" I whispered to Annabeth.

She nodded and put her fingers to her lips. I turned my attention back to the play.

Two and a half hours, lots of mistaken identity and scurrying through the woods later, Puck appeared onstage for the final time.

"...Give me your hands, if we be friends,
And Robin shall restore amends."

The audience clapped on cue. He bowed from the waist, gave a wave, and the rest of the actors joined him onstage for their curtain call. The applause was polite as each actor took a bow, that is until Gary stepped forward and received what could almost be called a standing ovation. I say almost, because in all fairness, some of the people standing up were just stretching, while others were busy gathering their chairs, blankets and picnic baskets so they could get to their cars before traffic got bad. But still, of all the actors in the play, Gary got the most recognition. True, his part was important, but he was good.

"Come on, Caryn," Sean said. "I'll introduce you."

"Uh…" I started a silent prayer to the Universe to somehow be excused from a very obvious fix-up, but before I could finish the thought, Sean had his hand on my back, steering me toward the gazebo. Annabeth was right behind me, so there was no hope of escape.

"The guy's harmless," my uncle whispered in my ear.

"Now you show up," I muttered.

"What did you say?" Annabeth asked.

I just shook my head and allowed Sean to lead me through the adoring fans over to Gary. He was smiling and chatting with an attractive thirty-something woman and some of his cast mates, and being that close, I noticed he was dripping with sweat. I guess it was to be expected since it was over eighty degrees out here and he'd been in full body makeup under spotlights. Still, not a good look.

"Hey, dude." Sean reached out and shook Gary's sweaty and probably slippery hand. "Excellent!"

"Thanks," Gary said. He even blushed, or at least it looked like he did. Maybe it was just the heat.

"Yeah, Gary," Annabeth said. "You were awesome."

I noticed she didn't try to shake his hand or hug him, or even get too close. Couldn't blame her.

"Dude," Sean said, planting me in front of him, "this is Annabeth's friend Caryn Alderson. She'll be starting at Hamilton Liberal Arts next fall with the rest of us." Sean patted my shoulder. "Caryn, this is my soon-to-be roomie Gary Riddell."

"Nice to meet you." Gary stuck out his sweaty palm.

I cringed as I gave him a wimpy and very quick handshake. "Pleased to meet you," I mumbled. I surreptitiously wiped my hand on my skirt and reminded myself to do laundry the minute I got home.

The attractive older woman Gary had been talking to reached over and hugged Gary's shoulders. Just as I was thinking how creepy it was for a woman her age to be so friendly with a guy in his teens, one of those mini-flicks went through my mind. I relaxed a little. "Is this your mom, Gary?"

"Brenda Riddell," she said as she turned to me with a smile that lit up her face.

Despite Annabeth and Sean's efforts, I wasn't the least interested in Gary, but I liked his mother immediately.

Gary ran his fingers through his dripping bangs. "Come on, Mom, I gotta hit the shower."

Brenda nodded but stopped to speak to some other adults as Gary playfully punched Sean in the arm. "Thanks for the ride, Sean. And for bringing"—he glanced at me with either disdain or indifference, I couldn't tell which—"friends." With that, he gave Sean the universal fist to ear signal for "call me" and turned to leave.

But then he stopped mid-stride. I watched in amazement as Gary stared at a tree, then put his hands on his hips and spoke to…the tree? Huh?

I grabbed Annabeth's arm and pulled her back. "What's that guy doing?"

Annabeth followed my gaze and saw the same thing I did, but seemed a lot less concerned. She shrugged. "Rehearsing?"

Rehearsing? After the play? That made no sense.

****

Annabeth called me the next day. "Well, what did you think?"

"About what? The play or the fix-up?"

"Both," Annabeth said with a giggle.

"The play was okay," I told her. "Sean's friend was

18

good. But as for me and him..." I tried to think of a diplomatic way to say it. "Actors aren't my type. And he's weird."

"Weird how?"

"You know, the talking to the tree thing. Totally creeped me out."

"There's a reason for that, Caryn. See, Gary's..."

"Annabeth," I interrupted. "I'm leaving in a couple of days for Houston and I won't be back till mid-August. All I want to do is spend time with Dad and Michael, maybe see an Astros game or two, hit the pool and museums, and relax. I'm not interested in dating."

She let out a long, exaggerated sigh. "Yeah, okay. Maybe once we're all in college—"

I cleared my throat and she stopped.

"Have fun in Texas." Annabeth sounded resigned. "And happy birthday. I'll text you."

"Sounds good." I clicked off. My birthday was coming up soon, on July Fourth, and Dad always had something special planned. And what I told Annabeth was true. I just wasn't up for dating. Especially a guy who talks to trees.

Chapter 2

"Hey, Riddell. Did you hear that?"

"Hear what?" Gary asked without looking up from his laptop. He wished yet again that Sean hadn't insisted on bringing that fifty-two-inch TV into their dorm room. The only place to put the thing was on top of the built-in dresser on the longest wall in the room, making it too high, too big, and too much of a distraction. Gary preferred to study, listen to music, or maybe just sleep in peace, while Sean was constantly watching sports, campus TV, or the local news. Gary snatched the remote control from the nightstand between their beds, switched it off, and set the remote back down. "Whatever they're talking about on campus TV, you can read about tomorrow in the campus news rag."

Sean reclaimed the remote and turned the TV on again as he nodded toward the screen. "But this is so cool! Didn't you hear that announcement? Some woman has reached out to The Ghost Stalkers Club to investigate her family's old farmhouse." Sean stretched out his arm, using the remote as a pointer. "Look!"

Gary raised his head in time to catch a quick glimpse of the information crawling across the bottom of the television screen, just before it cut to a pizza commercial. He went back to his preparations for his Oral Interpretation midterm. "So?"

"So?" Sean repeated. "This woman needs help."

Gary shrugged. "You and your fellow club members are always going off on wild-goose—excuse me, ghost—chases. What's different about this one?"

"That farmhouse, it's over a hundred years old, and it's right here in Hamilton County. I've heard it's really haunted. We could use your help, man."

Gary groaned. "Seriously? No way." He turned his attention back to Shakespeare.

"Come on, Gary. It's just one night. Think about it?"

"No." Gary didn't have time to humor his roommate's interest in the paranormal, and ordinarily he wouldn't have even been in his dorm room for Sean to bug him, but he needed to rehearse this speech out loud. The librarians frowned on that.

Gary's first college midterms were a big deal, considering that the fate of his scholarship money depended on decent grades. Brenda had offered to pay for as much of his schooling as she could, a huge sacrifice for a single mother on a tight budget, but Gary wouldn't let her. "I'll figure it out, Mom. We've done okay all these years, just the two of us."

Brenda had guffawed. "Gary, I don't think you've quite grasped the concept of student loan debt. It can be killer."

Gary tried to focus on his script, but he couldn't. The TV was too loud. "Sean, I need to study. B average, remember?" He shoved his laptop aside and ran his fingers through his hair in frustration. "Hey, instead of channel surfing, why don't you do something useful? Go to the library. Or the gym. Go do laundry."

Sean muted the TV and sat up on his perfectly

made bed. He lifted an eyebrow as he pointed to the floor by Gary's bed, which was piled high with clothes. "Dude. You're the one who needs to do laundry. And you can't get rid of me that easily."

Gary thumped his fingers against his script. "'To be or not to be…'" he said in full voice.

"All you ever do is study." Sean hijacked Gary's laptop, punched in some keys, and pulled up the Ghost Stalkers Club website. "There," he said, pointing to the screen, "that's the information. Read up on it. You might change your mind."

"No, thanks."

Sean was silent for a rare moment. But the quiet didn't last long. "Could it hurt to just come with us and maybe have some fun for once? And in the process, do your thing?"

Gary let out an exasperated sigh. "Sean, I've got a full class load, a play to audition for, plus a part time job. Besides, you and your crew have all that expensive equipment. You don't need me."

"Yes we do. EVPs only go so far. We need the help of a medium."

Gary reclaimed his laptop from Sean. He lay down with his computer balanced on his stomach and stretched out on the dorm room's standard-size bed that barely fit his six-foot-five-inch frame. He peeked at the headline on the Ghost Stalkers' website: *Local B&B seeks help in getting rid of pesky ghost.* But Gary wasn't the least bit tempted. "For the last time, Sean, I'm not a medium. Mediums talk to crossed-over spirits. I can only talk to the earthbounds that get in my face. Why don't you snag that roommate of Annabeth's? Isn't she a medium?"

"She's too busy with the campus newspaper."

"Then you'll have to rely on your high-tech Electronic Voice Phenomenon," Gary said.

"Annabeth thinks this is a good human interest story, since it's local."

Gary shrugged. "Well, I'm not going ghost hunting at some run-down farmhouse, just so your club with its cameras and fancy equipment can get a feature story in the campus newspaper." He sat up again, readjusted his laptop on the bed and got back to Shakespeare, even though he was pretty sure the wheels inside his best friend's head were still churning.

"Fine, man," Sean said as he pulled himself off the bed, sat down at his desk and opened his own laptop. "Be that way."

****

The next morning Gary walked from his dorm room across the small Hamilton Liberal Arts College campus, headed for the Thomas Belford Performing Arts Building, named after the town's founder. Late October in Indiana was usually mild, with the added bonus of the leaves changing colors from green to vivid reds and oranges, but today the air was crisp with a hint of frost. Gary thought about going back to his dorm for a heavier jacket, but a quick glance at the clock tower told him he was short of time, so he just pulled up the hood on his Colts sweatshirt and shoved his hands in the front pocket.

The Commons, the open grassy area in the center of the campus that was surrounded by all of the classroom buildings, was already decorated for Halloween, with bales of hay and carved pumpkins strewn about. Gary remembered the first time he had come here. It was just about a year ago when his mom had insisted they do some campus visits during his high school fall break, even though neither of them really knew at that point how they were going to pay for his college education.

"Gary, look how quaint," Brenda had said, pointing to the historic buildings as she read from the campus guidebook. "This used to be a military post until the 1880s. And that," she said, stopping in front of what appeared to be a nineteenth century residence, "was where the post's commanding officer lived."

"Well, he left behind one of his soldiers," Gary replied, tilting his head in the direction of a hundred-year-old oak tree.

Brenda's eyes followed her son's. "We've got a ghost?"

Gary shrugged. "He's gone."

"Did he say anything?"

"No, thank God."

Brenda smiled and patted her son's arm. "A campus that was once a military outpost probably has a few lingering spirits. It's part of the charm." She spun herself in a complete circle, admiring all the old buildings as she twirled, then abruptly stopped when she noticed a group of students staring at her. "Come on, let's go. I didn't mean to attract attention."

"You always attract attention, Mom." At age thirty-three, Brenda was still what his friends called a "hot babe."

Brenda had blushed, and the two of them had moved along on their campus tour. Despite the expense of a private school, his mom had talked him into applying for admission. "Their theatre department is one of the best in Indiana."

"And just how do you propose I pay for it?" Gary had asked her.

"You want to be a Shakespearean actor? This is where you need to be. We'll figure it out."

After some online research, Gary had to admit his mom was right about the theatre department. He also liked the small campus itself, especially The Commons area with its manicured lawn and huge clock tower in the center, which chimed every hour. The clock was striking now. Gary looked up and realized he was running late for his all-important presentation in Oral Interpretation class. He'd practiced and practiced this monologue, the Hamlet ode to indecision, but it wouldn't hurt to run through it one more time as he hurried to class. "To be or not to be…" he said under his breath.

"Hey, watch it!"

Gary came out of his head just as he collided head-on with a girl who looked familiar, knocking her bag out of her hand and spilling all its contents. "I'm sorry," he said as he stooped down to help her gather her belongings. "I was…"

"Not looking," she said, hands on her hips. "Yeah, I got that." She reached around him and finished putting her stuff back in the bag.

One notebook had escaped and tumbled down the sidewalk, landing in a pile of green, golden and red leaves. Gary picked it up, dusted it off, and was about to hand it back to her when he caught a glimpse of its cover. "Journalism major?"

"Yeah," she said, snatching it and stuffing it back in her bag. "And you're an actor." She pointed to his attire.

He blushed in embarrassment as he looked down at his torn jeans and paint-stained sweatshirt. "Well, I was running late and…" Just because he was wearing the clothes he'd worn when painting the backdrop for Midsummer Night's Dream last summer at Shakespeare in the Park was no reason this girl should stereotype him. He didn't always dress like this. He shifted his oversized backpack onto his other shoulder. "Gary Riddell," he said, extending his right hand.

She didn't extend her hand in return. "Yes, I know. Caryn Alderson. We met last summer. Apparently I didn't make much of an impression."

He self-consciously pulled his hand back and wiped his sweaty palm on his jeans. "Oh, yeah. Annabeth Walton's roommate?"

"Yeah. And you and Annabeth's boyfriend—" She broke off with a shrug.

"Right. I can't believe this is the first time I've run into you on campus." Gary rolled his eyes when he realized what he'd just said.

Caryn didn't react to his pun as she checked her bag to make sure she had everything.

Well, she looks the part of an aspiring newspaper woman, Gary thought. She was medium height, meaning a good deal shorter than him, with shoulder-length brown hair that she'd pushed back with a headband, revealing tiny pearl stud earrings. Her crisply starched jeans were paired with a tailored corduroy blazer, and carrying that Coach bag knock-off made her look like a woman most definitely headed to corporate America. "Nice to see you again, Carolyn," he said. "Gotta go. Late for class." He turned his back and hurried off.

"CarYN!" she called after him.

He rushed into his classroom just as Dr. Danson stepped to the podium at the front of the room to address the students. "Sorry I'm late." Gary slid into his seat and quietly pulled out his laptop as the instructor raised an eyebrow at him.

"Ladies and gentlemen, before we begin our presentations today, please keep in mind the two minute time limit." Dr. Danson glanced at his tablet. "Mr. Riddell, I believe you're first."

Gary pulled himself up out of the too-small desk chair and walked to the front of the classroom. As prepared as he was for this interpretive piece, a familiar churning in his belly gave him pause. All great actors get butterflies, he told himself in positive pep-talk style. Yeah, but who said you were a great actor? his negative ego answered back. He swallowed hard.

"Come on, Riddell, we haven't got all day," shouted Foster Benning from the back of the room.

Foster was a fellow freshman, an African-American scholarship student from an urban theatre arts charter school in Indianapolis. Since he was rumored to be the next student director for the fall production, Gary didn't want to get on his bad side. He shook off the sudden case of nerves and pulled himself up to his considerable height, faced his audience aka his classmates, cleared his throat and began.

"Hamlet's soliloquy is probably one of the most well-known in literature, certainly the first speech that springs to mind when Shakespeare's tragedy is mentioned. Hamlet's dilemma is not only his dissatisfaction with life and its many torments, but he's unsure and even frightened by what death may bring, including the damnation of suicide.

> *To be, or not to be, that is the question:*
> *Whether 'tis nobler in the mind to suffer*
> *The slings and arrows of outrageous fortune,*
> *Or to take arms against a sea of troubles*
> *And by opposing end them. To die—to sleep,*
> *No more…*

Gary stopped mid-soliloquy and blinked a couple of times at what was standing at the back of the classroom, right behind Foster. "What" pretty much summed it up. The ghost looked like she'd probably walked in this building when it was new. She was wearing a tight-fitting blue satin shirt-waist jacket that matched her skirt with its huge bustle in back, dangly earrings, a weird bun-type hairstyle and a small hat sitting precariously on top of her head. She appeared to be in her early twenties, making Gary a little sad that she had died so young. But she was dead and had been for a long time. She was trying to say something, so he shut his eyes and attempted to tune her out. "Bad timing, lady," he muttered.

"Uh, Mr. Riddell," Dr. Danson said. "You've hardly used up your two minutes. And to my recollection, there's no reference to a lady in Hamlet's soliloquy."

"Oh, uh…." Gary gulped. He lowered his head a moment, cracked an eye open as he glanced toward the back of the room, and the apparition was gone. He finished his speech, but unfortunately not with the skill and pathos he'd practiced it. He cringed when Foster smirked and wrote something on his notepad.

The class finally ended. After watching classmate

after classmate give flawless presentations, Gary was humiliated and couldn't wait to escape the building. He berated himself yet again for letting his attention be distracted. After all the preparation, and knowing what was riding on his midterm grades, he wanted to kick himself for not ignoring the ghost. He saw them all the time, so why he'd let this one throw him off, he had no idea.

Gary rushed out onto The Commons, squinted as the afternoon sun shone into his eyes, and finally took refuge under the large shady oak tree that was its centerpiece. Pathetic, he chided himself. He wished the ghost world would just leave him alone, let him have some semblance of a normal life. For as long as he could remember he'd been hounded by the undead, sort of like that kid in the movie Sixth Sense. No, he didn't see bloody or mangled corpses lumbering along zombie-style, but seeing normal-looking ghosts, and yes, hearing them, was almost as bad.

Gary's first memory talking to a ghost was at age five, a little boy about his age who looked so sad and just wanted to play. Gary was all dressed for his first day of kindergarten in the clothes his mom had laid out—brand new jeans, a clean white golf shirt, and new red sneakers. He heard her calling repeatedly from the kitchen to come eat his breakfast, but when he hadn't responded, Brenda had come to check on him and found her son in an animated conversation with the wall.

"Gary, what are you doing?" Brenda had asked him.

"Talking to my new friend."

"Oh. An imagin—a new friend." Brenda had

29

smiled indulgently, taken his hand and led him out of the bedroom.

Even though Gary was just a little boy at the time, years later Brenda told him how she'd been afraid for his mental state as the 'imaginary friend' seemed to crop up more and more in their conversations.

Brenda, who was very young herself then, barely twenty-one, began poring over childrearing books and the Internet to find possible causes, none of them good: autism, ADHD, ingested toxins causing hallucinations, or even loneliness. She even took him to her employer, Dr. Paxton. The doctor assured Gary's mom that this was a phase that would pass. But it didn't. Gary kept telling his mom that the imaginary friend was hanging out in his bedroom. Brenda was at her wits' end, but she had no one to talk to, not even her parents. They wouldn't have understood, and his bio dad had never been in his life.

Finally a few weeks later, Gary said, "Don't worry, Mom. My friend's gone."

Brenda had seemed to breathe a sigh of relief. "How do you know?"

"I asked him if there were any kids to play with where he lived, and he said they were always trying to get him to cross over the bridge and join them. He just kept telling them he couldn't."

"Why not?"

Gary had burst out laughing. "He thought I was lonely."

After that, Gary continued talking to more and more invisible people, and not just in his bedroom. He even insisted to his mom that some of them were long-dead family members, like his great-grandpa.

Eventually, Brenda began to believe Gary really could talk to ghosts. She never made fun of him or tried to convince him it was his imagination, and always told him he was special.

As Gary got older, he didn't feel special at all. In fact, ghosts were constantly disrupting his life. By the time he got to middle school at age twelve, it was pretty embarrassing to be having conversations with the dead. When he'd stop mid-sentence to listen to something no one else could see or hear and kids looked at him funny, he'd laugh it off as no big deal.

By freshman year in high school he still hadn't gotten any better at handling the unexpected ghostly visitor. He'd be in the middle of class or in a conversation with friends and would mutter under his breath or swat at something next to his ear. Luckily for Gary, the high school drama teacher was convinced all that pantomiming represented theatrical ability, so Gary signed up for the school's drama classes and started auditioning for plays. After that, if he happened to be talking to dead people, kids just thought he was rehearsing. An added bonus was that he loved acting and was good at it.

Still, Gary hated being harassed by the undead with their otherworldly agendas. Their timing always sucked. And today another ghost had trashed his Oral Interp presentation. The chilly fresh air in The Commons was helping to clear his head after that disaster, but it wasn't making the reality of it go away.

"Now can you help me, sir?"

Gary blinked and saw the same nineteenth century lady standing next to him by the oak tree. His eyes darted around to see who might be watching. No one was near, so Gary thought he was in the clear. "Help you what?"

The ghost was wringing her hands. "Help me find my son. Have you seen my little Horace? He's only two years old."

Gary did some quick mental math. If her son was two in the 1880s and lived to adulthood, he most likely died in the mid-twentieth century. "When did you last see him?"

The lady shook her head and a wave of sadness flashed across her semi-solid face. "I was ill, feverish, and my husband kept Horace away, fearful of contagion."

Oh, okay, she died from whatever it was that brought on the fever and didn't realize time had passed her by. "Isn't there a bright light on your side?" Gary asked her. "I'm sure if you walk into it, Horace will be waiting for you."

The apparition turned around and looked off into the distance. She then smiled, lifted her arms as if to embrace someone, took a few steps and disappeared.

"Good riddance and thanks for nothing!" Gary called after her. He knew that was uncalled for, but the frustration still rankled. He turned around and there was Caryn Alderson, watching him from the other side of The Commons. She lifted her eyebrow and went on her way.

"Great," Gary muttered. "Not only does she think I'm clumsy, now she's convinced I'm a head case." He groaned, but didn't have time to think about it because he was already late for work at the bookstore.

****

There he was again, talking to a tree. Either he was

in the zone with his acting, or just zoned out. He shifted his book bag to the other shoulder, ducked his head, and hurried off.

"Uncle Omar!" I called out, then tapped my foot impatiently, waiting for him to materialize.

Uncle Omar finally appeared in front of me. "You bellowed?"

I opened my mouth to speak, but took a good look at him and burst out laughing. "You look like—"

He leaned against the same tree Gary had been talking to, folded his arms in front of his waistcoat, adjusted his top hat, and crossed one knee-high leather boot over the other. "Mr. Darcy," Uncle Omar finished for me. "I'm trying it out as a Halloween costume."

I must have looked really surprised, because my uncle gave me a mischievous grin. "What? You don't think we have parties over here?"

Pride and Prejudice is my favorite Jane Austen novel, and I had to admit my uncle made a dashing Mr. Darcy, but still... "I guess I never thought about it."

"So you needed something? I'm on my way—"

"Yeah, yeah," I said with a wave of my hand. "Remember that guy I met last summer? Gary Riddell? You told me he was interesting, but from where I stand he's a head case, talking to trees."

"One might think you're talking to trees yourself."

Ohmigod. I pulled my phone out of my pocket and plastered it to my ear. Back in high school when Uncle Omar first appeared in my life, I didn't have a cell phone and I always wished for one, if for no other reason than to keep people from staring when I talked to him or any other spirits that popped by. Once I finally got a phone, I discovered it was a good cover to avoid the kinds of looks that I had been giving Gary just now.

Uncle Omar smirked. "He's not talking to trees any more than you are. He's talking to ghosts."

My jaw dropped. "Ghosts?" I peered into my uncle's semi-solid face to see if he was joking, and when I knew he wasn't, I shook my head. "Can't be. I didn't see any ghosts. Today or last summer."

Uncle Omar stood up straight, hands on his hips. "You're a psychic medium, Caryn. Meaning you see and talk to spirits, those who have crossed over to the Other Side. You can't see or communicate with earthbounds. You know, the ones stuck here on Earth."

I gasped and took a few steps back, my hand with the phone in it dropping to my side. "That's not true!" It couldn't be! I've been seeing spirits all my life, and making predictions since I was in kindergarten.

"Sorry, kiddo," Uncle Omar said. "I thought you knew. Ghosts aren't your thing."

Now that I thought about it, the only spirits I'd ever seen were the crossed-over kind. I felt like a fraud, like I'd been lying to people and my paying clients for years, just now finding out part of the spirit world was off-limits to me. I stamped my foot like a toddler throwing a tantrum. A couple of students stepped around me on the sidewalk so I hurriedly put the phone back to my ear. "What the—"

"Language, Niece," my uncle warned.

I took a deep breath and thought through what I'd just learned about both Gary and myself. "Thanks for the news flash," I grumbled.

"If that's all, I'll be off." And just like that, Uncle Omar vanished.

My hand was shaking as I stuffed my phone back in my jeans pocket. It was pretty unnerving to find out something you've always taken for granted isn't entirely true. So now I knew I wasn't a ghost whisperer. Maybe I owed Gary an apology.

****

Gary rushed into the campus bookstore's back room. The store sold textbooks, offered a small selection of novels and nonfiction books, stocked school supplies, and even offered Hamilton Liberal Arts-embossed clothing and souvenirs. It also housed a popular coffee shop, which was always packed with students. Today was no different. Gary clocked in and grabbed his nametag off the employee bulletin board. He had lots of work to do, but instead of getting started, he logged on to the computer that not only stored the online inventory but also linked into the campus network.

"C minus." Gary cringed as he looked at his posted grade from the Hamlet speech. "Dammit."

"You've got a customer, Gary." Ellis Garrett, the student bookstore manager, tilted her head in the direction of a girl standing next to the cash register, tapping her foot impatiently. Ellis had run this store for eons—okay, since the nineties—and knew almost all the students by name, and also remembered some of their parents who had attended as well. She was sort of like a den mother to her employees, pulling them into a hug if they needed it, or scolding them if they needed that. Gary was too tall for her short, round frame to get ahold of easily, but that rarely stopped her.

"I'm on it." He logged out of his student account and headed to the register bay.

Just then Sean and Annabeth strolled into the bookstore hand in hand, and stopped by the counter where Gary was opening the cash drawer and cracking open a roll of quarters.

"Hey, dude, how'd your speech go?" Sean asked him.

He dumped the quarters into the cash drawer. "It sucked. I sucked. And that was my midterm grade." Gary glanced up from the register and thought he recognized the girl waiting to make a purchase. He couldn't come up with a name, but he knew he'd seen her around the dorm. She was gorgeous and very tall. "Aren't you...?"

"In a hurry," she said.

Gary would have liked to get to know her, but obviously this wasn't the time. He rang up her blue books and ran her credit card. "Have a nice day," Gary said as he handed her the receipt.

"Whatever." She shoved the receipt inside her bag and stormed off.

"Rude, Erica!" Annabeth called after her.

"You know her?" Gary asked, his eyes following the girl.

Annabeth nodded. "Erica Stone. She lives on the same floor as Caryn and me."

Sean waved his hand in front of Gary's face. "How'd that happen, man? Your speech, I mean. Last night you were spot-on. Go up on your lines?"

Gary's shoulders slumped. "I was the victim of a haunting."

"Ooo, do tell," Annabeth said with a giggle.

Gary knew all about Annabeth's love of ghost stalkers and mediums, including her roommate Caryn, who not only talked to spirits but could predict the future. Now that was creepy. He scouted out the bookstore one more time, hoping Erica hadn't left yet.

"What sort of ghost did you see?" Annabeth asked, leaning her elbows on the counter to get the scoop.

"You know this campus is a hotbed of paranormal activity, Annabeth," Gary said. "Isn't that why you enrolled here? To hobnob with the undead?"

Annabeth grinned at him and waved away his sarcasm. "I enrolled because of the J-school. So who was he? Or she? Details!"

Gary related his encounter with the nineteenth century dead lady as Annabeth hung on his every word. "Oh, and I bumped into your friend Caryn," he added. "Literally. And she thinks I'm nuts."

Annabeth shrugged. "She's had her share of people thinking she's weird. I can talk to her if you like."

Gary frowned. "What for? She's not my type."

Annabeth followed Gary's gaze and spotted Erica Stone chatting with some upper classmen in the coffee shop. "She's out of your league, Gary. And Caryn—"

Gary cut her off. "—wants nothing to do with me. Not that I care." Then Gary noticed Ellis giving him a disapproving frown from the other side of the bookstore as she pointed over his head to the history section. "I gotta get back to work."

"We're going for coffee," Sean said, jerking his thumb in that direction, "but I just wanted to know if you'd checked your email today." He let a sly grin slip out.

"I just looked at my online grades…"

"No, man, check your personal email. Might be something there."

Gary shook his head and hurried over to the history textbook section to help a bewildered-looking fellow freshman.

****

Exhausted after a long day, which included a bad performance on his midterm and demanding customers, including Erica Stone, Gary tossed his dorm room keys on his desk and collapsed onto his unmade bed. Just as he was about to drift off to sleep, he remembered Sean's cryptic comment about some email he needed to check. He yawned, opened his laptop and pulled up his inbox. One from his mom, several from fellow drama students wanting study or scene partners, a couple from professors with notices to check updated assignments, and then one that really caught his eye. Ghost-Stalkers Club was the subject line. "What now?" Gary groaned as he opened it.

Hey Gary,

Our member and your roommate Sean Paxton suggested we contact you. We have been invited to search for ghosts at the Pelson family's nineteenth-century farmhouse in Hamilton County. The building was being renovated as a bed and breakfast before the workers were scared off by supposed paranormal activity. We need a medium and hope you will agree to join us, at least for this one night. Please respond to this email ASAP.

Sincerely,

Barry Lansing, President, Ghost Stalkers Club, Hamilton Liberal Arts College

"Sean Paxton! I'm gonna kill you!" Gary shouted to the computer.

Chapter 3

Gary was so angry at Sean that if he'd actually spoken to him after opening that email from Barry Lansing, he might have ripped him a new one. So to avoid an argument, Gary ducked out of their dorm room and took refuge in the library. When it closed and he had to leave, he slung his overstuffed backpack on his shoulder and started walking aimlessly, ending up off campus at a twenty-four hour burger joint. He just wanted hot coffee, but when the waitress scowled at him, he ordered a burger that turned out to be a greasy slab of meat on a stale bun. With no place to go, he pretended to eat while watching people come and go, mostly students pulling all-nighters. Some of them appeared as lost as he felt. When he couldn't stand the smell of rancid cooking oil and soggy French fries anymore, he paid the tab with a small tip for the waitress, endured another scowl from her, and left. Then, to kill more time, he just walked around the empty streets of downtown Belford, peering into closed store windows.

Gary had forgotten how chilly late October nights could be. He pulled his jean jacket tighter around him and buttoned it up, angry at himself for just taking off without a thought as to where he was going or how he was dressed. He reached down to pull up his tube socks, then remembered he'd been unable to find any clean ones and had just stepped barefoot into his worn tennis shoes. Shivering, he stopped under a street lamp to check the time on his phone. 2:00 a.m. He hoped Sean was asleep by now and he could sneak back in without starting a conversation, or more likely an argument, but even if Sean was still up, it was too cold to stay out here any longer. He put his hands in his pockets and retraced his steps through downtown Belford and back toward school.

Once on campus, Gary inserted his dorm key card in the slot to buzz open the outer door and rushed into the warm lobby, blowing on his cold, red hands and stomping his feet to get some feeling back. He rode up the elevator, quietly opened the door and peeked in. Sean was sound asleep, so Gary tiptoed into the room, undressed in the bathroom without turning on the light, and then slipped under the covers.

Unfortunately he slept not a wink, to quote the Bard, still agonizing about how to avoid a big blow-up with his roommate over this Ghost Stalkers hunt. He must have dozed off, though, because when his alarm blasted on at 7:00 a.m. it jolted him awake. He groaned and pulled his blanket over his head.

"Dude. Get up." Sean shut off Gary's alarm and gave Gary's backside a kick as he yanked the covers back. "Staying out all night doesn't excuse you from classes, you know."

Gary knew. Walking the streets of Belford in the cold had left him feeling tired, achy, and yes, still angry at his roommate. He stumbled into the bathroom and got into the shower, letting the warm water roll over him. At least he'd put his time in the library last night to good use, because his English Lit midterm was this morning and he was ready. He needed to get a decent grade to offset the bad score he'd gotten on his Oral Interp presentation. Midterms factored into the grading equation that would determine his final semester grade and in turn, whether he kept or lost his scholarship money.

Since Brenda had insisted he apply here, Gary had put in his application for federal student loans and been approved, but then he'd never heard from HLAC. Despite glowing recommendations from his high school drama teacher, Gary assumed his mediocre SAT scores had disqualified him. So he forgot about Hamilton Liberal Arts and applied to other state schools. But then out of the blue he got a phone call from the HLAC admissions office.

"Mr. Riddell? We have some exciting news for you. Could you stop by our offices this week?"

Being called 'Mr. Riddell' was a weird feeling for an eighteen-year-old kid. Brenda got all worked up about this mysterious news and urged him to go hear them out, despite his misgivings. Gary didn't really know what could be so exciting about signing away the next twenty years of his life to pay off college loans, but to make her happy he went.

"Gary Riddell?" The admissions officer smiled at him as she shuffled through a stack of papers on her desk. "Ah yes, here it is." She shoved a document under his nose, handed him a pen and pointed to a blank line. "You're eighteen, right? Sign here."

Gary recoiled. "What am I signing? I filled out all my FAFSA forms online."

"Oh you won't be needing loans," she said, again pointing to the line requiring his signature. "This is a full-ride scholarship."

Gary's jaw had dropped. "What? How?"

The woman had smiled indulgently. "This is from a private anonymous benefactor, and the scholarship covers four years of tuition, books, room and board. The only stipulation is that you maintain a B average and complete all four years here. Transfer out and the money doesn't follow."

Gary's hand was shaking when he signed his name where she indicated, and then he rushed home to tell his mom about his good fortune. Brenda hugged him, popped open a bottle of sparkling water like it was vintage champagne, and toasted to the anonymous benefactor.

"I sorta feel like Pip in *Great Expectations*," Gary said. "Why me, anyway?"

Brenda shrugged and took a sip of her water. "Maybe he—or she—saw you in a play and wanted to encourage your talent."

Gary thought about that, and it made about as much sense as anything else he'd come up with. "I'll still have to work part time, though, for spending money."

"As long as you keep your grades up," Brenda warned.

"I started working when I was fourteen, Mom, bagging groceries. I'll be fine working part time during college."

Gary might be pissed at his roommate, but Sean was right. He couldn't risk losing the scholarship and disappointing Brenda. He still had to keep up his grades, and going off half-cocked like he did last night couldn't happen again. He finished his shower, got dressed, and headed to class.

****

I got interested in journalism after I was interviewed by a young reporter from The Indianapolis Star back when I was in high school. She wrote an article about me being a teen psychic, a topic I wasn't too keen to have publicized, but she handled it so well that it put me at ease. Her example inspired me to want to learn to write news stories, too, so junior year I joined the Rosslyn High School newspaper staff as a reporter. I kept in touch with the reporter, Serena, and she even let me shadow her for a couple of weeks that summer. Senior year I was named co-editor of the school paper. I guess I did okay, because at the senior awards banquet before graduation last spring, I was awarded some scholarship money from the Retired News Writers Guild to study journalism. I was thrilled, Mom was ecstatic, and all my dads were proud of me. I deliberately chose Hamilton Liberal Arts College because it was such a small school and I don't do well in crowds. I tend to psychically pick up too many random emotions from total strangers. At least here I wasn't bombarded with them as much as I would be at a school with thousands of students.

Annabeth and I were the only freshmen on the staff of The Hamilton Campus Herald. But in my application I mentioned my high school summer internship, which must have impressed someone because they brought me on board. And by "they" I mean our faculty advisor, Mr. Delwood. He was as dedicated to our small publication as if it were a big state university newspaper.

When I got here mid-morning the office was quiet.

Staffers who weren't in class were probably out covering their assigned stories. Being in here alone helped me focus on my work, without distractions like ringing phones or psychic hits.

Del usually assigned me breaking news and the fine arts scene. Janet Wilcox covered fashion and dorm gossip, Alex Bonham focused on sports and occasionally photography, and Sydney Marshall was part story editor, part news reporter. Annabeth was our main photojournalist. She had a head start on me in journalism, being on staff all four years at Willowby Prep's WP Gazette, where she had tons of fabulous feature pics and front page photos. One shot of a spectacular catch by a running back on their football team got thousands of hits on social media. As a result, Annabeth had her pick of colleges, including some Ivy League schools, but she chose Hamilton Liberal Arts. I'd like to think it was because of me, but I know it was really because of her boyfriend Sean.

The Herald offices were housed in the basement of the administration building in a large windowless room, furnished with a few desks and computers. There was also a tiny space that was once a storage closet, where Del managed to squeeze in a desk and used it as his office. We may be a small staff and work in a miniscule space, but we take pride in putting out a quality daily newspaper.

"Hey, Caryn, you here? Anyone here?" Annabeth called out, her voice echoing through the empty office.

I didn't even glance up from my computer. "Yeah, I'm here."

Annabeth dumped her book bag on the floor by the door and went to check the assignment board on the back wall, a large whiteboard where everyone—editors, staff, even our faculty advisor—either left notes or checked for weekly assignments.

"What's your assignment?" I asked her as I continued typing away.

"I'm supposed to be Sydney's photographer at that art display at the Student Union." Annabeth went to the cabinet where the cameras were stored, jiggled the handle and found it locked. "I don't suppose you know where Del is with the key?"

I kept my eyes on the screen, my fingers flying across the keyboard. "Yeah. Still in bed."

"You sure?"

I gave her a duh look, letting her know how I knew.

"Dang. I've got some free time right now and I'd like to get started." She tapped her foot impatiently, stared at the whiteboard, and then suddenly burst into a fit of giggles.

I glanced up from my computer. "What's so funny?"

"I hear you ran into Gary Riddell. Literally!"

That reminder ruined my concentration. "Ha ha." I stretched out my fingers and rubbed my neck. "He's weird, Annabeth."

She was still guffawing at her own joke, but she fanned her face and took a few deep breaths to get control of herself. "Oh, come on, Caryn. He's an artiste, you know? And they're always a little spacey, especially if they're trying to learn lines."

I lifted an eyebrow. "I already knew he was a theatre major. After all, we did see him do Shakespeare."

Annabeth tapped her cheek with a manicured nail. "Okay, right, but I'm dying to know what happened when you saw him on campus."

I threw up my hands in disgust. "He was rude! He acted like he'd never met me before. He called me Carolyn, if you can imagine."

Annabeth let out a last tiny giggle followed by a snort and a cough. She went to her book bag and pulled out a bottle of water. "He got distracted by a ghost. Maybe you could—"

I cringed. "Please please please don't start matchmaking again."

Annabeth took one last swig of water, recapped the bottle and stuffed it back into its cubby in her bag. "I'm just trying to help you get over your broken heart."

"I'm over it." I crossed my arms in front of my chest in full-fledged pout mode. I peeked out of the corner of my eye, hoping I'd been convincing, but Annabeth had that Yeah, right expression.

I slumped down in my chair and let out a long, huge sigh. "Quince called me last summer," I mumbled.

Annabeth rushed over to me. "What?"

I nodded. "Yeah. He started to ask me out, but when I told him I had clients...Same ol' same ol'. It always creeped him out whenever I mentioned any of that stuff."

"All the more reason for you to give Gary another look. He's been there done that, and he won't judge."

"Give it a rest, Annabeth. It took me most of the summer to get over one stupid phone call, and I don't need more aggravation."

She studied me closely for a minute but didn't say anything. Instead she peered over my shoulder.

"Whatchya workin' on?"

I relaxed a little, hoping she'd let go of the idea of matching me up with ghost whisperer Gary. I pointed to the keyboard. "Something that came in off the Info Line this morning."

"Okay." She scrutinized the screen.

"It's about the Ghost Stalkers Club." I grinned with amusement as that piece of information got her attention.

Annabeth bounced up and down on her toes. "You know I'm a member of that club, right? So what's up?"

"Haven't you checked the website lately? It seems the owner of that old abandoned farmhouse outside of town wants you guys to come figure out if the place is haunted."

"Is it?" Annabeth asked.

I shrugged. "Ask Gary."

She blew out a puff of air in frustration. "So do you at least have reliable sources? For the story, I mean. Sometimes the Info Line can be…"

"Unreliable, I know." I toggled back to The Ghost Stalkers website. "So I did my research. This is straight from Barry Lansing." I tapped my finger on his message to the club members.

Annabeth read silently. "Okay, so how can you already be writing your story? We don't even know if it's haunted yet."

"I Googled the house and its current owner. Seems Ms. Pelson is the last living member of the once-prominent family." I flipped back to my story. "So for right now, I'm writing background about her and the history of her home. I'll wait and see what the Ghost Stalkers Club finds out before I go any further."

Annabeth was thoughtful. "Hmm. This story involves a wealthy family, historical property, and ghosts. Could it maybe…?"

"Yes," I said as a little mini-flick raced across my mind. "It could possibly go viral and attract media attention from Indianapolis." I ignored her look of surprise and went back to work.

Annabeth's eyes lit up. "Hey, Caryn, why don't you go with us on the ghost hunt?"

My hands crashed onto the keyboard, making a mess of my story. I hurriedly deleted the inadvertent keystrokes and shook my head. "I can't."

"Why not? Sean and I will be there. And I think Gary—"

I put up my hand to stop her. "Don't say another word about Gary Riddell."

Annabeth groaned. "Sometimes it's frustrating trying to have a conversation with a psychic."

I turned to face her. "Sorry, but I'm still upset about what Uncle Omar told me this morning."

She grinned. "What did his hotness say that's got you so rattled?"

Annabeth, of course, has never seen my dead uncle, but I did show her the picture of him that Mom keeps on her dresser. "It seems being a psychic medium is different from talking to earthbound ghosts. Gary can apparently do something I can't."

Annabeth's eyes widened. "Seriously?"

I nodded.

"And you can't…?"

"No."

Annabeth was silent for a moment. Then she got that sly look on her face, the wheels inside her head turning. "Maybe you and Gary could, I don't know, work together. You get the psychic hits and he talks to the ghosts? Kind of a meeting of the minds."

I went back to my keyboard. "Don't you have work to do?"

She shrugged and re-checked the assignment board. "Ohmigod Caryn!" Annabeth squealed as she ran her finger down to the bottom of the board. "Did you see this? Del must already know about the Ghost Stalkers story because he's assigned it to you!"

"Wait. What?" When I got here this morning I went straight to work, not bothering to check the board. I darted across the room to have a look for myself. Sure enough, there it was.

"Now you have to go. Besides, it'll be fun. And look." She ran her finger halfway up. "I'm your photographer." Annabeth clapped her hands in delight. Then she looked up at the institutional wall clock. "Oops. I'm gonna be late for class! If Del comes in, tell him I'll be back for the camera." She grabbed her book bag and bolted out the door.

I went back to my desk and looked at the story I'd been writing about the historical background of the Pelson farmhouse. I read and reread it, sighed and hit Save. I nervously drummed my fingers on my desk, trying to decide what my next move should be. I silently offered up a little prayer to The Universe.

As if in answer, I heard Uncle Omar say, "If you decide to collaborate with Gary, you'll find more than just ghosts in that old house."

"Like what?" I asked him. But he was gone. Not being psychic about myself is so frustrating.

****

At least Gary's English Lit exam went okay. It was an essay and laptops weren't allowed. Students were required to write long-hand in blue books, for fear some enterprising student would download something from the Internet. The prompt was about Puck's last line from A Midsummer Night's Dream: "If we shadows have offended, Think but this and all is mended..." After last summer and Shakespeare in the Park, it was—Gary chuckled to himself—a walk in the park.

He stepped out onto The Commons and shivered. Note to self: break out the winter coat. The cold he'd experienced last night on his wanderings seemed to have settled in. He didn't have time before work to go back to the dorm, so he pulled up the collar on his jean jacket, shoved his hands in his pockets, ducked his head and started walking in long strides toward the bookstore.

"Sir, a moment of your time if you please."

Gary stopped mid-stride and turned to stare into the semi-solid face of a military officer, probably World War I era judging by his uniform. Great. Of all the campuses in Indiana, some rich benefactor had to choose this haunted one.

"You're dead, dude. Go to the light," Gary said, and hurried away. A quick glance over his shoulder told him the ghost was gone, wherever.

The bookstore was busy. Students were milling around the book stacks, grabbing HLAC-embossed hooded sweatshirts to ward off the chill, and of course stocking up on blue books and pens. "Yup, definitely midterms," Gary muttered to himself. He rushed to the back room, grabbed his nametag while simultaneously clocking in, and hurried out onto the floor.

The coffee bar was also crowded. The sudden cold snap gave students an excuse to linger over a hot beverage while reading or studying. Every table was occupied, but of course some students were just there to socialize. There were even a couple of professors on their laptops, hard at work grading or writing lesson plans or whatever professors do.

His boss Ellis Garrett was motioning for him to come to the check-out area, so Gary stepped behind the counter and started ringing up purchases. It was so busy he barely had a moment to look up. And then his register ran out of receipt tape. Perfect. He reached into the cabinet underneath and fished out a fresh roll.

"I can't find the flash drives," said a customer.

"They're over by the computer accessories," Gary said as he finished replacing the sales receipt roll, closed the cover and ran a test print. He tore that one off and threw it in the trashcan near his feet.

"Thanks. And by the way, this herbal tea is lukewarm."

Gary glanced up to see Caryn Alderson, carryout teacup in her hand. He shrugged. "Not my department." Ellis would kill him if he alienated customers, no matter how annoying, so with a level tone he said, "You'll have to discuss the tea with the barista."

Caryn stood there a minute too long, like she was on the verge of saying something else. Finally she shrugged. "Good talk." She turned on her heel and went off toward the computer accessories.

The girl's infuriating. "May I help you?" he said to the next customer in line.

****

Ghost-boy's infuriating! How hard would it have

been for Gary to just be civil? All I did was ask about a flash drive. Okay, and complain about the tea, but seriously. Like he said, not his department, so why did he get all huffy?

With no help from Gary, I found my flash drive and paid for it at a different register operated by a friendly-looking middle-aged woman. Out in the lobby, I took one more sip of the tasteless tea, grimaced and tossed it in a nearby trash bin. I was supposed to be on my way to the library to study, but I realized I was too honked off to concentrate. That Gary guy could sure make my blood boil.

I pulled my wrap sweater tightly around me, tied it at the waist, and started across campus. It seemed to be getting colder outside and I wished I'd worn a coat. But cold or not, angry or not, I had midterms to study for, and the best place for that was a quiet study carrel in the library.

Halfway there my phone buzzed with a text from Annabeth:

—*Don't make any plans for Thursday night. Big Ghost-Stalkers meeting!*—

Despite my misgivings, Del had assigned me the story and I knew I had to go, but…I texted back a reply.

—*Will Sean be there? Gary?*—

She replied that they both would be. UGH. Yes, I was happy that out of all the reporters on The Herald, Del had trusted me to cover this big story. Maybe he thought a psychic medium had a leg up, or maybe I was just the best one for the job. I didn't know, but I sure didn't want to run into Gary Riddell. Again.

****

Gary turned the key in his dorm room door and

52

stepped inside. It was after eleven p.m., he was tired and he still had to study. He tossed his keys on his desk and flung his jacket on the chair.

"Long day?" Sean asked. He was sitting at the built-in desk, working on his laptop, while half-listening to the eleven o'clock news on TV.

"Longer than yours, Mr. I-Never-Worked-a-Day-in-My-Life."

Sean's head jerked up as he frowned. "Mean, dude. I'm working every bit as hard as you are, trying to get a decent education here."

Gary kicked his shoes off and flopped down on the bed. "Yeah, okay, cheap shot. I didn't mean—"

"Wait," Sean said, putting up his hand to silence Gary. He upped the volume on the TV and turned to watch.

"We're continuing the story of Eddie Carson, an eighth grader at Belford Middle School, missing since this afternoon when he didn't return home from school. An Amber Alert has been issued," said the TV announcer. "His distraught stepfather, Clyde Seville, is asking for any information the public might have as to Eddie's whereabouts. 'All I want is my son's safe return,' Seville was quoted earlier today."

Gary didn't usually watch the news, but in this instance the story grabbed his attention as much as it had Sean's. "Poor kid." He thought the stepdad sounded a little insincere, but hey, what did he know about fathers?

Sean nodded. "Yeah, they've been talking about this all afternoon. One of the kid's friends said he saw him talking to some strange guy in a white pickup and then he got in the truck instead of the school bus. No one's seen him since." He turned his attention back to the news report.

"And in other news, Belford, Indiana, will soon be in the local spotlight when students from Hamilton Liberal Arts' Ghost Stalkers Club set out to investigate a reported haunting at the old Pelson Farmhouse. The property is currently owned by Clara Pelson, descendant of famed entrepreneur William Pelson. The farmhouse is located just outside of town near County Line Road, and Ms. Pelson had been planning to convert it to a bed and breakfast. According to the club's website, a local medium…"

Gary couldn't believe his ears. Surely they weren't talking about him? He snatched the remote out of Sean's hand and flipped the television off.

Sean lifted an eyebrow. "So I guess you heard from Barry, huh?"

"No thanks to you."

"Well? What did you tell him?"

"Nothing. I didn't reply to the email." Gary didn't want to get into this with Sean, partly because he was still mad and partly because it was late, he was tired, and he still had lots of work to do. He dug deep into his book bag, pulled out a script and thumbed through the pages.

"Why not? Gary, we really need you. All the EVP equipment in the world isn't half as effective as you talking directly to the ghosts."

Gary tossed the script aside. "Sean, for the last time, I'm not interested." He bit his tongue before he said something he couldn't take back.

Sean turned around in his desk chair and leaned his elbows on his knees. "Let me see the email Barry sent."

Gary reluctantly pulled his phone out of a pocket in his book bag and scrolled around until his emails came up. "Here," he said, shoving it in Sean's face.

Sean backed away a little in order to see it. "Sounds innocent enough," he said when he finished reading it. "Come on, man, just say 'yes.' What can it hurt?"

"It could hurt my reputation, that's what. I'm trying to establish an acting career here." Gary placed his phone on the nightstand between the beds. "I don't relish the idea of being interviewed by that campus gossip rag your girlfriend works on."

"That's your reason?" Sean was incredulous. "You don't want publicity? I thought that's what actors were all about."

"It's not just the publicity, Sean. You know I'm not a medium."

"So you've told me. Ad nauseum." Sean reached over and picked up Gary's phone. "But that's a fine distinction most people—and the media—don't grasp, that you can't talk to the happy spirits in Heaven like Caryn does, just the miserable ghosts stuck here." After a flurry of punched keys, he calmly handed the phone back with a sly grin. "Since I have to do everything for you, I—you—just accepted Barry's offer. And don't give me any of your tired excuses. You'll thank me later." Sean got up and slapped Gary on the back before turning the TV back on.

"I thought Caryn was the psychic," Gary grumbled.

"And anyway, the publicity could help your career. Your next theatre production will probably sell out, and who knows, HLAC might get a nice donation from the Pelson family after you scare off their ghosties."

Gary needed to wash this day away. "I can't believe you got me into this." He headed to the bathroom for a shower. "There'd better be some damn ghosts in that farmhouse."

Chapter 4

It's dark. Pitch dark. With trepidation I feel my way onto the porch of the rickety old farmhouse. There are cobwebs everywhere and I get an eerie feeling about the place. I don't want to go in, but for some reason I'm compelled to continue on. Just as I reach for the torn screen door, I sense someone behind me. Right behind me. So close, in fact, I can feel his hot breath on the back of my neck. Shivers run down my spine as I jump and turn to see who's there.

"Don't worry, Caryn, it's just me."

I breathe a sigh of relief. "Uncle Omar, don't scare me like that!"

"Don't tell me you're scared of ghosts!" he says with a chuckle.

I put my hands on my hips and scowl at him. "Of course not. Besides, you said I can't see them."

"Just a heads up, Niece. There's more than ghosts in this farmhouse. And Caryn..."

"Caryn. Caryn? Your alarm!" Annabeth reached over from her bed and hit the snooze button.

I opened one eye and looked at the clock. "Sorry, I was dreaming about..." My voice trailed off.

Annabeth rolled over onto her back and rubbed her eyes. "About what?"

I blinked, sat up, and looked around our dorm room as I tried to recall the dream. Finally I shook my head.

"I can't remember it now. Must not have been too important."

In late October it was still dark at seven a.m., so I got up and stumbled over my tote bag on the way to the bathroom. "We need to clean up in here," I said as I massaged my stubbed toe.

Annabeth mumbled something in agreement. Her desk on the far side of her bed was a little neater than mine, but it still had a stack of books piled high next to her laptop. Her school textbooks were neatly arranged on the bookshelf over the desk, offset by a considerable collection of paperbacks teetering on the edge of the shelf. I couldn't help wondering why they hadn't fallen and hit her on the head. At least Annabeth's closet was neat and organized. All her expensive designer shoes were lined up in pairs, and her couture clothes were arranged according to style, season, and color. In contrast, my closet was crammed full of off-the-rack or consignment store clothing I'd just shoved in. If there was no room for something, it landed on the floor or got stuffed into the built-in dresser drawers.

My side of the dorm room wasn't much better than my closet. There was an unwashed tea mug sitting on my cluttered desk. New and used blue books were piled on top of the laptop, along with a couple of overdue library books. School books were sitting on my shelf in no particular order, and I'd also put some of my beauty products up there. At least I'd started keeping my appointment calendar online, which freed up a little space on my study desk.

I picked up the tote bag at my feet and dug my phone out. Something told me my mom was trying to get in touch with me. Sure enough, she'd sent me a text.

I flipped on the bathroom light to read it.

—*Client desperately trying to reach you. Call or text when you get this.*—

I already had a busy week, and now I had a psychic client trying to track me down. Besides classes, I had a story to cover for the newspaper, and then there was that Ghost Stalkers meeting. I sighed and sent a reply:

—*I'll try to make time in a few days.*—

****

"Are you ready, Mr. Riddell?" Dr. Danson tapped his foot impatiently while Gary dug in his backpack for the script. He'd read it and reread it, practicing over and over the lines Mr. Darcy would say, even memorizing some of them, and now he couldn't find his script.

"Sorry, I—" He dug down to the bottom of his backpack, tossing out returned blue book essays, a syllabus for History, and his graded Acting 101 midterm test over stage terminology, an A- circled in red ink prominently displayed on the front.

That grade reminded Gary how relieved he was that midterm exams were over. Five courses, fifteen credit hours, and a lot of money at stake if he hadn't made his grades. Luckily his scholarship had survived this first serious round of tests. That unfortunate C- in Oral Interpretation was offset by an A in English Lit, since the essay question on Midsummer Night's Dream was a slam-dunk. Calculus was a little tough, but he'd earned a C+ on the exam, plus a B+ in History and that stellar Acting 101 grade.

"If you're not ready, we can go on…"

"Found it!" Gary pulled his now-rumpled copy of *Pride and Prejudice* from the bottom of his bag and held it up triumphantly. He hopped up onto the small stage, the one used for auditions, rehearsals and classroom presentations, and thumbed through his script. Tricia Palmer, who was reading for Elizabeth Bennet, was glaring at him.

The spotlight suddenly flashed on from the lighting booth at the back of the room, forcing Gary to shade his eyes with his hand and squint out into the seating area to try to spot the student director. Of course it was Foster Benning, just like everyone had predicted, and Foster always behaved as if Gary's acting abilities were subpar.

"Can someone please douse that spot?" Gary called out.

The student lighting coordinator turned it off. Gary blinked a couple of times till his eyes readjusted and he was able to locate the director and the Acting class teacher. Movement at the back of the room indicated there were a few other aspiring actors either coming in for their auditions or going out after, and there were also a couple of people whose faces he couldn't make out, just milling around.

"Tricia, Gary, go!" Foster said with an impatient wave of his arms.

Gary and Tricia turned to face each other, Tricia reading from her script and Gary holding his at his side, accessible for a quick glance if need be. He hoped the fact that he'd partially memorized this scene would impress both Dr. Danson and Foster.

Darcy: Miss Bennet—in vain have I struggled! My feelings will not be repressed! You must allow me to tell you how ardently I admire and love you!

Elizabeth: (Perfectly astounded) Mr. Darcy!

Darcy: Miss Bennet, I can well understand your

own astonishment at this declaration, for I am amazed at myself! My feeling for you has taken possession of me against my will, my reason, and almost my character!

Elizabeth: But Mr. Darcy—I have never desired your good opinion, and you have certainly bestowed it most unwillingly.

Darcy: And that is all the reply which I am to have the honour of expecting?

Foster let out a long, loud exaggerated groan. "Gary, aren't you a little off today?"

Gary cringed as he walked to the edge of the stage. "Off how? I thought..." True, this style of romantic comedy wasn't really his thing. In his heart of hearts he was a Shakespearean actor, but this was the play the drama department had chosen to do this semester. If he wanted to act, he'd have to bow to the will of the Jane Austen fans on campus and do his best.

"You memorized the words but forgot about the emotion." Foster Benning folded his arms and shook his head. "Never mind. Continue."

****

Gary a little off today? "Understatement," I muttered under my breath.

I'd been sitting in the back of the studio theatre watching this farce of an audition and taking notes for the school newspaper. Del must have thought I could do the story justice since I was such a big Jane Austen fan, because at the last minute he texted and asked if I could be here. Women all over campus were giddy with anticipation, wondering who would be cast as the most romantic hero in all of English literature. But Gary Riddell was no Mr. Darcy. I jotted down some notes:

Better suited to play Bingley, or Mr. Bennet, or maybe even that buffoon Mr. Collins.

I stuffed my notepad in my oversized handbag, slipped my coat on, and hurried out of the rehearsal hall. I had to get all these thoughts written down before I forgot what a bad actor Gary Riddell was. Like I could forget. Some things you just couldn't unsee.

I thought back to sophomore year in high school. I had a fantastic literature teacher who led our class step-by-step through *Pride and Prejudice*, kick-starting my love of all things Austen. Of course that class also kick-started my romance with Quince Adams. "Cut it out, Caryn," I chided myself as I pushed the thought of our breakup to the back of my mind. I opened the theatre building's door that led onto The Commons. And shivered.

"Brrr!" It was getting really cold outside. Even though I was originally from Houston, I'd managed to adjust to the Indiana climate. Still, it seemed winter was settling in way early this year.

I buttoned up my coat and dashed across campus to the newspaper office. Once inside, I wiggled out of my coat and tossed it on the back of my desk chair, pulled the notes I just took from the bottom of my handbag, turned on the laptop and began typing fast and furious.

"What are you writing?"

"Eek!" I jumped in surprise. I'd been really in the zone, venting my spleen about the poor excuse for acting I'd just witnessed. I paused to take a couple of deep breaths and slow my beating heart, but then something about being sneaked up on brought back my mysterious dream from this morning. Something about a scary old house and a warning from Uncle Omar. It was gone as quick as it came.

"Sorry," Annabeth said. She pointed to the screen. "What's this?"

"I'm expressing my outrage at the chutzpah of that drama department!" I told her. "It's an op-ed piece about the upcoming production of *Pride and Prejudice*."

Annabeth stepped around to my side and leaned down to look me in the eye. "I thought you were looking forward to that play."

"I was until I saw the auditions."

"Aren't you being a little premature? It's auditions, not dress rehearsal." Annabeth crossed her arms and fixed me with a curious gaze. "What's this really about?"

I turned back to my computer and tried to continue, but I was losing momentum. "Moral outrage on behalf of Jane Austen fans everywhere. Gary Riddell, reading for Mr. Darcy. Great part, worst actor ever." I threw up my hands in disgust as I got worked up all over again.

Annabeth frowned. "But last summer he was awesome! Maybe he was just having an off day?"

"That's what Foster Benning said, and he's the director."

"Spilling all that venom on the opinions page will just look vindictive, girlfriend. And Gary may not even get the part."

"He won't."

Annabeth groaned. "Since your sixth sense already told you that, why bother with the op-ed piece?"

"Because Del assigned me to write about the auditions, to capitalize on the fandom on campus." I stretched my fingers, rolled my neck, and bent over my laptop.

Annabeth continued reading over my shoulder. "Yeah, okay, but I still think you should tone it down."

"No way. That theatre department is in way over its head. They should stick to contemporary comedies. Gary Riddell wasn't the only bad actor I saw today."

"Your funeral." Annabeth shrugged and moved to her own desk, booted up her computer and began editing photographs.

****

Gary wasn't a morning person, to say the least. He regularly slept through his alarm and was frequently late to his first class of the day. Sean, on the other hand, was an early riser. He was always up, showered, and ready to greet the day while Gary was still hitting snooze. This morning Sean had literally dragged Gary out of bed, where he landed with a thud and a few expletives on the floor. Sean was always hungry first thing in the morning. At seven a.m., the most Gary could choke down was black coffee.

"It should be illegal for college kids to get up and eat at this ungodly hour," Gary grumbled as they walked into the almost-empty dorm cafeteria. "See? This place is like a ghost town."

Sean chuckled. "You would know."

Gary grunted his acknowledgement of his own pun. While Sean was going through the buffet line, Gary poured himself a cup of steaming black coffee, grabbed a free copy of The Hamilton Campus Herald from the stack next to the cash register, swiped his meal card, and ambled to an empty booth. Sean rejoined him, his plate piled high with eggs, sausage, and toast. The smell was enough to make Gary gag. He sipped his coffee and perused the paper.

Suddenly Gary read something that made him choke on his coffee. After a brief coughing fit he slammed the newspaper down on the cafeteria table. "Are ya kidding me?"

"What?" Sean asked around a mouthful of eggs.

Gary shoved the Editorial page underneath Sean's nose and poked the offending article with his finger. "An opinion on my audition! Seriously? She couldn't even wait to see if I got the part and then review my performance?"

Sean put his fork down and took the paper from Gary. "By Caryn Alderson." His eyes widened as he read it. "I guess she doesn't think you're right for the part." He tossed it aside with a shrug, grabbed his fork and continued his breakfast.

"Ya think? Geez. What did I ever do to her? She says here"—he began reading from the paper—"'*Gary Riddell would be better suited to play Elizabeth's crotchety old father Mr. Bennet, or better yet, work on the crew and stay off the stage altogether.*'"

"Ouch," Sean said.

Gary sighed and took a sip of his coffee. "Moot point anyway, since I didn't get the part. I'm playing Bingley."

"Well, that's good. Right? Solid supporting role?"

Gary shrugged. The more he thought about this article, though, the madder he got. How dare Caryn trash his acting career? Okay, it wasn't Shakespeare, but still. He grabbed his coat and book bag.

"Where ya headed?" Sean asked.

Gary didn't answer as he marched out of the cafeteria.

In fact Gary didn't know where he was going, but he was determined to confront the high and mighty Miss Alderson. He had no idea where he could locate her, where her classes were, where her usual hangouts were.

He pulled out his phone, punched a number and said with clenched teeth, "Hey, Annabeth, when you get this, give me a call. I'm trying to track down your backstabbing roommate." He shoved the phone in his pocket, glanced up at the clock tower and wondered what Dr. Danson would say when he arrived early for Oral Interp class.

Dr. Danson did seem surprised when Gary got to class on time, so he called Gary up to the front of the class for an impromptu reading from *To Kill a Mockingbird*. It was Chapter 20, the scene where Atticus Finch gives his summation to the jury at the end of Tom Robinson's trial. When he'd finished the reading, his classmates applauded and Dr. Danson gave him an imperceptible nod. Gary left class much more confident about his acting abilities than when he'd arrived, but he still checked his messages to see if he'd heard back from Annabeth.

—Newspaper office any time after ten this morning.—

"Does that girl ever go anywhere but the newspaper office?" Gary asked himself. Maybe that was why it was late October and until a few days ago, he hadn't so much as laid eyes on Caryn on campus. Even though their roommate situations created a sort of Six Degrees of Separation thing, he and Caryn obviously had nothing in common.

Gary realized he didn't even know where the

newspaper office was, so he headed to the administration building to consult the oversized campus map covering the entire wall in the lobby. He stopped and gazed up at the monstrosity, stepped back to get some perspective, scratched his head in bewilderment, and moved in for a closer look. This was a really old map, and parts of it were way outdated. In fact the date at the bottom of it read 1954. Since then buildings had been renovated, renamed, or simply torn down.

"I believe what you're looking for is in The Magazine," said a voice behind him.

Gary flipped around and didn't see anyone, although he did feel that recognizable tingling on the back of his neck. "What magazine?" he asked, hoping anybody within earshot thought he was just thinking aloud about the map.

"I said, THE Magazine, young man."

"Okay." Gary ran his fingers down the descriptions of the historic buildings, until he found it on the map key: The English and Creative Writing Building, originally The Magazine. Oh, that kind of magazine, Gary realized. The old-fashioned term for firearms storage.

And the newspaper office was in the basement of that building, all the way on the other side of campus from the theatre department. For once a ghost had been helpful. He checked the time to make sure she'd be there, but it was going on eleven, so he took off across campus.

He arrived winded from the exertion yet feeling warm despite the chill in the air. He pushed the "down" elevator button, tapped his foot for what seem like eons, then gave up and descended the stairs to the basement.

Gary found himself in a hallway of doors that all looked exactly alike and contained no markings except for consecutive numbers. The top floors of this building had been restored years ago, maintaining the solid wood doorframes and transoms that everyone said gave it character. But the renovation hadn't gotten down here because the basement was sterile and dank. Its walls were old-fashioned white plaster, all the doors were painted white, and there wasn't a window in sight. He walked up and down the corridor, trying a few doors that turned out to be locked, and was about to give up in frustration when he heard voices coming from the opposite end of the hallway. He followed the sound to an open doorway that actually had a sign, The Hamilton Campus Herald. He poked his head inside to discover a student newsroom. The staff members were crammed so tight into that tiny room, Gary had no idea how they got any work done. Desks with laptops were arranged in two narrow rows, closets and storage bins lined the walls, and there was a closed door at the far end that read Faculty Advisor.

Gary spotted Sydney Marshall and Annabeth with their heads together, one camera between them as they looked at some digital photos. He recognized Alex Bonham from his picture and byline in the sports section. There were a few other people Gary didn't know, but he was in no mood to make friends. He gathered his righteous indignation and stormed in, scouted out the room and easily located Caryn staring at what looked to Gary like chicken scratches on a white board.

"Thanks a lot!"

Startled, Caryn gasped and flipped around, but

relaxed when she saw who it was. "I take it you didn't care for my op-ed piece this morning."

Gary got up in Caryn's personal space and growled, "Duh. I guess you don't have to be psychic to figure that out."

She smirked, but backed away a little. "I only write what I see."

"What you saw," Gary said, crossing his arms in front of him, "was an audition. A tryout. Not even a rehearsal! How can you judge my acting abilities based on that?"

"I saw enough to know that you have no business playing Mr. Darcy."

"Well, thanks to you, I'm not!" Gary knew that wasn't really true, that her op-ed piece hadn't influenced casting, since he'd gotten the text from Foster sometime after midnight. But he was angry and it felt good to blame her anyway.

"Not my fault you were in over your head. Jane Austen is probably turning over in her grave."

Gary gaped. "What makes you such an expert anyway? Ever done any theatre? Ever written about it?" He felt his face flush, whether in embarrassment or anger he couldn't be sure.

"Yes, back in high school, I did write reviews of the school's plays." Caryn crossed her arms and glared back at him.

"And that makes you an expert? A few articles—" Gary's voice trailed off as he suddenly became very aware of all the attention they were attracting.

"Hey, Gary," Annabeth said, wedging herself between them, camera in hand. "How'd the audition go?"

"Bingley," both Caryn and Gary told her at the same time. They turned back to glare at each other.

"Cool." Annabeth aimed the camera and snapped a picture of Gary and Caryn glowering at each other. She stepped back and checked the digital image. "Besides, you don't have time to do the lead since you're going to be really busy ghost-stalking."

Gary pointed at the camera. "That better not end up in the paper."

"On the contrary, I think it makes a great human interest piece." Annabeth gave them both a big wide grin and ran her hand along an imaginary image in the air. "I can see the caption: Staff writer and student actor face off over artistic differences."

"I dare say, young man, you would have made a smashing Darcy!"

Gary cringed. Did Annabeth's mention of ghosts bring this one in, or was it the same disembodied voice he'd heard earlier? He looked over Caryn's head—not hard to do since he towered over her—and saw the ghost of a professor, probably from the 1950s judging by the fedora and the tweed jacket with elbow patches.

Gary could feel his face flushing. Anger? Embarrassment? He wasn't sure. "Dude, you're dead. Get off this campus and go to the light."

"How rude, young man!"

Caryn glanced quickly over her shoulder. "Why, Gary. You look like you've seen a ghost," she snickered.

"You mean to tell me you didn't see him? Aren't you some kind of psychic medium hotshot?"

Caryn tapped her foot impatiently. "Psychic medium yes, as in I see spirits. I'll leave the undead to you."

"Who was it?" Annabeth asked him, a little too eagerly.

Gary rolled his eyes. "Dead college professor. If he's still hanging around here fifty years later, he must have an agenda."

"Just seeing to it that students remain on task." The ghost grinned, took a puff of his pipe, doffed his hat and vanished into the ether.

Annabeth grabbed Gary's arm. "Walk me to class and you can give me all the details," she said as she dragged him out.

Gary caught a last glimpse of Caryn with an amused look on her face. He hadn't found any of this the least bit funny.

Chapter 5

Sean had left the TV on in their room when he went to class. Gary didn't bother switching it off, but he was only half-listening to the TV weather report while trying to memorize his lines for *Pride and Prejudice*. He looked up from his script to see the meteorologist waving his arms all over the Indiana map, talking about snow and freezing temperatures.

"That's right, folks, we're about to get hit with a possible record-breaking snowfall. We rarely get measurable snow this early in the season. The last time was in October of 1995 and we got less than three inches, but brace yourselves, because this storm's looking like six to eight inches."

Gary muted the TV. *No wonder it's been so cold.* Then he wondered about the Ghost Stalkers and if their trip to the farmhouse was still on for Halloween night. He hadn't heard, but the up side of the incoming bad weather was that it might force them to cancel. Gary wouldn't be upset about that at all.

Sean burst into their dorm room rubbing his hands together. "Crazy cold out there!"

Gary glanced up and raised an eyebrow. "Didn't your dad, the pediatrician, ever tell you to wear a coat in winter?"

"It's not winter," Seat shot back.

"Okay, record-setting fall cold snap. Why are you

going around campus in that thin leather jacket?"

"What are you, my mother?" Sean took the jacket off and hung it neatly in his closet. "It's all about fashion, man." He glanced at Gary who was shaking his head. "Yeah, okay, my winter coat's packed in a box in the dorm's basement and I haven't had time to get down there and dig it out. Who knew I'd need it in October?"

"They say a snowstorm's coming." Gary pointed his highlighter at the soundless TV before returning his attention to his script. "Hey, as long as you're here, wanna help me run lines?"

"Not especially." Sean flopped down on his bed, clasped his hands behind his head on the pillow, and watched the weatherman silently pointing out local weather alerts on the map. There was a crawler across the bottom of the screen announcing school and business closures and driving advisories. "I've got an Econ paper due Friday, and the professor wants hard copies, which means a long walk to the printing lab in the library. If it snows, he might—"

"Don't count on it," Gary said.

Sean harrumphed and continued to watch the weathercast. "Hey, wait." He sat bolt upright, took the remote from the nightstand and upped the volume. "Remember that kid that went missing, Eddie Carson? Still hasn't turned up."

Gary glanced up and then shrugged. "Oh. Too bad."

"Yeah, and they're running another interview with his stepdad." Sean listened intently as the reporter interviewed Clyde Seville about his stepson's disappearance and the ensuing search efforts, cut to a sound bite with the classmate who last saw Eddie before he got into the pickup, and then back to the anchor desk. "Doesn't look good," Sean said.

"Why do you care? It's not like you know the kid."

"It's creepy. Years of listening to my father talk about kids whose parents…" Sean shuddered. "Well, I just hate to think of a little boy out there in the cold, all alone and lost. Or worse."

Gary nodded. His father wasn't in his life, but he was lucky he'd had such a devoted mother. This kid's mom seemed to be MIA. "You're right about the dad," Gary said. "He seems shady, like he's all about the publicity." But he couldn't worry about a situation he knew nothing about and couldn't control anyway, so he put the highlighter to use marking up his lines. "Who knew Bingley would have so many scenes?" he muttered.

The newscast went on to the sports report, so Sean turned the TV off and rolled over on his side to face Gary. "Have you heard from Barry or Scott?"

"Who's Scott?"

"Scott Tildren," Sean said. "Ghost Stalkers Club faculty advisor, and head baseball coach of our Division AA championship Tigers."

Gary shook his head and kept on highlighting lines.

"Are you sure? Check your email."

Gary groaned, laid his script aside and booted up his laptop. "Yeah, there's a message," he said through gritted teeth. He read it silently and then turned the computer around so Sean could see.

—*Possible postponement due to inclement weather. But we're still going ahead with our meeting October 30, 7 p.m. in Room A, third floor of the Student Union.*

Plan to attend.—Barry Lansing—

"Whoohoo!" Sean shouted with a fist pump to the air. "It's on!"

"Did you not see the part about the postponement?"

"Possible postponement. This is Indiana, dude." Sean threw a pillow at Gary. "The weather changes hourly. And if it does turn bad, we can always reschedule. Ghosts haunt year-round." Sean watched as Gary nonchalantly closed his laptop and went back to studying his script. "Why aren't you more excited?"

Frustrated, Gary threw Sean's pillow back at him, hard, knocking Sean a little off-balance. Did his best friend not know him any better than that? Ghosts haunted his every waking moment, or at least it felt that way sometimes, so why would he voluntarily go looking for them? "This ghost stalking club is your thing, not mine."

Undeterred, Sean took his phone off his desk and fired off a text. In response to Gary's unasked question he said, "Annabeth. She's going not only as a club member but also as the school's newspaper photographer. I want to make sure she knows the meeting's still on."

"Just Annabeth?" Gary asked. "Not that crazy roommate of hers?" Gary felt an unfamiliar churning in his stomach. Was he hungry? No, he'd eaten dinner. Was he nervous about the play? Hardly, since Austen wasn't his idea of great theatre. He couldn't put a label on what he was feeling and he didn't have time anyway, because he needed to focus on more important things. He picked up his book bag and stuffed his script in it, zipped up the pocket and tossed it over one shoulder. Before Sean could open his mouth, Gary said, "Library. I need some peace and quiet to learn these lines."

Sean laughed out loud. "Peace and quiet at the library? Didn't you say that's one of the most haunted places on campus?"

Gary slammed the door on his way out.

****

Annabeth told me about the Ghost Stalkers Club planning meeting. She was all excited about both the club and this ghost hunt, and wanted me to join the club, too. I had no intention of joining, but since Del officially assigned me the story I needed to go to the meeting, which was being held in the Student Union. Room A was originally the school library, back in the day when Hamilton Liberal Arts only had a handful of students and all the classes met in one building.

I didn't want to make a big deal out of being there as a reporter, so I decided that if anyone asked, I'd say I was attending as Annabeth's friend. I had it all planned out: write a blow-by-blow description of the actual ghost-hunt itself, possibly interviewing club members on the spot like those "in the minute" segments on reality TV, and then afterwards do a well-written follow-up piece on the findings. If it turned out as I hoped, my story would get noticed outside of Belford, Indiana.

I arrived at the Student Union fifteen minutes early, which gave me a little time to look around. The dark oak-paneled walls around the room were lined with what were once glass-enclosed book shelves, now filled with a few old books and trophies. The whole atmosphere was very stately and dignified. I took a seat near the back of the room where I hoped to jot down some notes before the fun started.

The room was set up as if a guest speaker was coming, with institutional high-backed, armless cushioned chairs facing a podium with a microphone. People were arriving, taking seats and chatting, while others walked in, eyes glued to their phones. It soon became apparent that there weren't enough chairs, because close to fifty people had flowed into the room. Some of them were computer nerds I'd seen on campus who operated the technical equipment the club takes on all their stalks. But there were far more girls here than techie guys. I psychically picked up that some of those starry-eyed girls were less interested in ghosts and more into Barry Lansing.

And then in walked Barry himself, a senior and the club's president. He was something of a local celebrity, not only on campus but in Belford. Barry formed his Ghost Stalkers Club last year, initially starting with just a few close friends and some electronic video equipment, and with each well-publicized success it quickly grew to be one of the largest and most popular clubs on campus. Last summer Barry led a group that debunked some supposed hauntings at a history museum, and on their next hunt discovered what he claimed was evidence of paranormal activity at the county courthouse. I'd seen him swaggering around campus, but I had to admit he had charismatic good-looks. He was perpetually unshaven, sporting sophisticated glasses and always wearing his signature Ralph Lauren sweaters. As he sauntered into the room, doting eyes followed his every move, and he benevolently nodded greetings to his admirers.

Coach Scott Tildren, whom I recognized from his pictures in Alex's sports section, walked in right behind Barry, definitely overshadowed by the younger guy. He looked exactly as you'd expect a coach and former athlete to look—stocky, bald with a mustache encircling his chin and lip, one pierced ear, wearing jeans and a form-fitting fleece with the embossed HLAC logo. Coach had an elderly woman on his arm, whom he helped into a seat on the front row.

Every chair in the room was taken, with the exception of the front row that no one seemed willing to sit in. Some members gave up trying to find a seat and stood against the back wall, while a group of giggly freshmen girls sat on the floor as close to Barry as they could get.

I wondered what was keeping Sean and Annabeth. She'd been so insistent that I come tonight and yet she wasn't here. I sent her a quick text and a moment later she replied.

—*Sorry. Went to Tony's Pizza and lost track of time. On our way.*—

Great. I was stuck here by myself.

Barry Lansing stepped to the podium, tapped the mic with his finger, and spoke into it. "Ladies and gentlemen, if I could have your attention." That effectively stopped the chitchat, as all adoring eyes were trained on him. "We have a very special guest this evening." He indicated the woman seated next to Coach Tildren. "This is our homeowner, Ms. Pelson."

"Please, call me Clara," she said. She was probably in her fifties, plump with mostly gray hair pulled back in a ponytail, and wearing khaki pants with an oversized purple turtleneck sweater.

Barry scouted out the room. "Now all we need are Sean Paxton and that medium he promised us," he muttered, which was unfortunately picked up by the microphone.

Medium? I cringed and sank down in my seat at the back of the room. Did he know I'd be here? Or maybe he was referring to Gary. But Gary's not a medium, and for the life of me I couldn't figure out why they needed him anyway, since the Ghost Stalkers have all that EVP equipment. I shook my head, ready to be done with all this and get down to the business of writing the story.

Sean and Annabeth walked in, finally, hand-in-hand, just in time for Sean to respond to Barry's blurt. "Gary will be here, don't worry!"

"Pssst, Annabeth," I whispered as they sailed right past me.

Her eyes darted around until she caught sight of me. She grabbed my arm, pulling me out of my seat, and we followed Sean to the empty chairs at the front of the room, next to Clara Pelson and Scott Tildren.

I glanced up at the institution clock on the wall. 7:15. Despite Sean's assurances, whatever Gary called himself—medium or ghost whisperer—he was late.

Barry cleared his throat and didn't look too happy. "Well, folks, maybe we'd better get on with club business."

I tuned him out when he asked the recording secretary to read the minutes from the previous meeting, which had been held prior to their last ghost hunt at an old bar on Main Street. "Yes, folks," Barry said, "we have electronic evidence of a haunting in that old place."

Ten minutes later Gary appeared in the doorway, looking as unsure of himself as I felt.

Barry held up his hand to stop the reading of the minutes. When Scott spotted Gary, he got up and walked across the room to shake his hand. "You must be Gary Riddell. Scott Tildren." Scott indicated Gary should follow him to the front row.

"'Bout time, dude," Sean said.

"Play rehearsal, dude," Gary shot back as he sat down where Scott indicated, on the other side of Sean.

"I'm Barry Lansing." He shook hands with Gary. "And this is Clara Pelson, the owner of the haunted farmhouse." Turning to Clara he said, "Gary Riddell, our psychic."

I gasped loudly, which turned heads my way. I immediately faked a coughing fit.

"Uh, I hate to burst your bubble," Gary said, "but I'm no psychic."

"You can say that again," I muttered under my breath.

Scott waved away Gary's comment. "Medium. Barry meant medium."

Gary shook his head. "Maybe you guys have the wrong idea about me. I'm not a medium either."

Barry seemed a little put out. "But you can see them, right? Ghosts, spirits, whatever?"

"Oh, yeah, I see ghosts," Gary said as Barry visibly relaxed. "See them, talk to them, but they have to come find me. I don't conjure them up like a medium can."

I don't 'conjure them up' either, I thought. *I open my energy and wait to see who arrives from The Other Side.* I sighed as I glanced around the room at the puzzled crowd of ghost-stalking, EVP-loving camp followers.

Annabeth stood up and said to Barry, "If you're looking for a psychic and a medium, I've got the real deal for you!"

Uh-oh. Annabeth hooked her arm in mine and stood up, forcing me to stand up with her. I felt like a high school sophomore all over again, being outed by a big-mouthed friend.

"Who's this?" Barry asked. "We don't allow nonmembers at our meetings."

"This is my friend and roommate, and fellow Herald reporter, Caryn Alderson."

"We didn't invite reporters, either," Barry growled.

Sydney Marshall stood up from the middle of the audience and waved her arms to get everyone's attention. "Hey, guys, remember that brouhaha a few years back? Some kids at Rosslyn High School in Indianapolis staged a walkout in protest of school uniforms. Remember Caryn proving she was psychic on TV? Well, here she is in person!"

A few club members nodded, while others whispered and eyed me suspiciously. I tossed Annabeth a seriously dirty look and was about to bolt out the door when Barry approached me, all smiles and seemingly good humor. He was a better actor than Gary Riddell ever thought about being. "Any friend of Annabeth Walton's is welcome here. Are you planning to join our ghost hunt?"

Standing this close to Barry Lansing, I got a little weak in the knees, and for a moment I was as star-struck as those other groupies. "Um, well..." I took a step back, hoping for some perspective.

"Of course she's joining us. She's amazing,"

Annabeth gushed.

Gary stood up and tossed his bag over his shoulder. "Well, then you don't need me." He turned and started for the door.

Ohmigod. He's leaving and it's my fault, and they really do need him. "Actually, I…" I cleared my throat, and tried again. "I can't see earthbound ghosts."

Barry turned to me in surprise. "Wait. What?"

I lowered my voice. "Yes, I know things about the future, and yes, I can see and talk to spirits who have crossed over. But not ghosts. For that you need him," I said, jerking my thumb at Gary's retreating back.

Gary groaned. "Great. Just great." He was standing in the room's doorway, already halfway out.

"Gary, don't go," Scott said, hurrying over and putting a hand on Gary's shoulder. "Is Caryn right?"

Gary shrugged. "Yeah, I can talk to dead people." He locked eyes with me. "She gets to see happy, crossed-over spirits. All I see are anxiety-ridden earthbounds with unfinished business."

"So then we need you both. Two heads are better than one," Scott said, "since it seems you bring different things to the table."

Quite the diplomat, I thought. Yet somewhere inside, my sixth sense told me I could trust Scott. Barry I wasn't sure about, despite his good looks, but Scott Tildren seemed like a genuinely kind and caring man.

"So what we need from you during the hunt, Gary," Scott continued, "is to tell us if you see ghosts in the farmhouse, and describe them for the camera crew when the time comes. Naturally we'll have our equipment for verification. And Caryn," he said, turning to give me more unwanted attention, "perhaps you could take a different part of the farmhouse and give us any psychic impressions you get. That way we cover more territory. Agreed?"

Gary and I exchanged glances. Gary nodded. I went along with it, too, knowing this was really unprofessional. Journalistically unprofessional, that is. No reporter with any integrity allows herself to become part of the story, yet here I was, inserting myself into it.

"If that's all settled," Barry said, turning and giving Clara his full attention, "please tell us about your farmhouse and what you've been experiencing." He motioned for her to come to the podium and speak into the microphone.

Clara rose hesitantly, got too close to the mic and caused a squelch, backed up, cleared her throat and tried again. "Well," she said, "the Thomas Conner family helped endow this college, as you know. Mr. Conner built the farmhouse back in 1886 when Hamilton County was mostly farmland and a few little towns here and there. He and his family lived there until 1936 when Mr. Conner sold it to my grandfather, Arthur Pelson. Granddad raised his family there, but after he passed away, Grandmother didn't want to remain in the house. This was in the 1980s, so my father leased it out to a succession of tenants. The house fell into disrepair, was a haven for vandals and runaways, and no one wanted to rent it or buy it. It has been vacant since 1998. When Dad passed away he left me the house, so I convinced the historical society to back me financially so we could spare the farmhouse from the city's wrecking ball. I'm having it restored and plan to turn it into a bed and breakfast, which will boost the economy by bringing tourists to Hamilton County."

"And how are the renovations going?" Barry asked.

Clara frowned. "Three thousand square feet is a lot of house, so it would be a slow process anyway, even without all the disruptions."

"What sort of disruptions?" Scott asked.

Clara shrugged. "Noises. Rattling sounds in the basement, pipes being pounded on, lights going on and off, a cold breeze in the living room, the workmen's tools going missing…"

"I'm sure that's unnerving, Clara, but there could be rational explanations. We always check for those first," Barry said, glancing at the other club members who nodded in agreement.

"There have been reported sightings of a woman in white for years," Clara said. "Many of my father's tenants claimed to have seen her, but they all said she was harmless, mostly seeming to watch out for any children living in the home."

"She was a teacher," I offered. All eyes turned to me and I sank down into my chair. Note to self: Stay out of it. Just write the story.

"What happened then, Clara?" Barry prompted.

"Some of the workmen quit," she said. "Claimed they saw her, or heard things they couldn't explain, or found their previous day's work vandalized. I haven't been able to hire any new workers because of the rumors."

Barry and Scott exchanged meaningful glances. "Sounds like you've got something going on, that's for sure," Barry said. He turned to address the crowd. "So that's why we've agreed to help, to try to get to the bottom of things so you can move forward with your plans."

Scott held up his hand in caution. "But with the weather coming in, like Barry told everyone in the email, the ghost hunt may have to be postponed. As cool as it would be to hold it on Halloween night, we have to exercise caution. Barry will send out a text tomorrow when we know more about the storm."

"And I'll include the list of club members participating." Barry paused to let the grumbling die down. "We can only take a limited number, those with essential jobs."

Clara stood and Scott helped her into her coat. "I really appreciate all you're doing. People almost expect a restored nineteenth century B&B to be haunted, but they don't want to be confronted with murderous ghosts."

My jaw dropped. What was she talking about? I don't do ghosts, but really, they can't hurt people. Scare them maybe.

Even humorless Gary almost laughed. "Murderous ghosts?"

"We don't know anything yet, Gary," Scott said, "but between you and Caryn, maybe you can ferret out the ghosts."

"Ghost," Gary said. "Probably just the one, if you listen to past reports."

I stopped and stared off into space, tilting my head to one side as I watched the mini-movie flash before me. "Gary's right. Definitely just one ghost." But there was something else…

"I now declare this meeting of Ghost Stalkers closed," Barry said, snapping me out of my reverie. "Watch your email and texts for updates about tomorrow."

Everyone gathered their belongings and headed for the door, but Gary lagged behind and cornered me before I could make a clean getaway. "Who—or what—were you listening to?"

"Not listening. Watching." Before he could ask me anything more, I hurried out the door.

****

Gary didn't think that meeting would ever be over. The whole thing just made him uncomfortable, and then Annabeth's roommate showing up, the girl who always seemed to be looking down her nose at him. Just what he didn't need. Not only was he being coerced into a ghost stalking, now he had to contend with the high and mighty psychic-turned-reporter. Just as he was about to make his escape into the cold night air, someone tapped him on the shoulder.

"Gary, mind if we have a chat?"

Scott Tildren looked like he had something important on his mind, and Gary was in no hurry to head out into the bitter cold. "Sure. What d'ya need?"

"Coffee." Scott tilted his head in the direction of the student bookstore in the basement. It was near closing time, but Gary followed Scott down the back steps and into the store. Hey, a warm beverage might be just what he needed before braving the night air, and with any luck Coach Tildren was buying.

As they entered the deserted coffee bar, Gary offered a sheepish grin and half-hearted wave to Ellis and the barista. They didn't smile back. He should have known better than to come in at this hour. They were sweeping floors and wiping down counters, which was the last thing they always did before locking up the

86

store at night.

"What's your pleasure?" Scott asked as he walked to the order counter.

"The usual," Gary said, and then seeing the puzzled look on Scott's face, said to the barista, "Mary, I'll have what I always have." He watched her scowl as she rebooted her register to ring up the sale.

Scott shrugged and said to Mary, "Black coffee. High octane." He paid in cash for both cups and then turned back to Gary. "Come here often?"

Gary smiled. "I work here." He led the way to a freshly-cleaned table and they sat down.

Mary set down two black coffees. "Sorry, Gary, but since it's closing time, this is what's left." She winked at him before returning to her closing duties.

Gary blushed as he took a sip of his coffee, which was the dregs of the pot and boiling hot from sitting too long on the burner.

"Looks like you've got a friend." Scott grinned at Gary, took a tentative sip of his beverage and grimaced. "Ugh." He shook his head. "So…I usually like to get to know new club members a little before we take them on a ghost hunt."

Gary sighed, blew on his own coffee, and then poured a packet of sugar in to help cut the bitter taste. "I don't know how you got the idea I was joining your club."

"You said you were," Scott said. "In your email."

Gary rolled his eyes. "You know my roommate Sean Paxton, right? He took it upon himself to volunteer my services, and he's known to play fast and loose with the truth."

"Ah." Scott tapped a couple of packets of sugar

against the coffee mug, poured them in, and took a sip. "Does that mean you aren't planning to go on this ghost hunt after all?"

Gary blew on his own coffee, mostly to stall for time. Even though this whole thing had been Sean's bright idea, he was in too deep to back out. "No. I mean…" He shook his head. "Ghosts hunt me all the time. But I don't know anything about hunting them."

Scott chuckled. "We'll ease you along. Just be sure to bring along your ghost-whispering abilities."

Gary groaned. "If only I could ditch them somewhere."

"Look, Gary, I like you. You remind me of my teenage son in some ways, but…" Scott propped his elbows on the table and leaned in toward Gary. "But even if Sean stretched the truth, he was right that you can communicate with ghosts, and that's not a skill too many people have. We need you."

"Truth?" Gary said. Scott nodded, so Gary continued, "I don't like the notoriety, and I already got a taste of it tonight from all those Ghost Stalkers. And then there's Caryn Alderson. Makes me feel superfluous."

"Well, you're not." Scott shrugged and took another swallow of the stale coffee. "But this might all be moot, judging by the deteriorating weather."

Gary was relieved at that news. "Okay, great, so you'll let me know?" He took a swig of his coffee as he stood up and reached for his book bag.

Scott pointed to the chair. "Not so fast, Riddell. Just because we might not do the ghost hunt tomorrow night doesn't mean we're not doing it at all."

Gary plopped back down in the chair. Dammit, he

liked Scott and didn't want to let him down. He sighed. "I said I'd do it. If the lady ghost in that old farmhouse wants to chat, I'm game."

"What if there's more than one?"

"The only thing Caryn and I agreed on tonight was that there's just one ghost haunting that place," Gary said. "I don't know how she knew, but my clue came from Clara Pelson when she mentioned a cold spot. One cold spot. The rest of what she said sounded like your territory."

They both glanced over when Ellis cleared her throat to get their attention and put her hand on the light switch.

"I guess that's our cue." Scott smiled and stood as they prepared to leave. "In spite of Sean's little deception, I think we've got the right man for the job."

Gary shook Scott's hand and they parted ways. Even though they'd just met, Gary decided he liked Scott, even admired him for being the caring father he seemed to be. Tildren Jr. was a lucky kid. Gary admitted to himself that he was jealous, and wondered yet again why Ned Harrington couldn't be persuaded to share even a fraction of his wealth with his only son and the woman who gave birth to him. It was a source of constant anger and resentment that he'd tried to work through over the years, but nothing could alleviate the pain and rejection. Yeah, the ghost thing was a little weird, but he had other talents his father could've admired, like his acting, so why would it have been so hard for Harrington to spend an occasional afternoon with him? "Knock it off, Riddell," he chided himself, "it is what it is."

Before exiting the building, Gary wrapped his wool

scarf tightly around his neck, put on his gloves, and zipped up his down jacket. He told himself it wasn't that far to the dorm, but it would have been nice if he had some kind of transportation instead of being forced to walk the half mile or so across campus. He pushed the heavy glass door open and sucked in his breath at the blast of cold air. Once again he wished he owned a car—heck, any car, even a clunker. Brenda had offered to help him buy a car but he knew the expense would be a strain on her budget, never mind the insurance. And it still rankled that his father could easily have provided him with one.

He watched in amazement as his breath condensed in the air. He could almost feel the snow coming as the wind whipped around and chilled him to the bone. Gary reached a well-lit crosswalk and jumped up and down to keep warm as he waited for the light to change. "This sucks," he muttered as he realized he couldn't feel his hands. Just as the light in the crosswalk indicated he could go, someone in a sleek, late-model luxury sedan pulled up alongside him.

"Need a ride?"

Gary peered into the car, but the windows were tinted and he couldn't see the driver. "No, thanks, I'm fine," Gary said, and hurried along the sidewalk without waiting for the light. Some stranger offering him a ride. Creepy. He walked a little faster.

The guy lowered the passenger side window. "Come on. Hop in. It's freezing out there."

Gary stopped walking when he thought he recognized the voice, and then recoiled. "What the hell, Ned?"

Ned Harrington put the car in park, stepped out and

leaned over the hood from the driver's side, towering over the top of the car. Gary realized that they were approximately the same height, one more thing they had in common, and yet they had nothing in common.

"I just happened to be driving by and saw my son walking in the cold."

Son indeed. "What are you doing on this side of town anyway?" Gary demanded. He blew on his fingers to get the feeling back in them. "Slumming?"

Ned walked around the front of the car and approached Gary, but Gary stepped back. Ned sighed and shook his head. "Gary, I—"

"Like you said, it's freezing out here." Gary jaywalked across the street and started running toward his dorm. In the distance he heard his father's car roar off.

Chapter 6

Halloween morning had started out just like any other Friday. Sean had been wide awake and hungry, and Gary was jonesin' for caffeine, so the two of them had gone to the cafeteria for breakfast like they always did. At the checkout, Gary picked up a copy of the The Hamilton Campus Herald and brought it to their table. He unfolded the paper, took one look at the front page and choked on his coffee.

"You okay, man?" Sean pounded Gary on the back.

Gary shook his head and got up for a bottle of water. He coughed a couple more times and then took a few gulps of water. When he'd gotten control of himself, he straddled the white plastic institutional chair backwards and pointed to the offending picture on page two.

"It's enough to make even you lose your appetite," Gary said.

Sean scrunched up his face and took a closer look as Gary thumped the photo for emphasis. Half of the page was taken up with that photo Annabeth had snapped yesterday in the newspaper office, the one of Gary and Caryn mid-argument, staring each other down. The caption read "A Meeting of Minds" with a subtitle "Gary Riddell, Theatre Arts major, and Caryn Alderson, Journalism, face off over artistic differences."

Gary pounded the table, causing his mug of hot coffee to slosh. "I can't believe it! First Caryn's op-ed and now this."

Sean pulled a handful of paper napkins from the dispenser and gave them to Gary as he pointed to the byline. "'Photo by Annabeth Walton,' it says." He peered at it closely and beamed with pride. "It's pretty good, don't ya think?"

Gary wiped up the coffee spill, wadded up the napkins and tossed them on the table. "It's not the quality of the picture I'm upset about. It's like they're out to get me."

"Don't be so paranoid," Sean said as he returned to his half-eaten plate of pancakes. "This is a small campus, so something like a disagreement between two major players in different departments is gonna be front page news."

"I gotta go to class." Gary shoved aside his now-cold coffee. "Tell Annabeth she owes me big time."

"Hey, this is a big deal for her!" Sean called out as Gary sailed out of the cafeteria.

****

Halloween and snow don't go together, I thought. This was just crazy. Growing up in Houston, I'd only seen snow a handful of times until I moved to Indianapolis three years ago. Seeing everything white and frozen for months was a big enough adjustment, but this time of year I expected to see frost on pumpkins, not icicles on telephone poles. I had to keep my head down to avoid the blowing snow as I scurried across campus to the newspaper office after classes.

Everyone on staff must be lying low till the storm

passed, because Mr. Delwood was the only person there. His office door was ajar as he sat pounding on his computer keys. I noticed he had on his signature jeans and black turtleneck. Someone once told him he resembled Steve Jobs, so after that he dressed like the Apple guy did.

He glanced up and readjusted his glasses when I knocked. "Caryn. You're finally here. I left you that message hours ago."

"Yeah, sorry," I said. "I had some personal business." I had to call the psychic client my mom had texted me about earlier this week. I tried not to judge, but sometimes what seemed urgent to my clients was pretty mundane. Like this one. Luckily I'm as effective on the phone as I am in person, so after classes I went up to my dorm room for some privacy and gave Faith a call.

"Hi, Faith, it's Caryn. Mom tells me—"

"Oh, Caryn, thank goodness. It's about Miguel, you know, the guy at my church?"

I remembered that she'd talked about him before, but I rarely remember details about my clients' personal lives. So I opened up my energy and focused on Faith and Miguel. I could visualize him—good-looking Hispanic guy, high school senior, totally focused on his schoolwork, job, and…wait, this was new. The guy's an artist? A pretty good one, too, from what I was seeing. I've got a little artistic talent myself, but Miguel's work looked awesome.

As for Faith, she was one of those wallflower types. Not totally unattractive, but she didn't make the most of her potential. And she didn't have many friends, either, preferring to spend her time alone, writing stories or poetry. Maybe that was why she was constantly consulting a psychic about her love life.

"Miguel still hasn't asked you out, right?"

I could hear Faith sigh on the other end of the phone. "No, but I was hoping he'd ask me to the Fall Dance. Everyone at school is going."

I watched the scenario play out in my head and blew out a puff of air. "Faith," I said as tactfully as I could, "Miguel's got a lot on his plate right now." She giggled on the other end. "Oh, sorry, bad pun. He works in a restaurant, right? Anyway, you'll be going to the dance, just not with him. But don't give up because there's a chance for something later in the spring. Give it—give him—some time. And there's a classmate of yours who's going to facilitate the date."

Faith sounded disappointed when she thanked me and hung up. But even though the timing wasn't perfect for her, she and Miguel will one day be a couple. I knew that for a fact.

"Caryn? Did you hear me?"

"Oh, sorry, Del, my mind wandered. What did you say?"

"Well," Del said, swiveling around in his desk chair to face me, "I wanted to talk to you about…"

I nodded. "The Ghost Stalking's been called off."

"Yeah. How did you know?"

I smirked as I folded my arms and leaned against the doorway. "Some people say I'm psychic."

"Oh, right." Del reclined in his swivel chair.

I shifted my stance to the other foot. "Is it off for good?"

"I got the impression this was a postponement due to weather, not a cancellation."

I relaxed a little. As much as I didn't relish the idea of going toe-to-paranormal-toe with Gary Riddell, writing the story about a ghost in an historic farmhouse had the potential to be a show-stopper. "Okay, so what did you need to talk to me about?"

Del pointed to the whiteboard. "Since the ghost hunt has been derailed by snow, you and Annabeth have been reassigned for tonight to the open-campus frat party at the Sigma Zeta house."

I gasped involuntarily and then tried to cover it with a fake cough. Writing about cheesy Halloween costumes at what would surely be a drunken frat party was not exactly an elite assignment. "But you put Janet on that one!"

"Well, you're the better reporter, so Janet's now covering the pumpkin decorating contest in downtown Belford. Party starts at nine." And with that, Del turned back to his desk and resumed typing.

I stood there for another stunned minute, but Del's total concentration meant I'd been dismissed. I quietly closed his office door.

"Bummer," Uncle Omar said with a chuckle.

I glanced across the room and saw him leaning against the file cabinets, arms crossed, dog tags dangling, a wicked grin on his face.

I scowled as I walked over. "What are you laughing about?" I asked. "Me going to a stupid frat party?"

"Things happen for a reason," he reminded me before he vanished.

"Perfect!" I shouted, then grimaced, hoping Mr. Delwood hadn't heard me talking "to myself."

I was trying to process what Uncle Omar had said

when my internal radar started buzzing. Loudly. Alarm bells went off in my head, causing me to feel nervous, wary, and over-heated all at once. I held completely still as I tried to get a read on what it was, but it was just out of reach, and then it evaporated. I sighed. All I knew for sure was that something big was going down tonight.

I put on my coat. If I was going to a Halloween party tonight, I needed a costume.

Chapter 7

Gary walked out of the Fine Arts Building after his last class of the day and straight into the predicted snowstorm. He blew on his hands, put on a pair of gloves, and pulled a baseball cap out of his backpack. Some committee had gone to a lot of trouble to set up for Halloween. Carved jack-o-lanterns, scarecrows, and bales of hay had been placed decoratively around The Commons and dorm entrances. Too bad everything was quickly being covered in thick, wet snowflakes.

He pulled his phone out to check messages. Sure enough, he found the one he'd been hoping for from Barry, calling off tonight's ghost-stalking event. Gary was relieved. He'd heard about a big Halloween-themed frat party open to anyone on campus, and Gary wanted to go. Heck, he might even have some fun for a change.

Despite the weather, people were already getting into the spirit of the holiday. It was 5:30 in the afternoon and costumed students were everywhere. He gaped at a Count Dracula, watched a couple of Hunger Games wannabes hurrying along, spotted some 1960s hippies looking like they were dressed for a beach clambake rather than a blizzard, and then he came face to face with Beetlejuice.

"Hey, Foster," Gary said with an approving nod at the very authentic-looking black and white outfit, complete with ghoulish makeup and white wig. "Cool get-up. Where'd you get it?"

"Costume room." Foster looked Gary up and down with obvious disdain.

Gary followed Foster's gaze. "Haven't had time." Not that he owed Foster an explanation, but for some reason Foster's status as favorite son of the freshman theatre class intimidated him. Just as he was about to mumble some explanation about ghost hunts and late classes, he caught sight of one of the resident campus ghosts, strolling along as if he belonged in this world. Gary realized it was that same military ghost that he'd seen when he and Brenda toured the campus months ago.

Foster snapped his fingers in front of Gary's face to get his attention. "You going as boring college boy?"

"Ghost whisperer," Gary said. He hurried off, both to get away from Foster and to avoid the ghost.

"I don't get it!" Foster called after him.

Gary went back to his dorm room, dropped his book bag in the doorway, and started rummaging through his closet. He needed something to wear, and clearly he owned nothing that could be even remotely considered a Halloween costume, let alone compete with Foster's. Then it dawned on him. If Foster was brazen enough to borrow something from the costume room in the theatre building, Gary could, too. He hurried down the hall and rang for the elevator. When the door opened, there was Sean, about to step off.

"Where ya headed in such a hurry?" Sean asked.

"Since the ghost hunt's off, thought I'd go to that Sig Zeta party." Gary stuck his hand between the elevator doors to keep them from closing. "What about you?"

Sean shrugged. "Annabeth wants to go."

Gary stepped onto the elevator and pushed the button for the lobby. "See ya there?" The more he thought about it, the more eager he was to go to an open-campus party that would be crawling with attractive women. Between classes, working at the bookstore, play rehearsals, and dodging the undead, he hadn't been on a single date since he'd started college. Not that he'd had that many dates in high school, but he had fully intended to make a fresh start when he got on campus. "And tonight's the night," he said aloud, just as the elevator doors opened into the lobby. He blushed when two upper class girls who were waiting for the elevator burst into giggles. At his expense, he assumed.

"Uh, hi. I was just…"

Neither of the girls made eye contact as the two of them hopped on the elevator and pressed the UP button.

Bad start if you're looking for love, he told himself.

****

I had totally ransacked our dorm room closet, looking for something, anything, that I could turn into a last-minute Halloween costume. The last time I dressed up I was fifteen and wearing a Madame Wilhelmina fortune-telling costume. My friend Megan roped me into playing the part of a robe-wearing, crystal-ball-gazing cliché at the high school Halloween Carnival. I didn't still have the costume, but even if I did, the memories of how I embarrassed myself in front of my peers would keep me from ever putting it on again. So I had to come up with something else, hopefully something more sophisticated.

Nearly every outfit I owned was lying in a heap on my twin bed. Nothing. I sat down on the edge of the bed to think it through. Whatever I decided to wear, I had to come up with it quick, and it had to be something I could cobble together from what was in this room. I closed my eyes and tried some visualization. That didn't always work for me when it's about me, but hey, I was desperate.

Aha! Nope, no psychic insights, just a good idea. I jumped up and dug through the pile of clothes until I found my professional-looking business suit, the one Mom insisted a reporter must have, but tossed the matching pants aside as not quite right for what I had in mind. Hoped Annabeth wouldn't mind…I found a navy blue pencil skirt in her closet that was a little tight on me, but a close match to the jacket. With a white button-down shirt, my hair tied back in what I hoped looked like an old-fashioned, bun-style hairdo, I was ready. I grabbed my press badge dangling from the corner of the mirror, put it around my neck and surveyed my look.

"You need a cloche hat," a disembodied voice said.

I tilted my head to the side. "When did you become a fashion guru?"

"I've got access to all the biggies over here, remember?"

He never ceased to amaze me. "Thanks, Uncle Omar."

"Good luck tonight," he said with a chuckle.

My eyes widened. "Am I gonna need it?"

Naturally he didn't answer.

I don't have one of those hats Uncle Omar mentioned, and Annabeth doesn't own one either.

Despite vintage fashions coming back into style, I couldn't think of a single person who might have a cloche hat, nor could I get ahold of it now anyway. With shops in town closing early due to the snow, there was only one way to find the finishing piece for this otherwise-perfect costume. I put on my down overcoat with the hood, decided boots were more practical than pumps, even though the pumps would have been more appropriate for the time period I was going for, and headed out the door to the theatre department across campus.

I arrived cold and shivering, but when I tried the door I was relieved to find it unlocked. Inside, the building was deserted with the exception of the custodian, who was sweeping the hallway.

"Can you tell me where the costume room is?"

He looked up from his dustpan and frowned. "You a drama kid?"

"No, she's not." Startled, I flipped around to see Gary scowling at me.

"You a theatre student?" the janitor asked him. "Otherwise, the two of yous gotta go."

"Yes, I'm a drama major," Gary replied while giving me the stink eye.

I wasn't about to let Gary Riddell deter me. I turned my back on him and gave the janitor my most winning smile. "I need to borrow a hat. For a Halloween costume." I could tell that the janitor needed more convincing. "I didn't have time to go shopping, and now with the snow I'm outta luck. I promise to bring it back in the morning. Please?"

The janitor looked me over, exchanged glances with Gary, then shrugged and motioned for us to follow him down the hall. He pulled a large ring of keys from the loop on his belt and unlocked a door that revealed a classroom that had been turned into a massive walk-in closet. There were rows and rows of costumes, arranged in a kind of order that must make sense to actors but made no sense to me. I stared at medieval clothes, nineteenth century dresses—which made me wonder which one Tricia would wear as Elizabeth Bennet—men's frock coats, and finally mid-twentieth century outfits, both men's and women's.

Still overwhelmed by the sheer volume of costuming, I thanked the janitor.

He shrugged. "Door's gonna lock behind you when you leave." He turned and walked back down the hallway.

"Talk about chutzpah," Gary muttered under his breath as he perused the rows of men's clothing.

I scowled at him. Was he talking about me? Pretty nervy, since the guy was also here raiding the costume stash. "Del—Mr. Delwood, our newspaper faculty advisor—reassigned me to write about the frat party tonight and I didn't have time to go shopping. I just need one thing to finish off my costume."

He looked me up and down. "Right."

A man of few words. Acting seemed like an odd career choice for a guy who couldn't string two words together. "I guess since you're one of the elite theatre students, you can help yourself to whatever you want."

Gary didn't rise to the bait. He was too busy scouting out the storage closet. "I guess."

He was infuriating and I was over it. "I need a hat. If you could just point me in the right direction…" Gary didn't budge. Apparently asking nicely wasn't going to help, so I tried a different approach.

"What kind of costume are you looking for?"

"Something to top Foster Benning's costume." Gary ran his hands along the Regency frock coats.

"Not that," I said. Boy, was he wrong for anything Regency-era. "Maybe something that showcases your height?"

Gary seemed to give that some thought. While I had him distracted, I repeated my request. "Women's hats?"

He grunted and pointed to the back of the costume closet where accessories were stored on shelves. I left Gary to his browsing and headed over there. Some items were in labeled boxes while others had been tossed haphazardly onto the shelves. I ran my finger along the edges of the boxes, looking past shoes, capes, petticoats for various time periods, and finally came to the hats. They started with Shakespearean headgear for both men and women, and then abruptly switched to Jane Austen-era bonnets. I stretched on tiptoes up to my full five-foot-five inch height, but I couldn't reach any of them. I thought for a moment, and then pulled back some capes and searched the floor until I spotted a footstool shoved underneath. Standing on it, I could finally reach the boxes. I rummaged through a few labeled 1950s and at last found a cloche hat. It was pretty rumpled, but I smoothed it as best I could with the palm of my hand.

I went to the mirror on the closet's back wall to try on the hat. It wasn't a perfect fit, but hey, this was a Halloween costume accessory, not a fashion statement. I decided it would do and tucked it into my shoulder bag. I returned the stool to its place and retraced my steps. Gary was still staring at the racks.

So many choices. So little time. I needed to get going if I hoped to do justice to covering that frat party, but I didn't want to be rude to the guy who'd wrangled me a way in here. "Hamlet maybe?" I suggested.

"It's a little cold to go running across campus in leggings," he said.

He had me there. But an idea popped into my head, so I rummaged around through the robes, pulling out one that was so squished between other clothing that it was practically invisible. "Here. This is perfect."

Gary lifted an eyebrow. "Ghost of Christmas Future? Ha ha."

"Step out of character tonight and go as a ghost, not someone who talks to them." He looked skeptical in the extreme, but I needed to go and I almost felt bad leaving ghost-boy in there by himself. Not that he couldn't take care of himself, but for some reason he just looked like he could use a friend right now. But we were not friends, so I said the most reassuring thing I could think of. "It's just a long robe and it'll be warm."

Gary walked to the mirror and held the outfit in front of him. "It's a little short, but..." He shrugged, pulled it over his hooded sweatshirt and jeans, and tucked the mask under his arm. "Ready?" he asked as he held the door for me.

Which was rather chivalrous of him.

Once back outside, I realized the snow was coming down pretty fast, creating a sort of white-out condition. I groaned. "I wish I'd hitched a ride with Annabeth."

"Walking's not so bad," Gary said. "I do it all the time. And Fraternity Row's only about a block off campus."

Great. I had to arrive on foot with a guy I don't particularly care to be seen with. But there was no help for it, unless I wanted to walk across a deserted campus alone in the dark. Gary pulled his hoodie up over his head, I did the same with my coat hood, and together we pushed into the wind.

There was no mistaking which house was the Sig house, because the loud pulsating music emanating from the two-story building could be heard all the way down the block. It was just a house, though, sitting on a cul-de-sac among other houses that used to be a regular neighborhood in the mid-twentieth century, before ten of them were bought up by the University Greek System in the 1990s. This one was a white wood frame house with black shutters and a matching black front door. The minute I stepped onto the porch, that uneasy feeling I'd been having off and on all day washed over me. For sure I wasn't going in till I focused, so I stopped mid-stride.

Gary stepped up onto the porch right behind me and nearly bumped into me. "What are you waiting for?"

That blew my concentration. "Nothing now." I reached into my bag and pulled out the borrowed cloche hat.

Gary donned his mask while I adjusted the hat and we walked through the screened door, which had been left open, letting in the cold. Once inside, though, I understood why. Not only was it loud, it was really hot from all the bodies crammed in there. If the Fire Marshall should come by, I was sure the fraternity would get a code violation. And naturally all the lights were turned off with the exception of the red emergency exit lights glowing in the entry hall. Crowds like this set me on edge. Psychic overload.

I looked across the room and over the heads of some girls dressed as cheerleaders in tight mini-skirts, and watched as they danced with guys in football jerseys. One couple in particular was looking cozy, but sure enough, I saw their whole future relationship play out in my head. He was going to dump her right after football season in another month or so, and she was going to be broken-hearted. That was the kind of random stuff I hated picking up on, because even though I didn't know either of them, I knew what it was like to get dumped. I thought about cluing her in, but she probably wouldn't believe me. Boy, did I ever not want to be here. Too many variables. If I didn't have a job to do, I'd bail right now.

I surveyed my surroundings from the vantage point of about three feet into the entryway. All the rooms seemed to open off the main hallway, but a couple of walls had probably been knocked down years ago to construct a dining room big enough to accommodate all fifty or so members of the fraternity. As for the Sigma Zeta entryway, a fake candle flickered on a side table and the dark wood paneling, a throwback to another decorating era, was positively gothic in the dim light. Cheesecloth spider webs complete with plastic spiders dangled from the ceilings, and paper bats flew back and forth, blown about by a ceiling fan. A paper skeleton dangled from the ceiling, and in the corner by the ornate wooden staircase was a black plastic cauldron with smoking dry ice. Gary shoved the flimsy skeleton aside and stepped back to let me precede him into the large living area off to the left, which was where the party was happening. I guess somebody taught this guy some manners. His mom's face popped into my head. She may have been a young mother, but she taught him well.

A guy in a Spiderman costume staggered toward me and shoved one of his two beers at me. I backed away and shook my head. "Alcohol and psychic abilities don't mix."

Spiderman furrowed his brow like he was trying to grasp what I'd just said. I guess he didn't get it because he shrugged and said, "Coat room's down the hall."

"Want me to take your coat?" Gary offered.

"I'll do it. Feel free to go mingle. I'm here to work, not party, so maybe I'll find some interesting"—I caught sight of a girl in a naughty nurse costume draped all over a guy dressed as a doctor—"people to interview." I cringed. Del owes me big.

Gary took the beer from Spiderman and wandered off. I unbuttoned my coat and elbowed my way through the crush of mostly drunken revelers, retracing my steps back through the living room and into a different hallway. Must be the public part of the house, because there were restrooms labeled Men and Women, and of course a line was forming outside the Women's. I spotted a closed door with flickering lights from a television flashing under the door, and an image of a woman in her mid-sixties with a calico cat sitting on her lap zipped through my mind. "House Mother," I mumbled. I hugged the wall as I squeezed past the girls fidgeting uncomfortably as they waited for the restroom, and finally found the coat closet. Not a room turned into one, but an actual closet. Hangers were in short supply, so coats, jackets, sweaters and blazers were tossed in, one on top of the next. I sighed and shoved my coat in, too, and just hoped I'd be able to find it later.

The sooner I got to work and collected a few interviews, the sooner I could get out of here and back to the dorm before the storm got any worse. Now what was Del looking for when he took this story from Janet and gave it to me? It was going on the fashion page, so I guess that meant I needed to ask about costume choices. Boring. Just the thought of writing this article, let alone reading it, was putting me to sleep. I dutifully headed back to the living room full of Halloween partiers in all stages of inebriation.

"Jell-O shots?" a girl asked. She was dressed like a 1940s cocktail waitress, with the tray suspended around her neck on a strap, displaying her selection of colorful but deadly concoctions.

"No, thanks." But hey, she looked kinda cute and her outfit seemed almost authentic, so I asked, "How did you come up with the idea for your costume?"

"Borrowed it from my aunt."

Right then I could have used Annabeth's help, because she was the skilled photographer, but I didn't see her, so I snapped a photo with my phone. "Cute. And you are…?"

"…remaining anonymous," the girl sniffed, and moved along, her tray swaying back and forth.

I blew out a puff of air and was scouting the room for more pliable interviewees when someone tapped me on the shoulder. "Who are you shupposhed to be?"

I turned to see an obviously over-served Beetlejuice weaving back and forth. Gary was right about Foster's clever costume, but I didn't have a chance to give it a close look. I had to step back to avoid his alcohol breath and flailing arms. "Hey, Foster," I said as I waved away the stench.

"Hey, baby." He leered at me, got in my face and made kissing noises.

I pushed him away, totally grossed out with both his obvious pass and his drunken state. Even if I was interested in jumping back into the dating pool, I'd rather stay single than date this jerk. But like a good reporter, I made note of his movie-inspired costume.

"Caryn!" Someone called out. I turned to see Sean waving from across the room.

Seeing a friendly face alleviated my anxiety somewhat. "Sean!" I motioned him over.

Sean, dressed in cowboy boots, tight jeans with a large belt buckle, and a Stetson, pushed his way over to me. "Where's Gary? I saw you come in with him."

I raised an eyebrow and gave his faux Texas costume a frown. As a native of the Lone Star State, I can say with authority that his costume was a worn-out cliché. "I didn't come with him, we simply walked across campus at the same time. I'm here on assignment."

Sean gave me a Yeah, right look and took a couple of Jell-O shots off the faux waitress's tray as she sauntered back by. "So you decided to hang out with us Halloween revelers?" he asked as he swallowed them.

"Like I said, I'm working. And speaking of work, what have you done with my roommate?"

"Annabeth's around here somewhere." Sean was pretty tall, not as tall as Gary, but he was able to see over my head. "She's over there, chatting up The Grim Reaper."

I followed his gaze and sure enough, there was Little Red Riding Hood aka Annabeth Walton. "That's Gary," I told Sean. "He's the Ghost of Christmas Future. You know. *Christmas Carol*?"

"Looks like the Grim Reaper to me." Sean gave me the once-over. "Is that supposed to be a costume?"

I felt deflated. "How can you not get it?" I did a full three-sixty turn for him.

"I jusht ashked her that," Foster slurred. He tried to drape an arm over my shoulder, missed, laughed and then fell on the floor.

Gross! "I'm Lois Lane, of course." I readjusted my borrowed cloche hat and moved my shoulder bag around to free up my right arm so I could take notes. I needed Annabeth, but she was still absorbed in her conversation with Gary, and I didn't even see her camera. My phone would have to do. I snapped a picture of Sean reaching down to help Foster back to his feet. I wondered who was helping whom as they both staggered a bit.

"This Daily Planet reporter just got her first scoop."

Sean looked dubious. "Scoop?"

"Well, party-pic then." And as interesting as it was catching the theatre department's star scholarship student behaving badly, I moved on. There had to be better stories somewhere.

****

Gary was beginning to regret his choice of Halloween costume. Why had he listened to Caryn?

"The Grim Reaper?" Tricia Palmer lifted an eyebrow as she assessed his attire.

"I'm not..." Gary pulled his mask off in

frustration. "It's supposed to be that character from *A Christmas Carol*. You know, Ghost Number Three."

"Huh," Tricia said.

Gary blew out a frustrated puff of air. "I see you borrowed Elizabeth Bennet's evening gown," he said. "Not too original on your part either."

Tricia smoothed her empire skirt down and dramatically tossed her hair back. "Good advertising."

"Tricia," said a Holly Golightly wannabe, "who's your Grim friend?"

Gary turned to see a tall, slender girl who was the spitting image of Audrey Hepburn in Breakfast at Tiffany's, puffing on an e-cig through a very long cigarette holder. He'd seen this girl at both the dorm and the bookstore and remembered thinking she was very attractive, not to mention height-appropriate. "Gary Riddell," he said, offering his hand to shake. "Aren't you—"

"Erica Stone," she replied as she declined to shake hands. "Pre-med."

"Gary's a freshman drama major," Tricia told her.

"Freshman, huh?" Erica wrinkled her nose, turned and left.

Puzzled, Gary watched her walk away. "What just happened?"

"Girl's out of your league, Riddell. Seventeen year old upper-class genius." Tricia scouted the room. "There's someone more your type." She pointed to a girl in 1940s cocktail waitress attire. "Third semester freshman, majoring in party."

"You obviously don't think too highly of me," Gary said. "But hey, Foster Benning's on the loose. Maybe he's your type."

Tricia snorted. "Not a chance. I've got my eye on him." She pointed to an Asian guy who was helping himself to Jell-O shots.

Gary pulled his mask back into place and turned on his heel. Erica was the hottest girl he'd seen all night and he wasn't giving up that easily. Even Caryn wasn't as attractive, and anyway she was entirely too short for his liking.

A few couples were slow dancing in the middle of the living room floor, despite the loud, fast-paced rock music. Sean in his cowboy get-up and Annabeth in her very short skirt and red cape were dancing *this* close. Gary didn't feel like pushing through the other dancers, loiterers and drunks to go join them, since he didn't know what he'd do when he got there except interrupt a private moment. Then he spotted Erica in a dark corner of the room, cuddled up to one of the varsity football players. Gary took his mask off and approached her, hoping she'd give him another chance.

"Hey, Erica, I think we may have gotten off on the wrong foot. I thought maybe—"

"Back off, buddy," growled football guy. He put an arm around Erica and balled up his fist like he was defending his territory.

Gary put his hands up in surrender and backed away. Anyway, his stomach suddenly growled long and loud. He vowed to try to talk to Erica Stone later, after she'd ditched her beefy athlete, and instead went in search of the kitchen.

After stepping into a couple of wrong rooms, Gary located the kitchen behind a set of saloon-style swinging double doors off the dining room. There Gary spotted Caryn taking cell phone pictures of Foster and

Barry Lansing, who were drunkenly mugging for the camera. Foster was trying to get a Jell-O shot into his mouth, but he was staggering so badly that he missed and landed with a crash on a nearby empty service cart. Barry was a little less drunk, but not by much.

Gary moved the cart aside. "You guys are gonna so regret this in the morning."

Barry shrugged. "Not like there was anything else to do." He reached down to help Foster off the floor, but Foster was too bleary-eyed and disoriented to stand. "I'm gonna go find this guy a bed and toss him in," Barry said. "Then I'm outta here." Barry hoisted Foster with an arm around his waist and the two of them staggered out of the kitchen.

Caryn glanced up at Gary, lowered her phone and sighed. "I'm done. The newspaper can only print so many pictures of drunk students before the administration gets on our case."

"I'm ready to bail, too," Gary said. The idea of finding Erica and trying to strike up a conversation was still in the back of his mind, but he figured that was a lost cause. At least tonight. "Can I walk you home?"

"I'm not your date," Caryn reminded him.

"Okay, fine. But the least I can do is leave you with Sean and Annabeth. They were dancing in the living room last I saw. After you."

Gary followed Caryn through the dining room, occupied by a vampire and a witch making out, down a deserted corridor and back to the living room. To Gary's surprise, the music was still playing loudly, but the crowd had disappeared. The only people left were Sean and Annabeth, and they'd moved to the sofa for some serious kissing.

"Weird," Gary said to Caryn as he surveyed the room.

Caryn stopped moving and visibly shuddered. "Uh-oh. I knew it."

"Knew what?" Gary asked.

Caryn shook her head. She hugged her arms tightly around herself as her eyes darted around the room.

"Seems kinda early for a Friday night holiday party to break up," Gary said. "Must be the weather."

"It's not the weather," Caryn insisted.

Gary studied her for a minute, but couldn't figure out what was going on with her. He never could understand women anyway. "Sean, Annabeth!" Gary called to the two lovebirds. "Come on, let's go. I guess the party's over because of that freak snowstorm."

Annabeth came up for air. "Killjoy!"

"I just told you, it has nothing to do with the weather!" Caryn stamped her foot, but then stopped and cocked her head to the side, listening to something only she could hear. She nodded and said, "Okay, it's partly the weather. But I'm not getting the whole story yet."

"About what?" Gary asked again.

Again she didn't answer, just kept staring off into space. She reminded Gary of when he was talking to a ghost. It always looked really weird to outsiders.

"You're both wrong," Sean said with a goofy grin as he pointed outside. "Party's not over. It's just relocated!"

Gary stepped to the large bay window that was the room's focal point, with Caryn right behind him. He peered out into the night and was astonished to see underdressed college students congregated on the cul-de-sac. "What's going on?"

"Someone said something about a snowball fight," Sean replied.

"Now we've got a story!" Caryn exclaimed. "Annabeth, got your camera?" Annabeth nodded and pulled it out from under her red cape. Caryn hooked her arm through Annabeth's and pulled her outside, Sean and Gary following close behind.

The snow had stopped falling, the clouds had cleared and the full moon was shining brightly, illuminating the piles of slushy snow that covered everything. The four of them stopped when they heard yelling and screaming coming from the end of the block.

The cold was biting. Gary pulled his robe tighter around himself and then glanced over at Caryn. "You need to go back inside and get your coat."

"No time. I don't want to miss this!" Caryn and Annabeth took off running in the direction of the increasing crowd noise.

Gary and Sean hurried after them, dodging slush bullets kicked up by the stampede. The crowd was moving en masse from the edge of the fraternity row cul-de-sac toward campus, with kids laughing, screeching, and throwing snowballs at the nearest human target. Gary ducked when Tricia tossed a handful of loosely packed snow at him. Erica Stone picked up a handful of slush and lobbed it at a staggering Barry Lansing. To get Erica's attention, Gary grabbed some snow, packed it down a little— enough to hold it together but not so tight it would hurt—and fired it straight at her.

"Hey!" she cried, turning around laughing. "You are so dead!" Erica was about to return his volley when she got hit again, this time by Spiderman. "And so are you!" She took off after him.

Gary groaned and watched his newfound crush chase off after another guy. He and Sean were still following the crowd, which was congregating on The Commons, when Kevin Michaels began pummeling Gary with loose snow. The guy can't even form a snowball, Gary thought, and frowned again when he remembered how he'd lost the part of Mr. Darcy to this idiot.

Gary stepped back and surveyed the scene. It may have started as a fun snowball fight with a few students getting drenched in melted snow, but it had quickly evolved into a whole-campus brawl. Snowballs were flying in every direction, stirring up a cloud of dusty mist that looked like a scene from a Peanuts cartoon. Gary did a full turn until he spotted Caryn next to Annabeth, who was clicking one shot after another from every angle. However, Annabeth wasn't the only one taking pictures, because cell phones were out everywhere, flashing like so many fireflies.

"Annabeth," Caryn shouted over the din, "hurry up and post as many shots as you can, before some of these amateur pics end up on social media!"

Gary got hit in the back with a well-aimed shot thrown by Erica. He grinned, happy to see her back again, picked up a handful of snow and returned fire. To Gary's chagrin, Sean jumped between them, scooping up ice and flinging it in her direction.

Erica threw up her hands and shouted, "I'm done!" She hugged her arms to her thinly-clad and now drenched body and ran off in the direction of the dorms as fast as her four-inch heels would carry her.

Gary sighed, but thought he might have made some headway with her.

At first the main snowball shooters were the fraternity guys still in Halloween costumes, but a few members of the basketball team had joined the fray and knew how to aim a shot, even if it was made of ice. Their main targets seemed to be a group of girls from one of the sororities. The girls fired back, giggling and squealing every time they got hit. Gary was one of the few students dressed for the cold, but with all the frenzied activity, he doubted anyone was noticing the frigid temperatures.

The full moon provided plenty of light and the snowball fight was escalating. Gary winced when Barry Lansing got smashed in the face with a zinger thrown by the softball team's star pitcher and one of his Ghost Stalkers club members, petite Karla Hansen. For a girl who screamed at every shadow and couldn't possibly be useful on a ghost hunt, her pitches packed a wallop.

"It's on!" hollered one of the Sig Zeta guys from the far end of The Commons. They united with the basketball guys, grabbing what snow hadn't already been tossed or melted, and drove the sorority girls back up against the wall of the administration building.

Soggy and exhausted students began yelling and egging on the combatants, anger replacing the fun. Caryn adroitly ducked when a snowball whizzed by her ear and then ran over to Annabeth's side, all the while dictating play-by-play commentary into her phone. Suddenly there were sirens and flashing lights moving toward them.

"Cops!" someone shouted. Students started running.

Sean and Gary came up behind Annabeth and Caryn. "Time to go," Gary said. "I mean like now!"

"Come on, Annabeth, he's right," Caryn said. "We've got enough for a front-page story."

Sean put his arm around Annabeth's shoulder and pulled her away. Students who hadn't already run for their dorms were backing away from the chaos as well, shaking snow out of their hair and dusting off their clothing. It looked like the impromptu fun was about to come to an end when Tricia Palmer screamed, long and loud. "Look! On the roof! A shooter!"

Caryn froze in place, staring at the spot where Tricia was pointing, which wasn't actually the roof but the dorm's twelfth floor open deck patio. "Ohmigod," she whispered.

Gary followed Caryn's gaze, but from where he stood he couldn't tell who was out on the balcony. There were shouts of "Run!" or "This can't be happening!" and "I'm too young to die!" Kids were covering their heads, running, screaming, and most of them getting nowhere due to the slippery mess all over the grass and sidewalks. The snowball fight that had started in fun quickly turned into mass panic. Everyone was pushing, shoving, and screaming, trying to get out of the way of the sniper on the balcony. The campus police—all five of them—were shouting through a bullhorn for everyone to get off The Commons.

The campus cops must have had the sense to call for backup, because seemingly out of nowhere the city's police force appeared in full riot gear. Gary grabbed Caryn and pointed to his phone, which had pinged with a campus-wide text alert.

—*Sniper on campus. Everyone take cover.*—

119

Caryn nodded as she checked her own message. She looked up onto the balcony again where Tricia had claimed to see a shooter, but no one was up there now.

"Sean? Annabeth?" Caryn screamed, visually searching the area.

Gary didn't see them either. "I'm sure they're..."

"Over there," said a voice behind him. Gary turned to see his "friend," the professor ghost from the 1950s, pointing to the bushes near the administration building. Sure enough, Gary saw Sean with his arms around Annabeth, both of them cowering in the corner.

"Thanks," Gary said.

Caryn was shivering, so Gary put his arm around her, pulled her in closer and hustled her over to where Annabeth and Sean crouched in fear.

Annabeth was white as a sheet, and Sean was in no condition to run for his life. He slowly stood up, wobbled, and then puked into the bushes. Gary's eyes darted all around but he didn't know which direction to go because the sniper could still be nearby, police were everywhere, and a helicopter with search lights was now circling low over the campus.

"Hold it right there," a voice behind them said. All four of them froze as they found themselves on the business end of an assault rifle.

Chapter 8

At least they didn't put us in a jail cell.

The four of us—me, Annabeth, Gary and Sean—were sitting in the police station lobby, all wearing our wet and bedraggled Halloween costumes.

The Belford SWAT team hauled in dozens of students after the snowball fight, but most of them were released within the hour, sent home to dry off and rethink their impulsive behavior. But I made the big mistake of opening my mouth based on a psychic hit I got, which was why we were cooling our heels in the waiting area.

Having a police officer point a high-powered rifle at you is unnerving, to say the least. "What are your names?" he'd asked us, a light shining right at us and his gun at eye level.

Of course we told him.

"Did you see the shooter on the roof? Can you describe him?" the officer had asked.

Gary, Sean, and Annabeth all said no, but that was when I'd stuck my foot in my mouth. "Tricia Palmer claims to have seen someone on the upstairs balcony, but she was just caught up in the moment. Trying to be dramatic."

The officer moved in a little closer to me. "And you know this how?"

I gulped but couldn't squeak out another syllable.

121

That, and Annabeth shot me a warning look, probably from years of hearing her attorney father tell clients to clam up.

A police station would have been an intimidating place under the best of circumstances, but at three o'clock in the morning it was positively creepy. Old-fashioned wooden chairs were lined up against a plaster wall that was painted institutional gray. The desk that the sergeant on duty sat behind was more of a barrier than a reception area, and he only looked up from his laptop when he had to answer the phone. A mug of coffee sat next to his elbow on top of an old newspaper. At least I thought it was old. Otherwise why would it be so crumpled? I would assume that there were other people around, those who worked the overnight hours, but if so, we didn't see them.

I whispered a few words of supplication to the Universe, to Uncle Omar, to anyone Up There who might be listening. Nothing. And I was seriously scared. Facing down the barrel of a rifle will do that to you.

Seemed like Sean was sobering up, but the number of Jell-O shots he'd consumed kept forcing him to sprint for the men's room down the hall, his cowboy spurs jangling. Little Red Riding Hood aka Annabeth dutifully went with him every time, standing outside with her ear pressed to the door.

I was over it. The stupid frat house Halloween party, the drunken make-out sessions, the impetuous snowball fight, all of it. It was a fiasco and all I wanted to do was go back to my dorm for a warm shower and bed. I was exhausted and cold, since I'd refused to take Gary's advice and go back for my coat in the fraternity house. And I was facing a long, cold walk back to campus. Sean was in no condition to drive, Gary didn't drive at all, and Annabeth's car was parked on campus. I leaned my head back against the hard, cold plaster wall to rest, and that was when I realized the borrowed cloche hat was gone, lost who knows where. I groaned in frustration.

"Excuse me," I called to the desk sergeant. "Are we under arrest?"

"No," he replied without even looking up from his computer. "But we can't let you go till your attorney gets here."

"Why do we need a lawyer if we haven't been arrested?"

The officer looked square at me. "You are a person of interest." Gulp. You'd think I would learn when to keep my psychic impressions to myself. Just then his phone rang. He picked it up, mostly listened since he was only able to get out an occasional "Yes, dear." He shook his head and hung up.

"So that was your wife reaming you out for holding innocent college kids in the police station all night. Right?"

The sergeant's head snapped up, that oh-so-familiar look of surprise on his face. "Uh…"

I smirked at him. Score one for the psychic. It didn't get us out of here, but it made me feel better.

"I'm never doing Jell-O again," Sean moaned as he returned from his latest trip down the hall. He collapsed into the chair next to me and leaned his head on Annabeth's shoulder.

"Good." I got up and moved to the chair on the other side of Gary to distance myself from Sean. The guy reeked of alcohol and vomit. I almost felt like gagging myself.

Gary turned to Annabeth. "Why isn't your dad here yet?"

"My father's out of town," she told him, causing me to groan inwardly, "but he said he's sending another attorney from his law firm to straighten out this mess." Annabeth threw her red cape over one shoulder, dug her phone out of a pocket and checked for a text. She shook her head in answer to everyone's unspoken question and was about to fire off another one, when the front door opened with a cold blast of air.

Eyes forward, Sean's father stormed up to the desk sergeant. "Where's my son?"

"Over here, Dad."

Dr. Paxton furrowed his brow as he turned to see the four of us sitting against the wall. "Sean, thank God."

"What took you so long?" Sean asked, wobbling to his feet.

Dr. Paxton hugged his son, then held him at arm's length with a scowl on his face. "I guess you aren't hurt since your sense of entitlement is intact, but we're going to have a long talk tomorrow about underage drinking." The doctor took a closer look at the broken blood vessels around Sean's eyes.

Sean blinked a few times and nodded.

Dr. Paxton walked over to the desk sergeant. "Is there any reason these kids are still here?"

Before the sergeant could answer, the front door opened yet again to admit a man with an air of authority about him. And I recognized him. Worse yet, he recognized me. He froze in mid-stride with that deer-in-the-headlights look on his face, and his body language pleaded with me to keep quiet. He was a client, so of course I'd respect his privacy.

Gary had been slumped in the chair next to me, but he glanced at the newcomer and stood up, jaw tight, fists clenched.

They're the same height, I thought to myself. My client had been dressed casually the day we met last summer when I did that reading for him, and tonight was no different. Or should I say this morning? He still looked fairly put together in starched jeans and a corduroy blazer, considering the ungodly hour. And then it hit me. Hard. I glanced at Ned, then at Gary, and then back. That was the son he was so concerned about, the one he was estranged from. Gary looked like a younger version of his dad, slender build, light blond hair, the same blue eyes. Maybe part of Ned's discomfort was not because he saw me, but because he saw his son. And judging from Gary's expression, he wasn't happy about seeing dear old dad, either.

Ned strolled to the sergeant's desk. "I'd like you to release my clients."

"And you are…?" the officer inquired.

"Their attorney. Ned Harrington."

Now Gary looked like he was the one who was gonna puke.

****

What the hell is he doing here? Of all the law partners Mr. Walton could have sent, why Ned Harrington? Gary was still in shock from having gone to an innocent Halloween party, gotten caught in a sniper's crosshairs, and then landed at the police station. And his father shows up to represent them? He pulled his Ghost Number Three robe over his head and tossed it on a chair in disgust.

The sergeant picked up his phone, spoke into it, and then calmly went back to his laptop. Gary figured it must be one fascinating game of solitaire. You'd think the guy would want to get in on all the excitement, considering the most serious crimes in small-town Belford, Indiana, were car break-ins and petty theft. Now Belford and Hamilton Liberal Arts College had a bona fide sniper, one who hadn't been caught yet. Gary still couldn't wrap his head around that one. And he and his friends had been sitting here for hours because of it. Wait. Is Caryn my friend? He didn't have time to think that through because a hall door opened and out walked Tricia Palmer in a now-soiled and rumpled empire dress, hand-in-hand with the Asian guy she'd shown interest in at the party. Tricia blew everyone a kiss with a sly smile and waved as she and the guy waltzed out of the police station.

Great. She sets off all the furor and then gets off scot free.

Another officer, dressed in a uniform and sporting a bullet-proof vest, appeared around a corner, spoke to the desk sergeant, and crooked his finger at them.

One by one they fell into line as he led them down the hall to an empty office. The officer stood aside to let everyone pass, then came into the room and shut the door. "I'm Captain Albers," he said, motioning for everyone to have a seat around the desk. "I was called to campus this evening to investigate the report of a sniper."

Ned remained standing. "Captain Albers, I can assure you that none of these young people are snipers.

You have no reason to detain them."

Captain Albers eased himself onto the edge of his desk, one leg dangling off the side. "Your clients were in the wrong place at the wrong time, Mr. Harrington."

"So were lots of other people, if the news reports are correct," Ned said.

"But we detained them because this young lady," the detective tilted his head toward Caryn, "was a witness."

"Mind if I record this?" Caryn asked, pulling out her phone and flashing her press badge. "I'm a reporter for the Hamilton Campus Herald."

Gary wondered why she wasn't more upset about being hauled in as an eyewitness to a sniper attack.

The Captain shrugged, so Caryn set the phone to record. "Your clients, Mr. Harrington," the Captain continued, "were brought here after Miss Alderson intimated that she had information pertaining to the shooter."

"And did she?" Ned demanded.

Gary figured Caryn had gotten some kind of psychic insight about that snowball fight, but he decided not to mention it. He was way too uncomfortable being in such tight quarters with his bio dad to want to stick around the police station one minute longer than necessary.

Caryn spoke into her phone and then held it out toward Captain Albers. "What have you discovered about the, uh, 'shooter'?"

The officer shook his head, a grim expression on his face. "I'm afraid what we had was a case of false reporting. Too much partying, an out-of-control snowball fight, and then mass hysteria with kids imagining things in the dark."

Ned crossed his arms, his feet firmly planted as if he were interrogating someone on the witness stand. "Who made this alleged false report?"

Captain Albers flipped open a notepad with handwritten notes and read from it. "A student by the name of Tricia Palmer. She claims to have screamed out that she'd spotted a shooter on the roof of the dorm, causing hysteria among the students and a number of 911 calls. Turns out she was referring to a snowball shooter by the name of Jake Chung. He'd gone to the balcony to take better aim at his classmates."

"Then I assume my clients are free to go," Ned said, relaxing his stance.

"Mr. Harrington's right, Captain. It's late," Dr. Paxton said, "and I need to get my boy home."

Captain Albers stood with arms crossed, frowning at Caryn. "Miss Alderson, you gave a statement to the officers that Miss Palmer was..." he flipped a few more pages in the notebook, "...being dramatic. How did you know that?"

Caryn held up her hands in mock surrender. "A girl recognizes a drama queen when she sees one. It was just my opinion."

"Be careful from now on when you voice your opinions," the detective warned.

Caryn nodded and put her phone away. Annabeth turned to her as they stood to leave the room. "Where's your coat, girlfriend?"

"Long story," she replied.

Annabeth lifted an eyebrow. "Then it's a good thing I called a cab." The two of them left for the lobby.

Dr. Paxton put a steadying arm around Sean's

shoulder and led him out. Gary was beyond ready to go, but he waited till Ned was at a safe distance ahead before venturing down the hall. He wanted to get out of the police station, yes, but he also wanted to avoid any further contact with his erstwhile dad.

"I've got my coat," Annabeth told Caryn, "so I'll go wait by the curb. You keep a watch for the taxi."

Caryn nodded and planted herself by the glass entryway. Ned walked up to her and quietly said, "Thanks for your discretion."

Discretion about what, Gary wondered, and how could they possibly know each other? He'd have to ask her another time, because right now he was fried.

Caryn shrugged but kept her eyes on the street. "Just don't forget you've got problems from another relationship to deal with, too."

Gary was stunned. "Hey, Caryn," he called out, "can we talk—"

Her cab must have arrived, because without another word, she was out the door. That left Gary and Ned standing in the lobby of the police station, staring at one another. Gary was tempted to just leave without a word, but his mother had taught him to be polite. He figured that included the father who had abandoned him. "Thanks for your help." Gary picked up his Halloween costume and turned to walk out the door.

"Wait, Gary," Ned said.

Gary stopped and turned around. "What?"

Ned now seemed very uncomfortable, completely different from the self-confident lawyer Gary had just seen. "I just thought..." Ned's voice trailed off.

"Thought what?" Gary looked his father in the eye, easy enough since they were nearly the same height.

"Could we go somewhere and talk?" Ned cast a sideways glance at the desk sergeant. "Privately?"

Gary was exhausted. It had been a very long night and this chance meeting was the last straw. Did Ned think he could just waltz in, save the day, and then expect all kinds of gratitude? Gary was angry at all the years he and Brenda had just scraped by while his father lived in the lap of luxury. Angry at all the time he could have spent getting to know his dad if only Ned had shown any interest. And now, according to what he'd overheard Caryn say, Gary was even angrier that Ned had another girlfriend somewhere and was more interested in her than in what should have been his family. Well, as far as Gary was concerned, it was too late. "No thanks," he growled, and started again for the door.

"Wait. Do you need a ride, son?"

Son? That tore it. "As far as I'm concerned, Ned, you're just a sperm donor." Gary could feel his face turning red and the veins in his neck about to pop. With a steely glare, he shoved open the glass door and walked out into the early morning air.

Chapter 9

Even on Saturdays, Gary didn't usually sleep in, preferring to use his free time to catch up on his studies. But after last night he'd made an exception. He yawned, stretched, and looked out his dorm room window. Miracle of miracles, the sun was shining and the snow was quickly melting. He glanced at the bedside clock. He didn't have much time before he had to get to *Pride and Prejudice* rehearsal and then to work at the bookstore. He needed a shower, strong coffee and some food before he could face any of it.

Gary had expected the dorm cafeteria to be nearly empty by this late on a Saturday morning, especially after last night, but instead it was freakishly crowded. Students were huddled in groups reading the campus newspaper, sipping coffee and whispering as they read. Gary went to the food line and poured himself a large cup of coffee and put in a to-go order for bacon, eggs and fruit. The bin that housed free copies of the newspaper was empty, so he had to look around to find a discarded one, on top of a sticky table as it turned out. Gary sat down, took a sip of his coffee and read the headline: SNOWBRAWL HOAX!

So that's what had captured the attention of so many students. And sure enough, there was Caryn's name just under the headline. Everything they'd been told at the police station last night—or rather a few hours ago—was detailed in her article. How she'd gotten the story written and into the paper so fast, he had no idea. It continued on the next page, complete with professional-looking photos by Annabeth Walton and a few that Caryn had snapped on her cell phone during the chaos.

"Not too shabby if I do say so myself."

Gary turned around to see a bleary-eyed Annabeth peering over his shoulder. "Think it's going to go viral?" he asked her.

"Already has."

Gary nodded and took another sip of his hot coffee. "Bad news travels fast in the social media age."

Annabeth plopped into a chair. She started to lay her head on the table but recoiled at the sticky filth. "Yeah, and it's generated a lot of chatter from kids who were actually there. The media even picked it up and were all over the college sniper story, but they dropped it fast once they got ahold of Caryn's story about it all being a hoax."

Gary offered up a toast with his coffee mug. "Seems like Caryn scooped them all. How very Lois Lane of her." He rolled his eyes at his own joke.

"I'll tell her what you said." Annabeth gave him the thumbs up sign. "But hey, don't forget we've still got that ghost hunt coming up. It might be an even bigger story."

Gary grimaced. "I was hoping that was postponed indefinitely."

"Unlikely," Annabeth said with a yawn.

"Your pictures are good." Gary pointed to the one she'd snapped just as Tricia had screamed "Shooter" and started the student panic.

"Yeah, pictures turned out great, and so did Caryn's article. She went to the newspaper office about five a.m. this morning." Annabeth winced at that thought.

"At least Caryn wasn't confronted by a deadbeat parent last night."

"Oh, you mean Ned?" Annabeth said. "Sorry 'bout that. I honestly thought Dad would send one of the junior associates, not a partner. How'd that go, anyway?"

Gary shook his head. "It didn't. I couldn't get out of there fast enough. Had to walk three miles back to the dorm."

Annabeth reached out and patted Gary's arm. "Sorry. Why didn't you say something? Dr. Paxton would've given you a ride."

"Order number seventy-three," a voice called over the PA.

Gary checked his receipt. "That's me," he said. "Speaking of Paxton, have you heard from Sean yet?"

"No. Probably sleeping it off at his parents' house. I'll text him later. Like me, he's eager to get that ghost hunt set up."

Gary groaned. Why had he thought the ghost hunt thing might just go away? He went to the register to pick up his food, swiped his card and left.

Gary couldn't believe play rehearsal hadn't been called off. Poor Foster Benning was wearing sunglasses indoors, had a baseball cap pulled low over his forehead, and took frequent sips from his water bottle. "Let's start from the top of Act Two," he croaked.

Gary didn't really feel too sorry for the guy since he had no one to blame but himself. Even though this rehearsal in the middle of Saturday morning had been scheduled before last night's fiasco, Foster didn't look like he was going to make it through. Gary sat down in the middle of a row of seats in the rehearsal studio, glancing at his *Pride and Prejudice* script between bites of his breakfast. Feeling confident enough about his lines, he stuffed the script into his backpack and tossed the heavy bag and the empty Styrofoam box on the floor by his feet. They landed with a dull thud, causing Foster to flinch and chug more water.

Gary hopped up onstage. The scene was with Tricia Palmer as Elizabeth Bennet, Delia Ferguson as her sister Jane, Gary himself as Mr. Bingley, and the arrogant Mr. Darcy, played by Kevin Michaels. Delia knew most of her lines, but after last night Tricia didn't appear to be in much better condition than Foster, and was still reading from the script.

"Tricia," Foster said in a barely audible voice, "isn't it time you were off book? Opening night is in a couple of weeks."

Good news as far as Gary was concerned. In a little over two weeks he'd be done with this Jane Austen farce. Well, Brenda was proud of him and would be in the audience, like she was for every play he'd ever been in, and he guessed Sean and Annabeth would be, too, but otherwise Gary hoped attendance was sparse. Despite all the pre-play hype, and some bad publicity no thanks to Caryn Alderson, it wasn't looking to be a runaway hit.

Tricia shaded her eyes from the glare of the spotlight. "I had a bad night, Foster. I'll get there by next rehearsal."

"Let's take a break," Foster said, just before

dashing out the door.

Gary sighed as Tricia and Delia sat down on the stage floor to run lines. He glared at Kevin Michaels, who was leaning against a wooden frame that was posing as the fireplace mantel, perusing his script. How that guy ever got the lead was a mystery. Kevin stood about half a foot shorter than Gary and was a little overweight, so he hardly looked like the handsome leading man all the girls were expected to swoon over. Maybe with the right costuming... Gary shrugged. He went back to his seat and thought about getting out his copy of the play, but decided not to bother, since he was way ahead of his fellow actors.

And he'd just found out some good news. Gary had stopped by the theatre department's bulletin board on his way in and had seen a call out for a January production of Macbeth. That was what he'd been hoping for, a lead in one of Shakespeare's tragedies. As far as Gary was concerned, that part was as good as his. Tryouts were right before Thanksgiving break, so he had a couple of weeks to get this silly rom-com behind him and focus on what was important.

Someone tapped him on the shoulder. "Mind if I join you?" Caryn didn't wait for an answer but sat down in the seat next to Gary and pulled out a notepad.

"What are you doing here?" Gary eyed her suspiciously, because the last time she'd shown up here, he'd found himself the focus of a very unflattering op-ed piece.

"I need to interview Tricia about last night." She said that loud enough that everyone turned to stare. Tricia put her script in front of her face, like that would hide her.

Gary breathed a sigh of relief. Caryn was out to get someone else this time.

"Oh, by the way, how did it go with your father last night?" she asked.

"You're the psychic. You tell me." To avoid letting any emotions show, he kept his eyes facing front toward the stage.

Caryn didn't say anything for so long that Gary was sure he'd gotten to her with that zinger, but finally she replied, "Since you asked, it didn't go well. And it won't, not until some other information comes to light."

"Like what?" Gary said a little louder than he intended.

"Can we please have quiet?" Foster growled as he ambled back into the studio.

Caryn smirked and put her finger to her lips to shush Gary. "If I tell you that," she whispered, "I deprive you of the fun of finding out."

Fun, huh? Gary couldn't imagine what could be fun about bumping into a father whose only contribution to his life had been disappointment. Not to mention how much Ned had hurt Brenda. That was unforgiveable.

"Gary, Kevin, let's go!" Foster called, then winced at his own loud voice and put the bottle of water to his forehead to relieve the throbbing.

Gary scouted out the rehearsal hall as he walked up onstage. "Benning, I think Kevin left," he said. "Want me to go ahead without Darcy?"

Foster threw himself into his director's chair, looking pale and sweaty, and buried his face in his hands. "No. I'm calling it. Let's all get back here tomorrow and start fresh."

"Fine by me," Gary said. He reached to the floor next to Caryn, hoisted up his backpack and threw it over one shoulder. "I have to get to the bookstore before Ellis fires me."

Caryn playfully poked Gary's shoulder. "I think we may have been the only two sober people at that party last night, and—"

"—and speaking of," Gary said, "what happened to that hat you borrowed?"

She sidestepped around Gary. "Hey, I gotta go grab Tricia. I'll see you next weekend at the ghost hunt."

Gary was thunderstruck. "Next weekend?"

"Check your email," Caryn called over her shoulder. "Hey, Tricia, wait up!"

****

Timing was perfect, since I didn't want to explain to Gary about that cloche hat. After leaving the police station, I'd changed clothes in my dorm room to the dulcet tones of Annabeth's snoring, before heading to the newspaper office to write my story. I guess I shouldn't have been surprised that the campus was eerie-quiet, but of course it was five a.m. after an all-night party turned-snowball fight-turned sniper hoax. Since my heavy winter coat was still at the frat house, I had to wear my lined jean jacket, which I'd pulled tightly around me as I walked across The Commons. Stray gloves, abandoned stocking caps, a lone snow boot, and a glittery cape were left strewn around, abandoned when the fight took an alarming turn. As I had picked my way through all the debris, I looked down and there it was—the borrowed cloche hat. I snatched it up, dusted the mud off, and stuffed it in my shoulder bag, hoping I could clean it up before

137

returning it. I truly felt bad about borrowing something from the theatre department with no one's permission, and then letting it get damaged. I wasn't Gary Riddell's biggest fan, but this wasn't his fault and I didn't want him to get in trouble for vouching for me.

I caught up to Tricia in the hallway, just before she darted through the main door that led out onto campus, probably to avoid me if I had to guess. I shoved my phone in her face. "I've got a few questions—"

"Yeah, I'll bet you do." Tricia had a scowl on her face as she reached for the door.

"So can you tell me—or I should say tell the readers of the Hamilton Campus Herald—exactly what you saw on the dorm's patio balcony last night, and how your comments were misconstrued?"

"'Misconstrued' huh?" Tricia snarked. "I saw what I saw, I said what I said, and if you want anything else, go talk to that police detective who took my statement."

"I already did. But I'd like to quote you directly."

"Look, Caryn," Tricia said, one hand on her hip, the other on the open door, "I'm not trying to be your ticket to big-time newspaper fame. So back off."

"Well, if you don't answer my questions," I said with a steady gaze, "maybe I'll just write about how you deliberately started that riot."

Tricia gasped and her eyes got real wide. "How would you know that?"

I smiled as sweetly as I could, considering all the trouble the girl had caused, and offered my hand as if to shake. "Caryn Alderson, psychic medium, at your service."

"What kind of newspaper reporter claims to be psychic?" Tricia huffed as she went out the door, but then leaned back in. "You and Gary the ghost whisperer are a coupla weirdos."

I blew out a puff of air and put my notebook away. I'd just have to go with the information I already had, which I'd mostly gotten from Captain Albers. I psychically knew that Tricia had deliberately chosen her words to elicit a reaction from the crowd, although I don't think she'd thought through the ramifications. But she was right about one thing—psychic hits didn't translate into news stories unless there were facts to back them up. Maybe it was time to let this particular story slide to the back pages.

That ghost hunt at the haunted Pelson Farm was looking like a better story opportunity. And then I remembered Uncle Omar's warning, that we'd find more than ghosts there. What could he mean?

****

Gary fervently hoped he didn't have to hear one more word about that stupid ghost stalking. He had too many balls in the air right now and he couldn't justify wasting time on it. Since it hadn't happened on Halloween, which seemed like the whole point anyway, he didn't see why the Ghost Stalkers couldn't just go hook up their EVP equipment and check out that old farmhouse on their own.

He hurried into the bookstore, clocked in and put on his apron and nametag. There was no hurry about helping customers, since the bookstore was practically deserted, so Gary took advantage of the relative quiet to pull up his emails on one of the computers Ellis reserved for checking inventory.

Sure enough, just like Caryn said, there was an email from Barry Lansing with the subject line "*Ghost*

Stalkers redux."
Gary:

Ghost Stalkers has rescheduled the Pelson ghost stalking for next Friday night. We're all meeting out there at nine p.m. Since so many people have seen The Lady in White on the premises, we need your expertise if our equipment doesn't pick up anything. Let me know ASAP.

Sincerely,
Barry Lansing, President

Gary sighed. He hit reply and said he'd be there since he'd already promised. There goes another perfectly good Friday night, he thought. He logged out of his email and went to the theatre arts department's online bulletin board. He pulled up the *Pride and Prejudice* rehearsal schedule and saw that he was called for a brief run-through next Friday afternoon. Hopefully Foster would dismiss early so he could get to whatever party he was going to and let the rest of the cast have their evening free.

Ellis came up behind him and tapped his shoulder. "What are you reading?"

Gary quickly switched the screen to the store's inventory spreadsheet. "Just checking what supplies to order."

Ellis lifted an eyebrow. "And the play practice schedule, too, I suppose." She grinned. "Relax, Gary, I'm not mad. It's not busy here today."

"Thanks, Ellis. I don't know what I'd do without this job."

"That scholarship money would have to stretch a lot farther, I guess," Ellis said. "It's a good thing I don't have you scheduled on Friday, because I hear the Ghost

Stalkers Club has you roped in as resident medium."

Gary sucked in his breath. "Ellis, how did you—?"

"Know you're a medium, or know the Ghost Stalkers pressed you into service?" She waved toward the coffee bar. "I read the campus newspaper and listen to the gossip."

"Ellis, I swear I'm not a medium," Gary said.

"Maybe you should quit arguing about semantics."

Gary's eyes opened wide when he realized Ellis didn't say that. Was there a ghost in here somewhere, or maybe he just imagined it due to lack of sleep? At first he wasn't sure, but then he caught sight of her for a second before she vanished. If this was a new ghost, newly dead or just one he hadn't seen before on campus, she looked to be about his mother's age. That gave him cold shivers.

He quickly averted his eyes, hoping Ellis couldn't tell something was bothering him. "I'll be straightening the storage room if you need me."

****

I'd been running on nervous energy for nearly twenty-four hours, so I was totally wrung out when I got back to my dorm after my aborted interview with Tricia Palmer. I finally had time to shower and then, spying my muddy clothes from last night that I'd stuffed in a plastic bag, reminded myself to drop them and the cloche hat at the dry cleaners when I woke up.

Annabeth was long gone, having gotten a reasonable amount of sleep, I guess. I hung up my jeans and sweater, pulled on some sweats, and collapsed onto the bed. It wasn't long before I drifted off.

I take hesitant steps as I approach that rickety old farmhouse. I gather my courage and get past the front porch and into the house. I brush aside cobwebs and nearly trip on buckled floorboards.

Music's playing. Not eerie music, but rock music. It's coming from…

"Back again?"

I turn around to see Uncle Omar. "What's going on here?" I demand.

"It's coming from the basement, Caryn. It's coming from…"

I jerked awake. I sat up, rubbed my eyes, and tried to remember the dream, but just like last time, it slipped away before I could get a handle on it. So frustrating.

I went to the bathroom and splashed water in my face, then returned to my bed. Instead of going back to sleep, though, I picked up my phone and punched in Mom's number.

"Caryn! What a surprise," she said.

"Mom, I'm worried. I keep having these dreams, weird dreams, but then when I wake up I can't remember a thing."

Mom was silent a moment. "Are you sure there's not something that sticks out in your mind?"

I sighed. "Nothing. Just a creepy feeling."

"Did you ask Omar?"

"I tried. He basically said it involves my life so I'd have to wait it out."

She chuckled. "Well, there you are. From the mouth of my very smart, dead brother."

I decided to just let it go, since I was too tired to try and puzzle it out. "Mom, did you see my byline in the Herald?"

We chatted about that adventure for a few minutes and then hung up. I was almost afraid to drift back to sleep for fear of having another nightmare. Almost.

****

When Gary got back to his dorm room at the end of his work shift that night, he found Sean sprawled on the bed, watching some sports recap on TV.

"You're looking a little better than the last time I saw you," Gary said. He tossed his backpack on the floor next to his bed, kicked off his boots and collapsed on top of the unmade covers.

"Dad gave me some crazy hangover cure. Tomato juice, Worcestershire sauce, a raw egg." Sean shuddered.

"Sounds disgusting." Gary stared up at the ceiling. He was so tired he could barely keep his eyes open.

"It was gross, but it worked. So did the long, boring lecture about underage drinking."

"I'm dead tired, Sean, so if you don't mind—"

"No problem." Sean reached for the remote and did some last-minute channel surfing, but just as he was about to turn off the TV, he landed on the campus's in-house information channel. "Hey, look at that!"

Gary peeked open one eye, but try as he might he couldn't get his eyes to focus on the screen. "What?"

"You know that kid that went missing a week or so ago? Eddie Carson? The kid still hasn't turned up."

Gary grimaced. "That sucks, but I don't get why you're so fascinated with it. Maybe you should ask Caryn to get a psychic read on the kid."

Sean turned off the TV. "Maybe. But they're organizing a search party for him in Belford. That was a public service announcement asking for student volunteers."

Gary closed his eyes. "When?"

"Tomorrow morning. First light."

Gary pulled off his jeans and slipped under the bedcovers. "I feel bad for the kid, I really do, but if I don't get some sleep…" He drifted off.

Chapter 10

I shaded my eyes from the glare of the early morning sun. At least the weather had improved, because it was a good thirty degrees warmer than it was two days ago. And most of the snow had already melted. "I can't believe you dragged me out at this hour, Annabeth." I checked the time on my phone. Eight a.m. "Besides, the kid's not anywhere around here."

Annabeth's head whipped around. "You sure?"

"One hundred and five percent."

She aimed her camera at the gathering crowd of volunteers. "Well then, where is he? All these people here are hoping to find him." She lowered her camera. "Or his remains."

I could see Annabeth was upset about the fate of this missing child, so I concentrated really hard to try to find an answer. I sighed. "I don't know where he is, but I do know two things: he's not here and he's not dead. That's all I can pick up. But keep your camera ready because this is a good human interest story."

"Ladies and gentlemen, gather around." Scott Tildren was standing on the top step of the city courthouse with a bullhorn, addressing the volunteers.

There must have been over a hundred people here—college students, parents with Belford Middle School kids in tow, police officers, high schoolers—all ready to begin what would be an exhaustive, and as I unfortunately knew, fruitless search.

A command center had been set up inside a police van parked near the courthouse, equipped with electronic equipment, phone lines and computers, and parked next to it was the EMT ambulance. Near the ambulance was a school cafeteria-style table with yellow and red water coolers, the kind you'd see at a construction site, and energy bars for the volunteers. Piled neatly on the table were hundreds of copies of the Missing Child flyer for those who didn't actually know Eddie, featuring his most recent school picture.

"We have about ten hours of daylight to conduct this search," Scott told the crowd. "Eddie was last seen after school at his bus stop, where according to an eyewitness, he climbed into a late model white pickup truck with an unknown driver. The police have reason to believe Eddie met with foul play." Scott paused until the concerned murmuring died down. "We will be searching the areas around the school, the bus stop, the nearby park, and the wooded area behind the baseball field. Please stay with your groups, watch your text messages for updates, and report any and all findings to either your team leaders, the police or myself." He leaned down to listen to the man standing near him, nodded and said, "Eddie's stepfather, Clyde Seville, wants to let all of you know how much he appreciates the support of the community." Scott shook his head sadly and stepped down. "Okay, let's get going," he said, motioning for the various team leaders to gather their groups of volunteers.

I watched Coach Tildren become more and more emotional, and I felt bad for him, but then a happy family scene popped into my head: Coach playing baseball, first with a toddler, then an elementary kid, and then a high school boy about fifteen or sixteen. I knew that he was thinking of his own son and imagining Mr. Seville's fear. At least I knew Scott Tildren was a good father. I wasn't so sure about Clyde Seville.

"Where's Sean?" I asked Annabeth as I scouted the area for a glimpse of him.

She pointed off in the distance. "He's the team leader searching the park across from the middle school."

"And where's Gary?" a voice behind us asked.

Both Annabeth and I turned around in surprise. "Oh, hi, Brenda," Annabeth said. "I didn't know you'd be here."

Brenda nodded. "I had to come, although I'm afraid of what we might find." She frowned as she studied the copy of the flyer with Eddie's picture on it. "I know this is crazy, but this boy reminds me of Gary when he was that age."

That comment was a teaser, sort of a hint of a psychic insight, but nothing I could focus in on. I glanced at Ms. Riddell and knew I'd been right about one thing, though. She was very young to have an eighteen-year-old son. My mom was mid-forties and Brenda Riddell was probably early thirties. She was pretty, too—medium height and slender, so Gary probably, no definitely, got his physique from Ned. Brenda's hair was much darker than Gary's, shoulder-length and pulled back in a sleek ponytail, allowing tiny pearl earrings to peek out. She was dressed in acid-washed jeans tucked into fur-lined boots, and a form-fitting cable-knit sweater underneath one of those white ski-vest types of jackets.

I stepped closer to Brenda for a look at the flyer she was studying. Eddie's hair was dark brown and Gary's a blond. I shrugged. "If you ask me, all thirteen-year-old boys look alike."

Brenda shook her head. "No, there's something..." She stared at it a little longer. "Maybe it's my imagination," she said as she folded the flyer and put it in her coat pocket. "I'm probably just feeling bad for the family."

"The only family he's got is that stepfather," I said, pointing to where Clyde Seville was in deep discussion with Scott. "And he gives me the creeps." The man kept shifting his weight from one foot to the other, staring at the ground or out into the crowd, and he never once made eye contact with Coach Tildren. He looked like an angry bulldog, all muscle and scowl.

"Did Gary know you were coming?" Annabeth asked Brenda.

"I sent him a text. I thought he'd be here by now." Brenda pulled out her phone and tapped in a message. "I'll try again."

"Gary's probably dead asleep. It's been a long weekend." I was also sleep-deprived, but at least I got up and came to help with the search effort. Yeah, okay, I was there to document the search effort, even knowing it was a waste of time. That thought caused my mind to sort of wander off as I tried to hone in on where Eddie really was. I still couldn't see anything and I didn't know why. Maybe solving mysteries wasn't my psychic thing.

Annabeth snapped her fingers in front of my face.

"Caryn? Did you hear me? We're joining the group searching the school grounds and parking areas." She tried to suppress a shudder before adding, "And we might have to go dumpster diving."

That got my attention. I cringed. "Yuk. Let's get this over with."

****

Gary finally woke up on Sunday around noon, awakened by his buzzing phone. He reached over to the nightstand and checked the message, which was from Brenda. Actually, it was one of five messages from his mom. The first one said she was joining the search for Eddie Carson and asked if he'd join her. Then the others got progressively more insistent that he either come help or at least text her back. He groaned, stretched out in the bed with his feet hanging over the edge, and pulled the covers up around his neck. Sean's neatly made bed meant he'd gotten up early and gone to volunteer. Sean had a lot of empathy for kids, probably due to Dr. Paxton's influence.

By this time of day, the search had been ongoing for hours, so Gary decided to skip it. Besides, he had tons of other things to do, like homework, a script to look over, and more importantly, that audition for Macbeth to prepare for. He threw the covers off and swung his feet over the side of the bed, yawned and stretched as he tried to get fully awake.

"Gary, you have to go look for Eddie."

Gary nearly jumped out of his skin. He stood up and did a complete three-sixty to try to locate the source of the voice, even checking the door to the hall to make sure it was still locked from the inside. If Gary hadn't felt the familiar tingle at the back of his neck he'd swear he was imagining things.

He yanked the blanket off the bed and wrapped it around him. "Whoever you are, you've got a lot of nerve invading my personal space!"

She didn't materialize. "This is important, Gary. Please go help."

"Are you the same person, uh, ghost, I saw at the bookstore yesterday?"

"I need your help," she repeated.

"You need to go to the light," Gary replied. But then he sensed she was gone. He sighed, ran his fingers through his bed-head hair and picked up his phone from the nightstand.

—*Be there in half an hour*—he texted Brenda.

When Gary arrived at Belford's town square, he couldn't tell if the search was in full swing or winding down, because there was hardly anyone around. There was a table that had a volunteer sign-up sheet on a clipboard, the pages blowing in the breeze, next to a large water cooler with empty and crumpled paper cups strewn on the ground near an overflowing trash bin. A few unused cups were still on the table next to a couple of stray flyers with pictures of Eddie Carson as a geeky-looking seventh grader, complete with crooked grin and disheveled hair.

Scott Tildren was deep in conversation with Ellis Garrett, the two of them huddled near the water cooler. As Gary approached, Scott looked up. "Better late than never, Riddell," he said.

"Back off, Scott," Ellis said, walking over and giving Gary's shoulder a hug. "He's had a rough weekend."

"Yeah, I heard about the snowball fight," Scott said

with a wink.

Gary ignored the reference to the ill-fated frat party. "I'm sorry I couldn't get here earlier, but..." Gary decided excuses were unnecessary. After all, this was a volunteer event. "Any luck? Finding the kid, I mean?"

"We had over a hundred volunteers show up this morning," Scott said, "and six hours later, nothing."

Gary had a sinking feeling about Eddie's fate. "I'd still like to help out," he said. "Is there anything I can do?"

"I've got some deli sandwiches in my car," Ellis said, "a donation from the Student Union sandwich shop. I'm sure the volunteers are famished. Would you mind, Gary?" She handed him her car keys and pointed to a faded and dinged-up red hatchback parked illegally on the town square.

"No problem," Gary said, taking the keys from her. Just then his phone pinged with a text and he pulled it out for a quick peek. "It's from Brenda." He saw the blank look on both Scott and Ellis's faces and added, "My mom. She says she's with a group searching the grounds around the middle school." He keyed in a reply and put his phone away.

"I'll straighten up this table and Gary can get the food set up for the volunteers who will be trickling back in soon," Ellis said.

With Ellis's keys in his hand, Gary headed to her car. He beeped open the hatchback door to retrieve three large aluminum trays of sandwiches, which were each wrapped tightly in cellophane and stacked one on top of the other.

"Shouldn't you get someone to help you carry all

that?" asked a female voice behind him.

Gary groaned as he set the trays back down. "You again?"

"I told you Eddie needs your help," she said.

"And I told you to cross over. You know you're dead, right?"

He hadn't really seen her yet. She'd only been visible for a split second at the bookstore and didn't materialize at all in his dorm room, but this time he got a good look at her. She was early forties maybe, not exactly young but too young to die, and dressed in what looked like a designer business suit and expensive shoes, the kind people pay hundreds of dollars for. Gary scrutinized her, hoping to figure her out before she vanished again. Whatever she'd died from, illness or injury, she looked okay now, just worried. Well, ghosts were always worried about something, otherwise they'd go straight to the light and leave him alone.

Gary turned his back on her and focused again on unloading the large trays of sandwiches. He peeked over his shoulder once to see if she was still there. She was. "Since you won't go, what do you want?"

"I want you to help Eddie."

"But you haven't said why." Gary set the three large trays on the roof of Ellis's car with one hand, closed the hatchback with the other, and locked the car with the remote. "Are you related to him?"

"That's not the point."

Gary groaned in exasperation. "Then what is the point? I need to know why you're stuck here because otherwise I can't help you."

"Can you please just help Eddie?" she begged.

Gary almost felt sorry for her, she sounded so

pathetic. "Look, lady, the kid might be dead for all I know."

"He's not. But he's in danger."

Gary rolled his eyes. "Okay, so if he's not on your side, quit worrying because there are tons of people out looking for him. They'll find him."

"It has to be you, Gary," she said.

He couldn't imagine why, but he didn't want to get into a long-winded discussion about her motives. He gathered up the trays of food and walked them carefully back toward the table, all the while hoping Ms. Ghost would leave him alone. But he could feel her right behind him. He set the food down, making sure the full trays wouldn't fall off the table, and then after looking over his shoulder to see if anyone was watching, he said, "Since you're so sure I'm the one to help the kid, maybe you could tell me where he is."

"Need some help there?" Ellis came up next to him and eyed the placement of the sandwich trays. She lifted the plastic wrap from each one for a quick peek to make sure the food had survived. Each tray contained a different variety: turkey and cheese, veggie, and tuna salad.

Gary looked over his shoulder and didn't see the ghost, so he figured Ellis must have scared her off. "Good riddance," he muttered.

"What did you say?" Ellis asked.

"Um, I said the food looks good."

The search party was called off by mid-afternoon. The crowd of volunteers had thinned considerably since the morning, but the ones still left were disheartened by their futile search. They reconvened on the courthouse square in defeat, dived into the fresh deli sandwiches, and then went for cups of water from the cooler. Some even managed to throw their trash in the bin instead of on the ground.

Brenda, looking exhausted and frustrated, came walking slowly back with Caryn, Sean, and Annabeth.

"Hi, Mom," Gary said, giving her a hug and a peck on the cheek.

"Hey, hon, thanks for coming." Brenda returned her son's hug and held on for a long time.

"Better late than never," Caryn said. "But it doesn't matter anyway."

"What's that supposed to mean?" Gary asked.

"Hey, food!" Sean picked up a sandwich and practically swallowed it whole.

Gary frowned at Caryn but turned to his mom. "No luck, huh?" The look on his mom's face said no and he could tell she was disappointed. Still, after his conversation with the ghost, he instinctively knew that Eddie was alive somewhere, which was a good thing. Maybe Caryn knew that, too, and that's why she seemed so unconcerned. Now if only the ghost had told him where the kid really was…

"That boy's vanished off the planet," Sean said. "Not a trace."

"No, he's—" Gary started to say.

"No, Eddie's fine," Caryn said at the same time. She and Gary exchanged glances. "What do you know?" she asked him.

"Not much, just some ghost lady telling me Eddie needs my help." Gary stopped when he saw tears in Brenda's eyes. She wiped them away with the back of her hand. "Mom? Are you okay?"

Brenda shook her head. "I don't know why, but for

some reason this missing boy has hit me hard. Maybe it's because he reminds me of you at that age."

"I don't see it," Annabeth said, picking up a flyer off the ground. "But middle school pictures are typically poor quality photography."

Caryn peered over Annabeth's shoulder. "That's some bad lighting," she agreed, stepping back, "but the kid will turn up."

Brenda turned to Caryn. "You keep saying that. How can you be so sure?"

Gary jerked his thumb at Caryn. "Mom, this is Caryn Alderson from Indianapolis. Psychic extraordinaire."

Brenda's eyes widened as she rounded on Caryn. "So do you talk to ghosts, too?"

"No, Mom," Gary said, eyeing Caryn, "but she does seem to know stuff."

"Folks, may I have your attention?" Scott Tildren stood up on the top step of the courthouse again to address the crowd with his bullhorn. "Clyde Seville, Eddie's stepfather, would like to say a few words to all the volunteers who came out today." He motioned for Clyde to join him.

Gary got cold chills just looking at the guy, who seemed less like a worried parent and more like an opportunist as he shifted his eyes and shuffled his feet. He was in his late forties, stocky muscular build, bald with a Fu-Manchu mustache, and wearing worn jeans with a faded flannel shirt over an old army fatigue-style T-shirt. Worse, Clyde was puffing on a cigarette, something that completely turned Gary off.

"That's Eddie's dad?" Brenda whispered in Gary's ear. "He looks…"

"Shady?" Gary finished. She nodded.

A camera crew from a TV station in Indianapolis shoved a microphone in Clyde's face. Caryn nudged Annabeth, who took aim with her camera, snapping shot after shot of the seemingly worried parent, while Caryn pulled out her phone and began recording.

"I'd like to thank everyone who turned out today to search for my poor missing boy," Clyde said, making eye contact with the camera a bit too long. "Please keep us in your thoughts and prayers."

"The man never prayed a day in his life," the female ghost said into Gary's ear.

Gary didn't turn around. "I take it you know him," he said to her.

"Who are you talking to?" Brenda asked.

"Some ghost who won't leave me alone. She's attached to Eddie somehow."

"Really? Do tell!" Annabeth's eyes lit up as she turned her camera toward Gary. She started to take a photo, thought better of it, and tapped her foot as she waited for him to fill her in on the ghostly details.

Gary ignored Annabeth, and instead turned to his mom. "I'm starved. Want a sandwich?"

Brenda shook her head. "This is too depressing," she said with a head tilt toward Clyde still mugging for the camera. "I need to get out of here. How 'bout Pizza Palace?"

"Sounds good," Gary said, getting nods of agreement from Sean and Annabeth. "Caryn?"

Caryn hesitated and looked like she was about to beg off, but Annabeth grabbed her by the arm. "She's coming. We'll meet you guys over there."

****

156

It had been a long, depressing day, and I was in no mood for pizza with Gary Riddell, but Annabeth hadn't given me any choice. We'd driven to the search in her car, and unless I wanted to either walk back to the dorm or call a taxi, I was stuck. And besides, my stomach was growling.

Annabeth started the motor, turned on the car's heater, and then cranked up the volume on the radio, which was tuned to a hard rock station. She flashed me a grin as she pounded the beat on her steering wheel while she drove down the four-lane, tree-lined boulevard through the residential neighborhood.

"Watch out!" I shouted.

Annabeth's head jerked back to the road just in time to correct her steering and avoid a head-on collision with an SUV. The driver blared his horn and flipped her off. "Oops," she giggled.

I reached over and turned down the volume. "What's got you so distracted?"

"Gary's new ghost, and I'm dying to hear all about it."

Of course. Annabeth and her obsession with the paranormal. I reached over and turned up the music again and we rode the rest of the way in silence. Verbal silence, that is, because the sounds coming from the radio were anything but quiet.

Annabeth easily found a parking spot right in front of Tony's Pizza Palace and shut off the engine. We were on the south side of Belford, an older part of town I'd never been in before. The pizzeria was in the center of a strip mall with a sign that should have read Mohawk Landing, but actually it said "Mo awk" because the h had fallen off, and the sign itself and the metal poles supporting it were in bad need of repainting. Next door to the pizza restaurant was a dog-grooming business, and on the other side was an empty storefront. It was early Sunday evening and most of the shops were closed, but then again, many of them were permanently out of business.

I got out of the car and surveyed the restaurant. "Are you sure this place is okay to eat in?"

"Yeah, it's got great food," Annabeth said. "My dad discovered it ages ago. It's a family owned place and we've been coming here for as long as I can remember." She linked her arm into mine and led me inside.

I looked around at the small space. "Kind of a stretch to call it 'Palace.'" However, the aromas were enticing, and I saw that the restaurant was clean and orderly. On a counter at the back was displayed a list of the day's specials handwritten on a chalkboard. The half-dozen tables were each covered with a clean red and white checkered plastic tablecloth and adorned with artificial flowers next to salt, pepper, and a shaker of parmesan cheese. Despite my initial hesitancy, I got a warm and cozy feeling about the place. In the corner by the window at two tables dragged together, I spotted Gary, Brenda, and Sean. My stomach rumbled loudly as I followed Annabeth to place our food order.

"Hi, Anthony," Annabeth said with a wink to the guy behind the counter. "Caryn, this is…"

"Tony, Jr. Yeah I figured."

"The usual?" Tony asked.

Annabeth nodded, but then turned to me. "I know you don't eat meat, but I always order the veggie pizza anyway."

I nodded. As hungry as I was, I would almost be willing to eat pepperoni. Well, almost, because that pepperoni used to be…

"Extra mushrooms, too," Annabeth told him. She pulled her credit card out of her back pocket.

He swiped her card and handed it back to her with a flirtatious grin. "It'll be right up."

"He likes you," I said as I followed Annabeth to the table to join the others.

Annabeth giggled. "I know. And he always gives me a discount, so I flirt."

We each pulled up a chair. Annabeth sat next to Sean, and I was forced to squeeze in between Gary and Brenda. I was beginning to get used to Gary, but I didn't really know his mom.

Brenda leaned on her elbow to face me. "Now, can you tell me how you know Eddie's okay?"

So we were back to that again. Sometimes when people find out what I can do, they won't let anything drop. I guess that's the life of a psychic. But for once, I didn't really have a good answer for her. "Just a feeling, that's all."

Brenda's face registered surprise. "How do you even know that much? I mean, how do you get your information?"

People were forever demanding to know the hows and whys of my psychic hits. It was just so hard to put into words, to explain how it happened, and even harder when they were nonbelievers. But maybe Brenda wasn't a nonbeliever, since her own son talked to the dead. "What happens is I get a churning in my stomach, a buzzing in my right ear, and then when I close my eyes there's a movie running on fast forward in my head."

"Sorta like how I know there's a ghost nearby," Gary told his mom. "The feeling on the back of my neck."

Brenda seemed to give that some thought.

Annabeth giggled and punched Sean in the ribs, who winced. "This is so cool. I'm used to Caryn's sixth sense, but now there's two of them."

"Annabeth," Sean said, rubbing his side, "you know Gary's not psychic."

"Yeah, but it's still fun to watch the two of them do their things."

Gary and I exchanged puzzled glances. "Our things?" I asked Annabeth.

Brenda put up her hand to halt the fan adoration, for which I was grateful. "Caryn, I can imagine it's not easy to explain. I've heard Gary try to put it into words all his life. Could you just tell us what you're seeing about Eddie's whereabouts?"

Okay, I decided to try again. I closed my eyes, opened my energy, and focused in really hard. This time I got something. "It's a small room. Really small. All white, no decorations or anything. There's a bed, or really just sort of a cot. No windows, cold but not unbearable, with only one door in and out."

Brenda gasped. "Has he been kidnapped? Can you tell if he's been harmed?"

I shook my head and opened my eyes. "I'm sorry, but that's all I got."

"Here you go, Annabeth," Tony said as he set her pizza down in front of her. "Order for Paxton?" He set another large pizza, dripping with greasy pepperoni and sausage, in front of Sean, Gary and Brenda.

"That used to be a pig you know," I said, wrinkling my nose at the meat-laden pie they were about to dive into.

Gary smirked as he picked up a slice, pretended to toast me with it, and took a large bite.

Brenda rolled her eyes. "I know, right? Boys. It's what they always order when they come here."

"Here, have some of ours," Annabeth said, shoving the veggie pizza toward her.

Tony returned with plates, napkins, and five sodas, and winked once more at Annabeth. "Enjoy."

The food was hot and delicious, and handmade with skill. I wondered how I'd never heard of this place before. I also enjoyed talking to Brenda Riddell, who was smart and could talk about anything from sports to Shakespeare. It was obvious how close she was to Gary. Sort of like my mom and me.

Then I remembered Ned Harrington and how dejected he was at not having a relationship with Gary, and I felt bad for both Gary and Ned. I didn't know what I'd do if I didn't have all three of my dads in my life. It crossed my mind that maybe there was something I could do to get the two of them talking, but right now I couldn't think of what that would be. Besides, we were all having so much fun eating, talking about school, Colts football, and the upcoming Thanksgiving holiday, that I forgot all about their father-son estrangement.

Chapter 11

The next week was hectic for Gary, so crazy in fact that he lost track of the days. He was either in class, in the library, at work or at a rehearsal. Even lunch breaks were sporadic. The cafeteria lines were too long and he couldn't spare the time, so he'd started hitting the vending machines in the Student Union between destinations. One good thing about this frenetic schedule was that he was too busy to let any ghosts bug him. He'd seen a couple on campus but had ignored them and they'd been polite about it. And since that persistent ghost from last Sunday hadn't been around, he hoped maybe she'd taken the hint and crossed over.

But after days of this nonstop activity and hit-or-miss eating, the rumbling in his belly forced him to slow down and seek out a proper midday meal. He got in the queue line at the dorm cafeteria, and while he waited he whipped out his *Pride and Prejudice* script to read through his lines for this afternoon's run-through. Opening night was one week away, and even though he had his part pretty well in mind, it never hurt to review. Unlike his ease with all things Shakespeare, Gary still felt uncomfortable with this formal nineteenth century dialog.

"Hey, buddy, you're holding up the line." The cafeteria server impatiently tapped her metal spoon on the serving dish.

Gary's head snapped up from his script. "Oh, sorry," he said. "I'll take the hot meatloaf sandwich. Lots of gravy."

He shoved his script in his jacket pocket, took the plate of food from the server, and scooted his tray to the end of the line to swipe his meal card. He scouted the room for an unoccupied table while picking up eating utensils and a bottle of water.

It was Taco Friday, meaning the cafeteria was packed with Tex-Mex lovers, and Gary didn't see anyone he knew well enough to crash their table. He was about to give up and ask for a to-go box when he spied Caryn Alderson sitting alone, way too close to the front door and its chilly wind to his liking, but it was a place to sit. Gary just hoped she wasn't saving the empty seat. He walked over and tapped her on the shoulder.

"Mind if I join you?"

Caryn looked up from her phone. "Uh, okay, I guess so." Empty dishes of tacos and guacamole were on the table, but she quickly gathered them up and stacked them on the tray in front of her. "Actually, I was done, so…"

Gary set his food tray down and pulled out the chair across from her, which made an annoying scraping sound on the linoleum. "Got a one o'clock class?"

Caryn glanced at the time on her phone. "Yes, and I've still got tons to do before we go tonight."

Gary took a bite of green beans, decided they were too mushy, and shoved them aside with his fork before tucking into his open-face meatloaf sandwich. "Where are you going tonight?" He didn't even make eye contact. He hadn't realized how hungry he was.

Caryn lifted an eyebrow as she watched him devour his food. "You must have skipped breakfast," she said. "That mystery meat…"

Gary held up a hand to stop her while he swallowed his food and chased it with a healthy amount of water. "Yeah, I know, it's not Mom's, but any port in a storm."

"Your mom's a good cook?"

Gary nodded. "Self-taught gourmet. She spent a lot of time watching The Food Channel in the middle of the night when she was trying to do schoolwork with a cranky baby on her lap."

Caryn rested her arms on the table and leaned in a little closer. "Do you have sibs?"

"No. I used to wish I had a little brother, but it's just Brenda and me. You?"

"Nope."

Gary went back to his food. "Where's your dad?"

"In Houston. He's an actor," she said, as Gary gave her two thumbs up, or rather one thumb, one fork. "Luckily his partner has a decent job, 'cause when my dad's not working, he's a waiter at a country club." The smile drained from her face. "I miss him. I only get to see him once or twice a year."

"At least your father cares about you. My bio dad lives in the same town and I never see him."

Was that a sympathetic look Caryn just gave him? Gary couldn't tell. She stood up, rewrapped her scarf around her neck, and picked up her tray to return to the conveyer belt. "I guess I'll see you later."

Gary set his fork down. "Why would you see me later?"

Caryn rolled her eyes, and Gary realized the aloof, investigative reporter Caryn was back. He sort of liked Vulnerable Caryn better.

"Ghost Stalkers?" she said, her voice turning the statement into a question. "At the Pelson farmhouse?"

Gary slapped his forehead. "That's tonight? I've been so busy this week I completely forgot." He groaned and ran a hand through his hair. "I have a rehearsal this afternoon that might run late."

"You can't weasel out now, Gary. There's something big going down and you have to be there."

Gary gave her a puzzled glance. Was that a psychic prediction or just a reminder that the Ghost Stalkers needed him?

"Text Sean for a ride," Caryn said over her shoulder before she sailed out of the cafeteria.

****

As I walked across campus, I went over that last remark I made to Gary. The punch-to-the-gut images in my head had barely started before I blurted that out. When I was younger, I was always spouting psychic stuff before thinking it through, but as I've gotten older and more comfortable with my abilities, I've been able to keep a lid on it better. But telling Gary he was about to be involved in something big tonight felt like the old, immature and insecure Caryn. Why did I do that? Especially since I didn't know the whole story yet. I shook my head and kept walking.

Photography wasn't my favorite class, to say the least, but it was a requirement for the journalism degree, and at least I had Annabeth in there with me. I'd always considered myself a pretty decent artist with paints or charcoal, but my photographs never measured up. Luckily Annabeth was always willing to give me pointers, or better yet, edit my shots so they might actually make a presentable portfolio for the class's final project.

"I can't believe there are only four weeks left before finals," I said as I dropped my bag on the floor next to the desk where I always sit.

Annabeth was already in her seat, notebook and pen ready to take notes, and passing the time by flipping through some recent shots on her camera. "Yeah, the semester's gone fast." She put her camera aside and readjusted the beret on her head, stuffing a few stray brown hairs back under it. "Are we still picking you up tonight?"

I took off my faux down jacket and hung it on the back of the chair. "If you don't mind. Have you heard from Sean?"

Annabeth shook her head. "Why?"

I dug my notebook and pen out of my bag. "I sorta had lunch with Gary. He needs a ride, too."

"How do you 'sorta' have lunch with someone?"

"Table shortage. He just hijacked the empty chair across from me. It's a good thing, too, because he'd forgotten about tonight. I had to remind him of his date with a translucent lady in white."

Annabeth burst out laughing, loud enough to draw the attention of a few students on the other side of the classroom and the professor who had just walked in. He scowled at her over his glasses as he set his briefcase on the podium.

"Sorry," Annabeth told him, stifling the rest of her giggles.

Once I was sure he wasn't watching us, I

whispered, "The only reason I'm going to this stupid ghost hunt is for the byline Del promised me. And the hope that you'll catch some unexplained orbs on camera. And maybe find out what's been psychically bugging me lately."

"That's three reasons."

"Yeah, okay. But otherwise I'd spend the evening in our room, catching up on old episodes of 'Monica the Medium.'"

Annabeth's eyes lit up. "Ooh, that girl's so cool! Wait till you see—"

The teacher loudly cleared his throat. "Ladies and gentlemen..."

Voicing my premonitions sent my radar into overdrive. I tried listening to the professor's lecture, but I couldn't concentrate. So instead of taking notes on correct lighting, I scribbled notes about my psychic impressions. I sketched out a farmhouse from the picture in my head and from my nightmares, drew a ghost hovering over it, and then shaded in areas to represent the night-vision cameras that the Ghost Stalkers Club would set up. I scrutinized the sketch and couldn't figure out what was missing. Then it hit me! There's got to be a basement in that house, and my senses were telling me that was where we'd need to look.

****

Gary hurried into his dorm room after his rehearsal, which did run late. It was seven forty-five and Sean had texted him to be out front of the dorm no later than eight if he still wanted a ride. He took a quick shower and threw on some old jeans and the paint-stained sweatshirt he always wore while working on the sets in the production room. Crawling around a dirty farmhouse was a good enough reason to wear clothes he wouldn't ruin, and besides, ghosts didn't care what he wore. But then he thought about how Caryn had turned up her nose at his attire the day they'd bumped into each other on campus, and for some reason that gave him pause. Gary didn't know if he was prompted by vanity or just the fear of what Brenda might say if she saw him dressed like this in public, but whichever it was, he hurriedly threw off his stained clothes and changed into a pair of almost new 501 jeans, a clean flannel shirt, and boots. He decided to forego his baseball cap in favor of a stocking cap to ward off the chilly autumn air, fished gloves out of his coat pockets, zipped up the jean jacket and headed out.

The elevator stopped on every floor on the way down to the lobby, picking up Friday night revelers. Gary tapped his foot and repeatedly pounded on the lobby button, as if that would make it descend faster. He thought about sending Sean a quick text but by then the elevator was so crowded he couldn't dig into his pocket for his phone.

"Yo, tall guy," a girl in three inch boots said. "Chill. We'll get there when we get there."

Gary turned around and recognized Erica Stone. Great. A girl he still hoped to impress, and here she was observing his display of temper. He only had a minute to undo the bad impression, but he smiled and decided to go for it. "Where ya headed tonight?"

"Girls night. What about you? Hot date with a ghost?" Erica gave him a very obvious and very rude once-over.

Gary could feel his cheeks flushing. "Uh..." He

was usually quick on his feet with conversation. Heck, he could quote Shakespeare on cue or chat up the dead like old friends, yet this girl left him tongue-tied.

Erica shook her head and whispered something to the girl next to her, and both of them burst out laughing. "How are you still single?" she asked with a roll of her eyes.

His heart sank when Erica and her friend marched off the elevator without giving him a backward glance. Gary tried to remain stoic so that no one could see that her last remark stung. She was really the first girl he'd found interesting since enrolling at HLAC, but maybe Tricia Palmer was right. Erica Stone was way out of his league.

Annabeth's car was idling in the loading zone, and when Gary walked out through the double glass doors onto the circular drive, he could see Sean sitting shotgun. He opened the back door of her compact sedan and slid in sideways, pulling in his long legs and scrunching them up behind Sean's seat, which was pushed as far back as it would go.

"You're late," Caryn said.

Gary glanced at the dashboard clock as he fastened his seatbelt. "Five minutes." When she didn't respond, he added, "Sorry, rehearsal ran late. We open next weekend, you know."

"I'm counting the days," Caryn muttered.

Gary glowered at her, then turned to the window. Silently staring into the night was preferable to being insulted about his acting. Again.

Annabeth checked her rearview mirror, put the car in Drive and pulled out. "Hey, Gary, Ghost Stalkers are counting on you to do some serious ghost whispering tonight."

Gary kept a steady gaze out the window. "Only if the ghost cares to chat."

Sean turned around sideways in his seat and peered around the headrest. "I don't know why you're so sure there's only one."

"There is only one," Caryn said. "We both already told you that."

Gary glanced over at her. One thing was certain: she seemed to have his back on this point at least. He had to admire that.

"Ooo, I hope you're both wrong," Annabeth said, fairly jumping up and down in her seat. "I want to see lots of ghosts."

"You don't see them at all," Caryn reminded her.

"Okay then, capture their orbs on camera," Annabeth huffed.

By the time they pulled onto Highway 38 it had started to rain, causing traffic to slow. They rode along in silence, broken only by the slap-slap of the windshield wipers, the whir of the heater vent, and occasionally the ever-chipper Siri. A couple of times Annabeth had to brake to keep her distance from the car in front or come to a complete stop as traffic backed up in the ensuing downpour.

Sean leaned as far forward as his seat belt would allow and wiped at the foggy windshield with the sleeve of his jacket. "We're going to be late, Annabeth. Any way out of this traffic?"

"Not that Siri knows of," Annabeth sang back.

Gary almost said "Who cares?" but stopped himself. He'd made a commitment, adjusted his whole schedule around this ghost hunt, so he wanted it done.

Sooner rather than later.

"Turn left in one hundred feet, onto Conner Road," Siri instructed.

Annabeth made her turn off the highway and onto the one-lane road. "See? No problem." The rain had slowed to a drizzle, but fog was setting in. She switched her headlights to bright and inched her way down the long driveway toward the farmhouse, which sat majestically overlooking several acres of land.

"You have arrived at your destination," Siri announced.

"Thank you, Captain Obvious," Sean replied.

There were lots of cars and SUVs already there, as well as a late model red sports coupe with the Ghost Stalkers' banner flying from the radio antenna. "Whose car is that?" Gary asked, pointing at it.

"That's Barry's," Annabeth said. "Nice, huh?"

I'll say. Gary drew his lanky frame out of the backseat of the compact car, shook out his legs and stretched his arms overhead. Caryn hopped out the other side. Gary glanced at her over the roof of the car, thinking he might strike up a conversation about…well, he didn't know what, but it didn't matter. She seemed distracted. Besides, they weren't here as friends, if their relationship could even be considered a friendship. They were just here to do a job.

Sean and Annabeth got out of the front seats and Annabeth beeped open the trunk. Sean grabbed two large plastic grocery bags filled with snacks, and held them aloft. "Fortification for a long night!" he said with a grin.

The sight of the junk food made Gary's stomach rumble. It had been awhile since his mystery meatloaf lunch and he'd never had time for dinner. Not that chips and cookies would fill him up, but it was better than nothing. "So who all is supposed to be here tonight? You've got enough empty calories there to feed a small army."

"Barry, of course. And Scott Tildren, 'cause the Ghost Stalkers' sponsor has to be here. And the production crew," Sean said. "Mike Donovan, Karla Hansen, and Sydney Marshall. They got here early to start mounting night-vision cameras in strategic spots along the walls, and set up the EVPs."

"Karla's here?" Annabeth seemed surprised. "She doesn't know the first thing about the cameras. And she screams at every little shadow."

"Barry thinks she's cute," Sean replied. "And he likes that her squeals make the ghost stalking seem spookier."

Gary blew out a puff of air. He hadn't realized this would be quite as big a deal as it was turning out to be. "All to chase off one stubborn old lady ghost?"

"That's not all that's in this house," Caryn said.

"Wait, what?" Gary wanted her to clarify, but she'd already darted ahead to the porch.

He hung back, squinting up at the house to get a feel for it. Back in the nineteenth century this must have been quite a showplace, but time and neglect had taken its toll. The only exterior light was one low-wattage bulb in a fixture on the porch, so all he could really tell was that the house was a large two-story wooden structure in the gingerbread style that was popular back then, and in bad need of repair. It must have had an elegant wrap-around porch at one time, but now most of the lattice work was either rotten or broken off. The wooden porch floor was uneven and had boards missing, and the three front steps were completely detached and probably unsafe. Oddly enough, the porch swing was still intact, although it needed a coat of paint and new chains to replace the rusty ones that attached it to the ceiling. The whole house could use a coat of paint, and it definitely needed new shutters, since the ones still there were hanging askew. Windows dotted both the main floor and upper floor, with torn lace curtains visible upstairs. Strewn around the property were unopened packages of roofing tiles and pine boards for repairing flooring, evidence of a construction project halted midway, probably because of the ghost situation. Gary hurried to join the others. He opened the door to let the girls go ahead of him and Sean, but Caryn balked.

****

This was the very house I'd been having nightmares about. In my dream it looked creepier, because dreams can distort the truth, but still, this was it. "Give me a minute, guys," I told them. "I need to commune with my…" I caught Gary looking at me askance. "My uncle," I said in a huff. Too bad if he thinks it's weird I have a spirit guide. Right now I need him.

The three of them shrugged and stepped into the house.

"Uncle Omar," I whispered. I glanced around to see if anyone else was watching me talk to the porch swing. Just in case, I pulled my phone out of my pocket and put it to my ear.

"You rang?"

Always with the jokes. "What do I need to know

about this place?" I asked him.

"Welcome to the Pelson Bed and Breakfast," Uncle Omar said. He materialized into full view, lounging on the porch swing, his feet propped up like it was a balmy summer day.

"What am I supposed to do?" I asked him via my phone.

He winked. "Stick with the ghost whisperer for starters. Everything else will fall into place." And he disappeared.

"Uncle Omar!" I stamped my foot and lowered my phone. "Will you at least stick around in case I need you?"

"Always," he said in my right ear.

****

"Not too bad," Gary said, surveying their immediate surroundings. "Looks like the workers got started on some of the renovations before the ghost ran them off."

After stepping in from the dilapidated porch, Gary, Sean, and Annabeth walked into a well-lit and warm front hallway. Off to their right was the living room, or family room, or parlor, or whatever they called it back in the day. Some demolition had taken place in there, too. The ceiling beams were exposed, the brick around the fireplace had been torn down, and the wooden mantel had been removed and was now propped against a wall, waiting to be reinstalled. The hardwood floors were in need of cleaning and polishing, but not buckled or broken or rotted. But Gary could see that a lot more work would need to get done before Ms. Pelson could open this place up to guests. After the ghost was evicted, that is.

"Everything okay?" Annabeth asked Caryn.

Gary turned to see her walking in the door, a grim expression on her face. She must have already sensed something, judging by the way she'd dismissed him on the porch. As for his own abilities, Gary had enough experience to know that no self-respecting ghost would materialize with all these people around.

"Fine," Caryn said.

"I'm heading to the kitchen," Sean said, indicating the snack-laden bags.

Loud voices were coming from down the hallway, so Gary, Caryn, and Annabeth followed the sound through the living area and into what had once been a spacious and luxurious dining area, with lots of wooden ornate trimmings on doors and windows. Now everything was covered in dust and the yellowed and flowery wallpaper was peeling off. There was no furniture to speak of, just some folding chairs and an old TV tray. Gary removed his stocking cap and gloves and stuffed them in his coat pockets. Caryn unbuttoned her jacket and shook the rainwater off her faux leather boots. Annabeth unwound her scarf to free up the camera dangling around her neck.

Out in the hall, Barry was supervising Mike, Sydney, and Karla as they untangled cords and plugged EVP recording devices into an old-fashioned outlet. Just as Gary was thinking that didn't seem safe, there was an ominous buzzing. Barry quickly dropped the extension cord and pulled his hand back from the electrical shock, shaking it vigorously to relieve the pain.

"You okay, man?" Gary asked.

"Damn knob and tube wiring." Barry growled.

"Try a different plug, guys," he told his crew. He walked over to the four of them, still rubbing his hand. "Hey, glad you could make it, Gary. We were afraid the ghosts would scare you off."

"Ha ha." Gary started to reach for Barry's right hand to shake, but that was the sore one. Embarrassed, Gary withdrew his hand and stuffed it in his jacket pocket.

Scott Tildren emerged from the kitchen with a travel mug of steaming coffee in his hand. He held it up and tilted his head in the direction of the kitchen. "There's a fresh pot if anyone wants any. Might be a long night."

Sean came out of the kitchen empty-handed. "And there's plenty of junk food if anyone gets the munchies."

Scott turned to Caryn. "And here's our campus psychic. Welcome!"

Barry folded his arms in front of his chest and shook his head. "She may be psychic, but officially she's here as press. We need media coverage, even if it's just the campus news rag."

"Gee thanks," Caryn said.

"The Herald is not a rag," Annabeth reminded them. "It's an old and respected publication."

"Respected enough for this story to get picked up by the wire services?" Barry asked with a glint in his eye.

Scott frowned at Barry and turned to Gary. "Is she your girlfriend?"

Gary and Caryn exchanged surprised glances. "No way," Gary said, as Caryn shook her head.

Barry watched them looking at each other. "Uh-huh."

Caryn scrunched up her face and turned her back on Barry. She started punching buttons on her phone, then held it up in the air, trying all angles. "No signal?" she asked Scott.

"The house hasn't caught up to twenty-first century technology," Scott said. "None of us can get any bars. I guess that means we're off the grid for the night."

"Well, that's just great," Caryn said, powering down her phone and shoving it in her pocket. "How am I supposed to file my story? The whole campus knows Ghost Stalkers is here, so our readers will be eager to read about it in the morning edition."

"Don't worry, Caryn," Annabeth said. "I'll post some photos on social media when we get back to civilization, and then you can write your story. It'll be online by breakfast."

Gary was starting to sweat in the overheated house, or maybe he was just getting nervous about this whole thing. They all expected him to conjure up the ghost and talk to her, possibly on video, and Gary knew that wasn't the way it worked. He took off his jacket and tossed it on a folding chair. "So what do you guys need me to do?"

"Right now you can just familiarize yourself with the house, because once we go dark it gets more challenging." Barry checked his watch. "And that should be soon."

"Annabeth and I are gonna stake out some places where she can get the best shots." Sean took her by the hand and led her down the hallway.

"Just keep it professional!" Barry called after them. "Gary, take Caryn with you and go see if you two get any psychic hits."

Gary could feel his blood pressure rising. These electronics-dependent amateurs just didn't get it. "For the last time, I'm not a psychic. And she's not a ghost whisperer."

Barry waved his hand in annoyance at both Gary and Caryn. "Semantics. Maybe you two need to figure out how to collaborate, because we have a job to do here. Ms. Pelson's depending on us. Capiche?"

"Got it," Gary growled. He put his hand in the small of Caryn's back and directed her toward the entryway. Once they were out of earshot, he said, "Sorry 'bout that. That guy just rubs me the wrong way." Caryn nodded her agreement. "We may as well go upstairs and see what we find. You ready?"

Caryn closed her eyes and stood perfectly still for a few seconds. "I'm all ears, so to speak. And you need to keep a lookout for the ghosties."

"Don't worry, they—she—will find me."

A staircase near the front door led up to what Gary assumed was the second floor bedrooms. "This way." He stopped halfway up the rickety stairs and turned to see Caryn hesitating at the bottom. "They creak but they're sturdy," he told her as he bounded the rest of the way up. "See? They don't build 'em like this anymore."

Caryn tried the first step, found it solid, and inched her way to the top, hugging the wobbly handrail all the way. Once at the top, they both peered down an expansive hallway, but it was hard to see anything with only one old-fashioned light fixture in the center of the ceiling. Its low wattage bulb cast eerie shadows on the walls. She shivered. "Gary, there's something in this house…"

Gary winked at her. "Don't worry. Ghosts only hurt people in the movies."

"No, that's not what I meant." She hugged her arms tightly around herself. "There's something human we need to watch out for."

Gary was reaching for the nearest doorknob, but he stopped to face Caryn. "Any idea what?"

She shook her head. "Not yet."

Gary went back to opening doors. Four of them led into empty bedrooms, one was a storage closet, and the last door opened onto a bathroom where something rustled under a pile of plaster that had fallen off the walls.

"Ugh! What is that?" Caryn squealed.

"Mice maybe?"

Just then a loud bang from somewhere below caused them both to jump. "And what was that?" Caryn whispered.

Gary shrugged. "Someone probably knocked something over downstairs." He took one last look around the dimly-lit hallway. "I say we go back downstairs and wait for the go-ahead to start the real stalking." Suddenly he felt the air get chilly and that familiar tingle pricked at the back of his neck. "She's here," he whispered.

"Where?" Caryn's eyes darted all around. "Is she saying anything?"

Gary stood still and waited, but the ghost didn't make her appearance. He shook his head. "She's gone. Maybe she's shy."

"Great. Dead and bashful."

"Come on, let's go." They retraced their steps back to the top of the staircase when there was yet another loud noise from below. Gary stopped in his tracks and listened intently.

"Hey, Gary," Sean called up from the bottom of the stairs, "did you guys hear that?"

"Yeah." Gary walked back down the creaky stairs with Caryn right behind him, tightly gripping the bannister.

Annabeth giggled and put her arm around Sean's waist. "Maybe the ghosts started the party without us."

"Hey, Barry!" Gary yelled out, his voice echoing through the house. "Did you guys drop something down here?"

Barry poked his head out of the dining room. "No, but we heard it. Sounded like it came from the basement." His walky-talky squawked. "Yeah, Scott?"

"Lights out in five minutes!" Scott said over the device.

"Good to go from here," Barry replied. He hooked the walky-talky onto his belt loop. "Gary, Caryn, you two go back to the upstairs hallway. Hopefully our elusive Lady in White will appear and get caught on camera."

"Absolutely not!" Caryn said.

Barry lifted an eyebrow and exchanged glances with Gary. "Say what?"

"If you want to make use of my psychic abilities, my radar says the action is in the basement." And with that, Caryn turned and headed down the hall, trying doors on the main floor that might open onto the basement staircase.

"I'll go with her," Gary said.

Annabeth checked her camera to make sure it was ready to go. "What about us?"

"Sean, Annabeth, since they're going downstairs, you two cover the upstairs hallway and then the family room," Barry said. "I've got Donovan and Marshall checking out the exterior around the house. Hansen's with me covering the kitchen and main floor living spaces. And Scott's monitoring the equipment in the van." Barry handed a flashlight to Gary. "It's go time!" he called out.

Then everything went black.

****

I was on a mission. I didn't know if ghosts were haunting the place or not, but that was Gary's department. Every fiber of my being was screaming that there was something in that basement and I had to get down there. The first door I tried in the main hallway was nothing but trash stuffed into what should have been a coat closet. I tried another door that turned out to be a butler's pantry. Kinda cool with all that built-in wooden shelving, but I had to bypass the architecture tour in favor of solving this psychic mystery.

Gary turned on the flashlight and aimed it at the door. "What are you doing?"

"I'm looking for the door to the basement. Duh."

"Oh, right," Gary said, surveying the now-pitch dark hallway. He beamed his flashlight to illuminate another passageway off to our left. "Maybe down this way?"

"Maybe." I led the way and sure enough, just before we got to the house's back door, there was one more unopened door on our right. I reached out and gingerly tried the old-fashioned metal doorknob and found it surprisingly easy to turn. "Shine the light down

181

there."

Gary did as I asked. "Yup, it's a basement all right."

Very funny, I thought, but I didn't have time for sarcastic repartee. I grabbed the handrail and started gingerly down the steep wooden steps, Gary right on my heels. And as soon as we arrived at the bottom of the steps, my radar went crazy. I stopped in my tracks, closed my eyes, and watched the movie in my head rerun the same scene from my dreams. I opened my eyes to get my bearings. "We need to search down here."

Gary ran his fingers through his hair. "Just what are we searching for anyway?"

"I don't know exactly, but it's related to those humans I mentioned earlier. And my sixth sense is telling me we can't leave this basement till we find whatever it is." But I knew my psychic skills alone couldn't do the job, so I turned to Gary. "Can you reach out to the ghost? Maybe between the two of us, we can get some answers."

Gary winced. "Sorry to disappoint you, but I can't just summon them. Her."

I hadn't realized just how different our skill sets were. When I needed Uncle Omar's help, I simply asked. But maybe Barry was right, that Gary and I could find a way to pool our resources. We'd have to try because this—whatever it was—was important.

The basement seemed to have about the same amount of square footage as the entire first floor, making it huge, dank and creepy. Off to one corner and under the stairs was the laundry area, with an old washer and dryer sitting next to one of those old-fashioned work sinks, now all rusty and covered with dirt. The boiler took up a good portion of the middle of the room and probably didn't work, because next to it was a more modern furnace. And by modern I meant twentieth century. Broken pieces of furniture and boxes were piled up in the opposite far corner, and there was a boy's bicycle with two flat tires and a bent rim next to the boxes.

I started feeling along the damp walls, tripping over some of the cardboard boxes. I shoved them out of my way, determined to keep moving. "Anything yet?" I asked him.

Gary did a survey of the musty basement, playing the flashlight around the walls as he did. Suddenly he stopped and shivered. "Okay, when I feel the hairs on the back of my neck stand up, that's my signal for a ghost. And I just felt it."

I stopped and whispered, "Do you see her?"

Gary nodded and held up a hand to let me know he needed to concentrate. "Who are you?" he asked the ghost.

Gary stared at the wall and nodded his head. I've seen him do this before and always thought it was weird, but this time I was fascinated. "What's she saying?"

"Her name is Miss Fairchild," Gary said, then stopped and listened again. "She was a teacher, and she lived in this house as a boarder. I guess that means renter. Looked after kids and stuff."

"Okay, so...?"

Gary raised his voice and addressed the wall. "Lady, you're dead. You need to go to the light."

"What does she look like?" I whispered.

"Dead," Gary replied. When I scowled at him, he added, "It's like everyone who's ever seen her says, long white dress, graying hair in a bun, old-fashioned glasses."

"But what's she saying?"

Gary was silent for a moment longer, then shook his head. "Weird. Something about," he made air quotes with his fingers, "a child." He shrugged.

Then it hit me, so hard in fact I sucked in a long, raspy gasp. I coughed a little and then said, "Ohmigod, I know exactly what's she telling us!" I grabbed the flashlight from Gary and began playing it around the basement walls.

I could hear Annabeth and Sean moving around above us, fumbling with the door, disrupting my concentration and probably Gary's as well.

"Shhh, Sean, be quiet in case Gary's speaking to the dead," Annabeth said, not so quietly.

"Annabeth, Sean," Gary called to the top of the stairs. "Down here."

Another flashlight shone around the room, feet clomped, and then Annabeth and Sean came to a dead stop on the last step.

Sean pointed to the ceiling where the night vision camera had been set up. "Is that thing working?"

Annabeth squinted up at it. "No green 'ON' light. So no." She adjusted the lens on her camera, took aim and began snapping pictures around the room. "Hey, Gary, do you think I might get some orbs on the finished photographs?"

"Maybe," Gary said, "'cause we definitely have company down here." He stuck out his hand for me to return the flashlight.

"Ooo, do tell!" Annabeth giggled as she snapped a photo of Gary, who blinked and cringed.

"Gary spoke to Ms. Ghost, and I got a huge psychic hit. We have to keep looking down here until we find…"

"Find what?" Sean asked. "Hey, does anyone feel like we're in one of those Scooby kids cartoons?"

"Thanks for the comic relief, man," Gary said.

"Gary, don't keep me in suspense, what did the ghost say?" Annabeth repeated.

"She was a teacher back in the day, then after she died she stayed around to keep an eye on kids who lived here, and now she's fixated on some kid. I guess that's why she won't cross over." Gary began poking around in the pile of discarded toys and furniture off in the corner.

"Caryn," Annabeth called out, "what's your radar saying?"

"I think I know what—who—we're looking for, but…" I was getting frustrated as I inched my way along the walls, kicking boxes, pushing aside old pictures and bed frames. And suddenly there it was, hidden behind all the debris. "Look!" I unfastened a latch on a door that revealed a pantry of some sort. In it were rows of old wooden shelving, and they were crammed with jars. I stepped in for a closer look. "What do you suppose is in these?"

Gary flashed his light on them. "Botulism."

Annabeth joined me and snapped photo after photo. "Looks like homemade canned goods. Some of them are really old." She wrinkled her nose as she pulled one off the shelf and blew the dust off it. "Aunt Sarah's homemade pickles, June 1958." She shuddered and put it back.

I ran my fingers along the rows of jars, stopping when I got to the end of the last shelf. "Hey, check this one out. It's a generic brand from a local grocery store. Expiration date: August 2019. Canned peaches." I picked it up and examined it. "And all this other stuff, too." I pointed to a row of modern-looking cans of tuna, vegetables, fruits, potatoes, and a number of those spaghetti-in-a-can types of meals.

Gary moved in behind me. "Your point?"

Sean flashed his light over Gary's shoulder. "Maybe it was the construction crew's lunch."

I put the can back on the shelf. "No." I stopped a minute and closed my eyes. "Uncle Omar?"

"Keep looking," my uncle said in my ear.

"He says we're not done searching, guys," I said.

Gary groaned. "Searching for what?"

"A room I saw in a vision a few days ago. It's down here, so there's got to be an opening somewhere." I went back to running my hands along the walls.

Gary was astonished. "We're frantically searching for something you dreamed about?"

"You guys have fun. I'm out," Sean said. He pointed to the stairs and was about to head back up when there was another loud crash right near us.

We all froze.

My eyes darted around the basement. "See? I told you! He's down here."

"Who?" Gary and Sean demanded in unison.

"This is so cool!" Annabeth exclaimed.

****

Gary began poking on the walls and flashing his light on the ceiling, trying to pinpoint the location of the noise they'd just heard. He took a second to analyze what he was feeling, and sure enough she was there. The Lady in White, standing off in a corner, pointing to a wall.

"Gary, is the ghost back?" Caryn asked in hushed tones.

Normally Gary didn't care whether he scared a ghost off or not, but this time she was their only source of information and he needed her help. He stood completely still, waiting to see if she'd talk, but she just pointed and then vanished.

"Over there." Gary's gaze followed the invisible directions back to the pantry. He stared at it, trying to figure out what the ghost had been trying to tell him. He felt along the wall next to the shelves, his hands mostly hitting the concrete bricks, but then he felt something. Gary pushed aside a couple of boxes piled up a little too neatly next to the shelves. Sure enough, there was a door behind them.

Caryn and Annabeth rushed over. "A hidden door!" Annabeth squealed with delight.

"Huh. We're officially in a Scooby Doo mystery," Sean said.

"Ha ha," Gary replied.

The door had one of those rope handles instead of a doorknob. Gary pulled on it and it opened with a squeak. Inside was a small room, probably once used as a storm shelter and lined with old-fashioned plaster instead of drywall. The one lamp in the room flicked off just as the four of them stepped in. Gary aimed his flashlight at an old army cot in the corner with blankets and a pillow, and an end table with books and opened cans of food and soda.

Annabeth shrieked when something moved on the bed. "Oh. My. God. Now I'm seeing a ghost!"

Gary was as astonished as she was. "What is that?"

Caryn calmly stepped in front of all of them. "It's not a 'what,' it's a 'who.'"

Gary reached over and turned the lamp back on. There sat a little boy, eyes wide, scooting himself as far back into the corner of the cot as he could, pulling the blanket around him as a barrier. "Who the hell are you?" Gary asked.

"Who wants to know?"

Gary thought the kid looked panicked despite his forced bravado, so he stepped back to give the kid some space. That's when he realized what Ms. Lady in White had been trying to tell him. "He must be the kid the ghost was talking about."

The boy smirked. "Yeah, I'm a kid all right. Good work, Sherlock."

"And he's not just any kid," Caryn said. She waved her arms with a flourish. "Meet Eddie Carson, runaway."

Gary felt like his head was about to explode. Could Caryn be right? He peered into the kid's face and saw the resemblance between the photos that had been all over the media and the flyers handed out at the volunteer search last weekend. "Yo, kid, people have been looking for you. Your dad's really freaked out."

"He's not my dad," Eddie snarled.

"Okay, stepdad," Gary said. "How did you get in here?"

"None of your business. Go away and leave me alone!"

Gary took a step toward Eddie but stopped when

the boy recoiled in fear. Instead he did a visual search of the tiny space they were all crammed into. "You must've planned all this."

"Ya think?" Eddie had a microwave in the corner on the floor, a stack of paper plates, a hand-held can opener and plates of half-eaten food tossed next to the bed, plus he had access to those cans on that pantry shelf outside of the room. On a wooden crate-turned-nightstand was a stack of books and a deck of cards, and a backpack peeked out from under the cot.

Gary lifted an eyebrow at Eddie as he read off the titles of some of the books. "*Moby Dick. The Never Ending Story. The Great Gatsby. Harry Potter* something. *The Complete Works of William Shakespeare.* Some pretty sophisticated reading here, kid. Looks like you're planning a long stay."

"Like I said, none of your business."

Annabeth aimed her camera at Eddie, who quickly put one hand in front of his face and held the other palm up to stop her. "Get that thing away from me!"

"Dude, there's been a massive manhunt for you," Sean told him. "Everyone thought you were the victim of foul play."

"Who says I'm not?" Eddie shot back.

Gary thought he saw a bruise peeking out from under the kid's sleeve. He and Sean exchanged glances. "Um, Sean, this kid might be a...a..."

Caryn lowered her voice. "That's exactly what he is. A victim of child abuse."

Annabeth sucked in her breath and lowered her camera.

"Who are you guys anyway?" Eddie asked.

Gary extended his hand to shake, but Eddie shrank

back so Gary withdrew his hand and wiped it on his pants leg. "Gary Riddell, and this is Sean Paxton, Caryn Alderson, and Annabeth Walton. We're here on a ghost hunt. You know this place is crawling with Ghost Stalkers, right?"

Sean laughed. "And to think, we thought this place was haunted by a real ghost."

"There is a real ghost here," Gary said. "She was the one who led me to Eddie."

Caryn crossed her arms in front of her chest and smirked. "And who was it led you down to the basement?"

Eddie glared at her. "What are you? Some kinda psychic?"

Caryn smiled. "Yes, that's exactly what I am. So tell us why you're hiding out here."

"Because, that's why. I thought it was an abandoned house. It was bad enough when the construction guys were here. Now I'm surrounded by ghost hunters and psychics."

Sean stepped out of the small room and flashed his light at the night-vision camera. "So you disabled the camera down here, right? And made those other loud noises?"

"I accidentally turned over the lamp. Twice." Eddie pulled his hoodie up over his head, crossed his arms, and planted a pillow in front of him as a barrier. "You just don't get it."

"Okay then," Gary said. He pointed to the edge of the cot for permission to sit and Eddie nodded. "Help us understand."

Eddie was silent, opened his mouth to speak, but then slammed it shut and scowled at them. "I'm taking the fifth."

Gary grinned. "This isn't a court room, kid."

Eddie curled up his knees and buried his face. "I can't let anyone know where I am. And you guys have ruined everything, so now I gotta go."

"Go where?" Sean asked.

"Anywhere. Out of Belford." Tears came to his eyes.

Gary sighed. He felt sorry for the kid. Whatever was troubling him, Eddie had gone to a lot of trouble to disappear. "Eddie," Gary said, "something's obviously wrong and we"—he turned to the others who nodded confirmation—"we'd like to help."

Eddie stifled a sob. "I can't go home."

"Are you in trouble?" Annabeth asked.

"I didn't do all this," he said, waving his arms around the room, "because everything was hunky-dory."

They were interrupted by loud voices just above them, and then the basement door opened to admit Barry and Scott. Gary noticed all the lights had been turned back on upstairs.

"Anyone down here?" Scott called.

"Yeah, we're here," Gary answered. The four of them scurried out of Eddie's makeshift bedroom and Gary pulled the hidden door closed behind him.

"Hey, we wondered where you guys got off to," Barry said, easing down the stairs and fumbling along the wall for a light switch. "Did you see the ghost?"

Gary hurried out into the center of the basement to keep Barry from snooping around any further. "Lady in White? Yeah, I saw her." He shone his flashlight on the switch Barry was looking for.

Barry flipped it on, causing all of them to momentarily blink. "What did she look like? Did you talk to her?"

Gary nodded, but he couldn't really tell them what the ghost had said without giving Eddie's whereabouts away. So he dodged Barry's second question. "Middle age, white dress, early twentieth century. You might have gotten some images on the upstairs cameras. The one down here isn't working."

"Nada," Barry said. "But we already knew ghosts could play havoc with electronics."

Caryn stepped to Gary's side. "He had a long conversation with the dead lady, but I don't think she's planning to cross over any time soon."

"And what about you, Caryn?" Barry said. "Any psychic hits?"

Caryn was quiet a moment, her head tilted to the right, listening to something. "My spirit guide says we did what we came to do. The construction crew can get back to work."

Gary glanced at her, their eyes met, and he knew she was also covering for Eddie. "The ghost is harmless and she promises not to cause any more trouble," he fibbed.

Barry visually searched the room one last time. "Well, we're done here. The next step is to go back to school and go over the footage and the EVP recordings to see what we got. You guys ready?"

"Yeah, in a minute," Gary said. "We found some…" *How do I finish that sentence?*

"Some interesting antiques to write about in our news story," Annabeth finished for him. "I need to get a few shots." In order to be convincing, she whipped out her camera and took aim at the shelf stocked with old canned goods.

"Well, don't be too long," Barry said.

Gary waited till Barry was safely back upstairs before turning to the others. "What are we going to do? We can't just leave Eddie here by himself." Gary suddenly felt that familiar tingle on his neck and he turned around, expecting to see The Lady in White, but it wasn't her. His jaw dropped when he spotted the younger woman who'd been haunting him lately, completely materialized next to the hidden door.

Caryn followed Gary's gaze and hurried to his side. "Is The Lady in White back?"

Gary shook his head. "It's a ghost all right, but not the resident ghost. This one hasn't been dead all that long and she's been following me everywhere."

"Who is she? What does she want?" Caryn asked.

"You have to help him," the ghost said. "My son needs you." And then she was gone.

Gary blew out a puff of air. "Hoo boy."

"What are you two whispering about?" Annabeth asked, and then suddenly shivered and wrapped her arms around herself. "It's really drafty down here. Can we go?"

"Gary saw a different ghost," Caryn told her.

"She says we have to take care of...her son," Gary said.

"What?" Annabeth and Sean exclaimed at the same time.

"Poor kid. Seems his mom died recently." Gary ran his fingers through his hair, trying to think through this problem. With Eddie's mom dead and his stepdad a creep, Gary knew Eddie was in trouble, but they couldn't just escort the kid upstairs and say, "Look who we found." Scott Tildren would be the adult and call the police. The media would eat it up, Eddie would be "reunited" with Clyde Seville, and the four of them would be called heroes. But Gary didn't want notoriety at the expense of a desperate kid. He knew there was more to this story because two different ghosts had asked for his help. "We can't let anyone know about Eddie."

"So how do we pull that off?" Sean asked.

"I've got an idea," Gary said. He went back to the hidden room and opened the squeaky door. "Get your stuff, kid. You're coming with us."

"No!" Eddie exclaimed. "You can't make me!"

Gary was losing patience. "Look, Eddie, I get that something's wrong at home, and we'll try to sort it out later. But you either come with us or we call the cops."

"Then you'd better have a genius plan to sneak me outta here," Eddie said, crossing his arms and sinking into full-on teenage sulk.

"Yeah, Gary, what is your plan?" Annabeth asked.

"Right now all I care about is getting those two ghosts off my case." He shot the kid a withering look. Eddie grumbled but pulled the backpack out from under the cot, stuffed in the books, and flung it over his shoulder.

"Caryn," Gary said, "any insight?"

Caryn nodded. "Something big to do with Eddie's family. I mean big big. And it's got to be you that helps him."

"So I've been told," Gary said. "Anything else?"

"Not right now."

Gary had already figured out that Eddie was afraid

of his stepfather, and after seeing how smarmy the guy was, he couldn't blame him. "Time for operation 'hide Eddie Carson,'" he said.

"I'll go upstairs and distract everyone," Sean said. "You know, ask to see the footage or hear what's on the EVP or something." He turned to Annabeth. "Then you say something about going out to warm up your car, or trying to get a phone signal. Whatever."

Gary put Eddie right behind him, and because he was so tall and Eddie was short and skinny, Gary was sure he could block him from view. Sean went upstairs first. Gary could hear Sean in the living room engaging Scott, Barry, and Karla Hansen in an animated discussion of what they'd seen or heard during the blackout, Karla squealing at every detail. Gary figured her hysteria alone would distract Scott and Barry so they could sneak Eddie out. With hands behind his back, he motioned Caryn and Annabeth up, who made their excuses and ducked out the front door. Then Gary went up to the top of the basement steps, took a look around to make sure everyone was occupied, and pushed Eddie in front of him and straight out the front door.

"Damn, it's cold out here!" Eddie exclaimed.

"Watch your mouth, kid," Gary whispered, and gave him a shove in the direction of Annabeth's car. "Get in the backseat and duck down."

Gary waited until Eddie was safely in the car and then went back into the house and slipped into his coat, still lying on the folding chair where he'd left it. "Sean? You ready?"

Sean gave Gary a questioning glance and Gary nodded, so Sean hurried out the front door.

Scott sauntered out of the kitchen and toasted Gary and Sean with his mug of steaming hot coffee. "Hey Barry," Scott called out. "Our ghost-whisperer's on his way out."

Barry Lansing reappeared from the hall. "Thanks, Gary. We'll get in touch after we go over the video," he said. "Might need your input on whatever we find."

"And Ms. Pelson will definitely want to hear about your conversation with the ghost," Scott added.

Gary dreaded that whole scenario, especially because the only conversation he'd had with the ghost—make that ghosts—was about Eddie. "Yeah, I'll be interested to hear what your equipment picked up." He shook hands with Scott, waved at the club members who were packing up equipment, and left.

"Drive," he said to Annabeth as he slid into the front passenger seat. He looked over his shoulder and saw Eddie crammed between Sean and Caryn.

"Hey, Annabeth," Sean said, "turn up the heat. It's freezing in this car."

"It's November," Eddie said. "It's supposed to be cold."

"Thanks, Einstein," Gary said.

"Close," Eddie said, causing Gary to look at him askance.

Annabeth pulled out of the long driveway and slowly drove down the pitch-black road that led back to the state highway.

"So how did you find me?" Eddie asked as he rested his head against the cushion.

"The legendary Lady in White who resides— haunts—the Pelson farmhouse," Gary said.

"A ghost ratted me out?"

Gary didn't want to talk about it anymore, especially the part about the ghost of Eddie's mom. That was a whole other issue that could wait. He pulled his phone out of his pocket, checked to make sure he had bars, and started scrolling down for Brenda's number.

Eddie sat up straight, his eyes wide. "Who ya calling? The cops?"

The kid was getting on Gary's nerves big time. He had no experience with middle schoolers and right now he wanted to strangle this one, but he took a deep breath and replied, "My mom. I need some advice. I have no idea what to do with you and she's the most level-headed person I know."

There was sort of a muffled sobbing, gasping, choking noise from the backseat and Eddie said, "At least you've still got one."

Gary eyed Eddie sympathetically as he exchanged knowing glances with Caryn. Just then his phone pinged with a text. "It's Brenda." He looked up from his phone at a worried Eddie. "My mom."

"So what did she say?" Eddie demanded after Gary read his text and put his phone back in his pocket. "Do I get out and start walking or what?"

Gary sighed, glanced at Caryn, and rolled his eyes. "It's two a.m, Eddie. Mom says to let you stay at my dorm tonight. But any stupid stuff and you'll find yourself on your daddy's doorstep."

"He's not my daddy," Eddie growled.

Chapter 12

I bit my tongue on the drive back to campus. I could tell Eddie was making Gary crazy, not to mention the rest of us. Gary and Sean were stuck with him for the time being, but Annabeth and I could go back to our dorm room for some peace and quiet.

I felt sorry for Eddie, though. I never go to horror films, but the movie running on fast forward through my head was scarier than anything Hollywood could come up with. There'd been some kind of argument between Eddie's mom and his stepdad Clyde, with Eddie witnessing the whole thing. I saw his mother crash her car into a tree. I saw her funeral, felt Eddie's pain, and then I saw Clyde yelling at the kid and knocking him around the house, causing bruises and a bloody nose. No child should have to live like that.

Annabeth made eye contact with Gary in her rearview mirror. "Do you want me to call my dad?"

"It's the middle of the frickin' night," Gary said.

"Well, yeah, but…" Annabeth's voice trailed off.

"Who's her dad, anyway?" Eddie asked.

"He's an attorney," I told him. "Maybe he can…" I didn't know what Mr. Walton might be able to do. I was pretty sure Annabeth thought she was helping by offering to get her father involved, but right now this was a case for social services.

We drove along in an awkward silence, the only

sound coming from the purr of the engine. "I say we don't make any decisions tonight," I told the group. "Let's just sleep on it. I'm sure a solution will present itself."

Gary glanced over the headrest at me. "Are you sure there's a solution, or just hope for one?"

I didn't answer, but I was positive about two things: I was going to sleep soundly, and sometimes answers come to me in my sleep.

****

"I guess the kid can have my bed," Sean said to Gary as he frowned at the mess on Gary's side of the room, "since no one in his right mind would sleep in yours."

"If he takes your bed, then where will you sleep?" Gary asked.

"Stop talking about me like I'm not here," Eddie said. He pulled his hoodie off over his head to reveal a dirty Metallica T-shirt underneath, tossed his overstuffed backpack on the floor, and collapsed on Sean's bed.

"I'll go crash on the lounge sofa," Sean said. "Hey, it's not like it's the first time someone didn't make it all the way to their room on a Friday night." He grabbed his pillow and a blanket off the bed, and quietly closed the door behind him.

Gary threw his jacket on the back of his desk chair and sat down on his bed to pull his boots off. He felt Eddie watching him and looked up. "What?"

"Uh, he took the pillow."

Gary wrinkled his nose. It was obvious the kid hadn't showered recently. He tossed his extra pillow to Eddie and then dug through the drawer under his bed for a clean bath towel. "Go hit the shower and then get some sleep." Gary waited while Eddie dug through his backpack for clean sweats, tossed the towel over his shoulder, and started for the bathroom. "And hey, brush your teeth!"

Eddie groaned and went back to his backpack, digging around till he pulled out his toothbrush, toasted Gary with it, and went into the bathroom. As soon as Gary heard water running, he flipped off the lamp next to his bed and fell sound asleep.

A mere five hours after Gary went to sleep, Sean stumbled back into their room and headed for the shower. Gary groaned, pulled his pillow over his head and rolled over to face the wall.

Sean came back out fifteen minutes later, got dressed and left the room, probably for the cafeteria if Gary had to guess. Gary pulled the blanket up over his ears and tried to fall back asleep, but he noticed that Eddie was up, that is if the kid had ever been asleep. He had the TV on mute as he flipped through the channels. Eventually he landed on a replay of last night's Belford High School vs. Melville High football game on a local channel. With no sound to disturb him, Gary rolled over and tried once more to go back to sleep, but every time he was about to doze off, Eddie would cheer at some game play.

Gary gave up trying to sleep once and for all when Eddie tossed his pillow at him. "Hey, ya got anything to eat?"

Gary pulled himself to a sitting position, a scowl on his face. "You're lucky I have a rehearsal to get to, 'cause otherwise I'd march your smart-aleck ass straight to social services."

"Food!" Eddie repeated.

Gary groaned. "I'll have to go to the cafeteria and bring you back something." He stumbled into the bathroom, turned the shower on and stepped in, letting the hot water pour over him while he tried to wake up. Lack of sleep had given him a headache, and nothing would fix that but a strong jolt of caffeine.

Showered and dressed, he grabbed his jean jacket off the desk chair next to his bed and was about to put it on when he remembered his cell phone in the pocket. He pulled it out and saw he had a text from Caryn. Caryn? Hmm.

—*Going to do research on Eddie.*—

Gary texted her back.

—*Let me know what you find out.*—

When Caryn didn't respond, Gary figured she must still be asleep, lucky duck.

"Eddie, get dressed and start straightening up around here. I'll be back in a few minutes."

Thankfully there were few people in the cafeteria. He ordered take-out, poured himself a large coffee, and headed back across campus. Back in his dorm lobby, Gary rang for the elevator and was relieved that it was completely empty when it opened. The last thing he needed was someone asking him about the ghost hunt, or Erica Stone and her crew teasing him about his affiliation with Ghost Stalkers. Besides, as Caryn had predicted, the hunt turned out to be more about the living than the dead, and Gary couldn't share that with anyone. The elevator stopped on his floor, so while he juggled the food in one hand, he unlocked his door with the other, sticking his foot in enough to push it open. He found Eddie sitting cross-legged on Sean's still unmade bed, thoroughly engrossed in a video game of Grand Theft Auto.

Gary rolled his eyes. "Hi, honey, I'm home."

Startled, Eddie jumped to his feet, his eyes darting around as if looking for an escape.

"Relax, kid, it's just me." Gary helped himself to a muffin before handing Eddie the carryout box of eggs, pastry and fruit. Gary sipped his coffee and munched his blueberry muffin as the kid tucked into his food. When was the last time he had a meal that didn't come out of a can? Gary wondered. "You're welcome."

"Thanks," Eddie said as he shoveled in another bite of eggs.

"Sean's gonna freak if he sees his side of the room like this." Gary picked up Eddie's wet towel from last night and tossed it on the pile of laundry in his closet. Then he pulled his phone out of his jacket pocket and punched in some numbers.

"Whoa! Who ya calling?" Eddie asked as he tossed the half-empty box on the bed, jumped off and grabbed for Gary's cell.

Gary yanked his arm back and held the phone out of Eddie's reach. "Relax. I'm just calling my mom."

The kid exhaled loudly. "Oh." He sat back down on the bed, retrieved his fork from where he'd tossed it on the blanket, and went back to what was left of his breakfast.

Gary put the phone to his ear, but Brenda's line went to voice mail. "Mom, call me when you get this. And don't just send a text." He disconnected and sat down on his own unmade bed. "Great. So now what am I supposed to do with you? I've got a full day."

"I don't need a babysitter. I'll just wait here till you

get back."

Gary raised an eyebrow. "I've got my job at the bookstore, tech rehearsal for the play I'm in, and at some point I gotta go to the library and study. I won't be back for hours."

Eddie shrugged and turned his attention back to the video game. "I can take care of myself."

Gary sighed, but he didn't have time to argue about it. Foster Benning had insisted that the entire cast of *Pride and Prejudice* show up on time this afternoon so they could do the lighting and sound checks. Still, this rehearsal would cut right into the middle of his workday, which was inconvenient for his fellow employees at the bookstore. He thanked his lucky stars for Ellis Garrett, who had been nothing but understanding and accommodating about his theatre schedule ever since she hired him. He reminded himself to thank her again when he saw her.

Gary grabbed his backpack and slung it over one shoulder. "Eddie, you can't stay here indefinitely. You're a thirteen-year-old child with an Amber Alert out on you. You've got to go home eventually."

"No!" Eddie's face screwed up as he pleaded with Gary. "I can't go back there. My stepdad hates me. I'll do anything you want me to. Clean up here, do your homework…"

"Do my homework?"

Eddie broke into a crooked smile. "Didn't I tell you? I'm a genius."

Gary was stunned. "I thought you were joking." He let that information sit for a minute and the lightbulb sorta went on. Being that smart would explain how Eddie was able to fake his own kidnapping, terrorize

203

Clara Pelson's construction crew, and hide from the police for a couple of weeks. And then there were all the classic books he'd taken along. Eddie must have really needed to get away from that stepdad of his if he went to all that trouble. Then Gary had another idea, so he grabbed his phone again and punched in more numbers.

"Calling Mommy again?" Eddie asked, his attention already back on the video game.

Gary decided the kid reminded him of himself at that age. Not the genius part, but definitely the smart-aleck kid part. "Her name's Brenda Riddell, and I'll thank you not to...Oh, hi, Caryn?" Gary gave Eddie a glance. "Yeah, he's here and I've got stuff to do. Any chance you're free this afternoon?"

He disconnected the phone, pulled on his jacket, and left without a backward glance. Hopefully Annabeth and Caryn would look after Eddie. Gary was already exhausted from dealing with the kid and he hadn't even gotten his day started yet.

Gary sometimes felt like his whole life was running. Running to class, running to work, running to rehearsals. He was on the move all the time. Sometimes he wished he could slow down and catch his breath, maybe even get a full night's sleep, but when he metaphorically looked behind him, all he could see were those scholarship requirements nipping at his heels. He'd have to cut his workday short to get to play practice. And if they didn't get finished with rehearsal in timely manner, he'd have a long Saturday night in the library studying. Would it never end? Yes, in about three and a half years he told himself.

Brenda texted back while Gary was dashing across

campus to work, but it was one of those *Really busy, I'll get back to you messages.* He'd wanted her to call, not text.

"He's safe, right? Eddie, I mean."

Gary stopped stock still in the middle of The Commons and stared at the ghost. It was her again, Eddie's dead mother. Gary knew he could just keep walking, but he decided to take a minute, put her mind to rest, and maybe then she'd move on. He quickly glanced around him to see if anyone was watching, but the campus was as deserted as the cafeteria had been. "Yeah, he's fine. And you are?"

"Lucy Carson Seville. I'd offer to shake hands, but…"

Gary chuckled. "Yeah, I don't wanna get slimed. So listen, lady, uh, Lucy, uh, Mrs. Seville…"

"Please, call me Lucy. No need to stand on ceremony now."

Gary's eyes widened. The ghost was quoting Shakespeare, sort of. Which reminded him that he had to get to work so he could get to rehearsal on time, and hopefully put himself in Foster and Dr. Danson's good graces when it came time for auditions next week for the coveted part of Macbeth. "Look, Lucy, I'll see to it that Eddie's okay. You need to cross over."

"No way. Not till I'm sure he's safe."

Gary shifted his backpack to the other shoulder. "Safe from what?"

Lucy was fading. Gary knew it took a lot of energy for a ghost to materialize, much less have a lengthy conversation, but he could tell she had more to tell him. When she'd completely disappeared, Gary sighed and started walking again. That is, until he felt the familiar tingle on the back of his neck. He stopped and turned around, thinking Lucy had come back.

"See here, Mr. Riddell, that woman has no right to occupy this space. She's not from this institution."

Gary frowned at the ghostly professor. "Seriously? Territorial ghosts?" He shook his head and hurried on. "You two work it out on your side and leave me out of it," he muttered.

"Late night, Gary?" Ellis asked as he walked into the bookstore.

He nodded. "Sorry I'm late, and thanks for understanding. Complications at the ghost hunt."

"Hopefully there aren't any ghosts around here today to keep you from your work."

Gary chuckled, did a quick glance around the store, and tossed off a lighthearted, "Not at the moment."

Mid-morning the store wasn't busy at all, except for a half dozen or so bleary-eyed students sucking down coffee. That was fine with him, because he had lots to do and not much time to do it. There was yesterday's shipment of books in the storeroom to unpack and place on shelves, inventory to check and reorder, and the bathrooms that always needed a good cleaning. He wiped down the counter with disinfectant, and then the cash registers, and went to work unloading the new books onto shelves back in the English literature section. That was when he noticed that a bunch of the existing stock was all out of order. Those English majors could sure paw through a lot of books, and then put them back in all the wrong places. You'd think they'd know alphabetical order.

Next he went into the restrooms to check their condition and restock supplies. When he opened the door to the unoccupied women's restroom he gagged, covered his nose with his hand, and went right out again for the bucket of cleanser and the mop. He was pulling them backwards through the door to the women's restroom when he ran smack into Sean.

"Uh, gender crisis, Gary?" Sean asked with a smirk.

"Very funny," Gary said.

Sean smiled and pushed open the men's room door, but stopped halfway in. "How's our 'house guest'?"

Gary shook his head and looked upward as if to say Heaven help us. "I left him playing one of your old video games. I called Caryn, and I hope she and Annabeth will go over and keep him out of trouble for a while."

Sean nodded. "Yeah, but Annabeth and I have a date tonight, and that kid can't stay in our room indefinitely. You got any kind of plan?"

Gary leaned on the mop to catch his breath. "Well, I was going to ask Brenda, but I can't get ahold of her. I have reason to think—"

"Reason, as in ghost?" Sean interjected.

Gary ignored him and went right on. "—that Eddie might have been abused. Any way we could get your dad to check him out?"

Sean shrugged. "Maybe. I'll text him and see what he can do."

****

More running. This time across campus because Gary was late to rehearsal. He pushed open the doors to the Thomas Belford Fine Arts Building and rushed down the hall to the stage.

Foster pulled up his sleeve to check his nonexistent

watch and frowned at Gary. "It's about time, Riddell," he called from the stage, his voice echoing in the empty auditorium. Foster was standing in for him as Mr. Bingley, rehearsing the scene with Delia Ferguson who was playing Jane Bennet.

Gary slid out of his backpack and took the steps two at a time onto the stage. "Sorry, but it got busy at work," he said. "Where are we?"

"Act Two," Foster said. He stepped away from Delia, shaded his eyes from the glare and called out to the light and sound techs, "Top of the scene you guys!" Foster jumped off the edge of the stage and sat down in the front row.

Gary went to his place next to the fireplace mantel. He leaned his elbow casually against it, mindful of the correct posture required to pull off a tight-fitting nineteenth century waistcoat, stretch pants, and boots, which would make him appear even taller.

Delia tossed him a dirty look and reached for her bottle of water hidden behind the satin-covered sofa. "Some of us actually want this play to succeed." She swallowed a gulp of water and glared at him.

Gary tried to overlook Delia's sarcasm so he could get into character. "Jane, don't you look lovely," Gary-as-Bingley said.

"That's not the line," Delia said.

Gary sighed, pulled himself up to his full height and this time spoke the correct line. "Miss Bennet, you are the most beautiful creature I have ever beheld."

Delia was suddenly Jane Bennet, all straight laced and nineteenth century proper. "Why, Mr. Bingley!" She batted her eyelashes and fanned herself with an imaginary fan.

Gary offered his arm to escort "Jane" onto the dance floor. "May I have this dance, Miss Bennet?" She took his arm and Gary started to walk her over, but then stopped. This was their first time on the stage they'd actually be performing on in five days. It was much bigger than the rehearsal stage, and up till now they had never done more than mark their places. Gary stepped to the footlights. "Just where exactly is this dance supposed to happen, Foster?"

"You act like you've never been in a play before, Riddell," Foster barked. "Get your head in the game."

Gary sighed, stretched his neck and back to get himself refocused, and faced Delia for the pretend dance. Tricia Palmer's Elizabeth was downstage from Jane, and Kevin Michaels as Mr. Darcy stood across from "Elizabeth." Two extra men and women filled out the dance set. They all bowed to their respective partners, Foster made a circular motion with his arm to signal the start of the music, and the English Country Dance began.

Gary lost all track of time inside the theatre as they went through the rest of the play. It wasn't Shakespeare, but he felt an obligation to do his best and perhaps prove his versatility. What seemed like a short time later, Foster gathered the cast for notes and then called it a wrap.

Gary pulled out his cell phone and saw that it was after seven. Unfortunately he'd missed a text from Brenda hours earlier.

—*Meet at Tony's Pizza Palace 6 pm.*—
Gary groaned and texted her back.
—*Sorry. Long rehearsal. On my way.*—
So much for the library.

****

Even though we'd promised Gary to look in on Eddie, Annabeth, and I were a while getting over there. After the long night at the ghost hunt, we'd both slept in, and then I had some research to do that wouldn't wait. I went to the school newspaper office, fired up my computer, and pulled up the archives of The Indianapolis Star so I could read up on the accident that had killed Eddie's mother. I pored over all the news coverage, but my radar told me there was more to the story than the official police report. By the time I tore myself away and met up with Annabeth, it was late afternoon.

Outside Gary and Sean's dorm room, Annabeth rapped lightly on the door. We waited for an answer, but it was really quiet inside. *Maybe the kid's asleep*, I thought, *or he's taken off again*. No, I shook that thought off.

"Hello, Eddie?" Annabeth called out.

"Shhh!" I whispered, glancing sideways at a couple of girls strolling past us in the narrow hallway. "You can't call out his name."

"Oops." Annabeth nodded a silent greeting to the girls and then she knocked even louder. "Yo! Sean! Gary! Open up!" The door opened a crack and an eyeball peered out at us.

"Let us in!" I hissed.

Eddie hid behind the door as the two of us walked in, and then hurriedly shut and locked it behind us. He was wearing a dirty and worn pair of ill-fitting jeans, the same hooded sweatshirt from last night, socks with a hole in the heel, and I spotted his mud-encrusted tennis shoes at the foot of the bed. "Great. Babysitters," he muttered. He flopped back onto Sean's bed on his stomach, retrieved the remote from among the covers, and resumed his paused video game.

Annabeth reached over his shoulder and hit the TV's off button. "We need to talk."

"Hey!" Eddie whined, sitting up. "I was winning!"

"Keep your voice down. We—" I suddenly got a cold chill, the kind I've heard people sometimes get when there's a ghost nearby. I can't see ghosts but I know a creepy feeling when I get it. I hugged myself tightly and let my eyes dart around the room.

"What's with her?" Eddie asked Annabeth, jerking his thumb at me.

Annabeth watched me closely and asked, "Do we have company?"

"Maybe, but you know I can't be sure." I slowly walked around the cluttered room, dodging books, clothes, and empty soda cans, and felt the unfamiliar energy increase with every step. And the closer to Eddie I got, the stronger the energy. I took a deep breath, listened intently, and then nodded. "Uncle Omar says Eddie's mom is here."

"What!" Eddie shrieked.

Annabeth winced and put her fingers to her lips to shush him.

Eddie took a deep breath and lowered his voice. "What about my mom?"

I felt bad for the kid. First he runs away from an abusive stepfather, gets discovered by a psychic and a ghost whisperer, and now I'm telling him—through an unseen third party—that his mom's ghost is in the room. It was enough to scare the daylights out of anyone, let alone a thirteen-year-old boy.

211

I sat down facing Eddie from the edge of Gary's unmade bed, and leaned my elbows on my knees. "Remember last night when I told you I'm psychic?" Eddie nodded, eyeing me suspiciously. I didn't blame him for being skeptical of my abilities. Heck, most people are. "Well, my spirit guide—my late uncle—says to tell you that your mother is here in this room. I can feel her but I can't talk to her."

Eddie folded his arms in front of his chest and glared at me. "Why the hell not?"

"Watch your mouth," Annabeth warned him.

"Eddie, I'm a psychic medium, so earthbounds—ghosts—are at too low a frequency for me to pick up." I expected him to ask me to explain, but surprisingly he seemed to understand what I was saying.

"Then what good are you?" he finally growled.

"Caryn, isn't there something you can do?" Annabeth pleaded.

"Wish Gary was here?" Neither of them seemed to appreciate the humor. "Okay, I'll try." I took a deep breath, closed my eyes and listened to what my uncle was saying. When Eddie opened his mouth to interrupt, I held up my hand to keep him quiet while I concentrated. Annabeth stepped back to give me space, since she's familiar with my process. Finally I opened my eyes, ready to put into words the video I'd been watching in my head. "Your mom died a few weeks ago in a car accident. Uncle Omar tells me she was angry, driving too fast on a two-lane road somewhere up in Melville, her brakes didn't grab, and she smashed into a tree."

Eddie sucked in his breath as his eyes welled up. Annabeth sat down to put an arm around him, which he shrugged off. "So, big deal," Eddie spit out. "I guess you read the papers."

"Yeah, I've read the news stories. But the part about her brakes wasn't in any of them," I said. "The press just said she lost control."

Eddie's head popped up at that and he gasped. Anger, hurt, grief, and disbelief were all reflected on his face. He balled his fists and clenched his jaw as tears started flowing. "I don't get why she was even in Melville."

I crossed the room and sat down on the other side of him. "She was filing divorce papers at the county courthouse. She and Clyde—"

"He's a jerk," Eddie said, wiping the tears from his eyes with the back of his hand.

Annabeth scooted away from him a little in order to look him in the face. "So when did you decide to run away? And how did you pull that off?"

"After the funeral, things got really bad." Eddie dropped his head into his hands. "My friend Jake Harris, his dad's the foreman on the construction crew working at that old farmhouse. Mr. Harris took us out there after school one day. Jake's into all that hands-on building stuff and I'm a history buff, so while the two of them were measuring or hammering or something, I went exploring."

So that's how he found an out-of-the-way place to hide out. "But the day you disappeared, your friend Jake said you got into a white pickup," I said.

Eddie lifted his head and gave us a crooked grin. "I used my birthday money to stock up supplies, and then I called Uber."

"Yeah," Annabeth said, "but your picture was

everywhere. Why didn't that Uber driver call the police?"

Eddie shrugged. "College guy. Stoned out of his mind. Kept staring at his phone the whole time, ignoring me." He sat up straight and looked me in the eye. "So what's my mom trying to tell me?"

And then just like that all the paranormal energy in the room simply evaporated. "I'm sorry, but that's all I know. We'll need Gary to get the rest of the information."

Annabeth's phone pinged and she pulled it out of her pocket to read the text. "Sean says to meet him and his dad and Brenda Riddell at Tony's. You guys up for pizza?"

I looked Eddie up and down, checking out his wardrobe. "Yeah, as soon as we find some decent clothes for this kid." I got up and brazenly rummaged through the closet. Gary was way too tall for any of his clothes to fit this short, skinny kid, so I pulled a pair of khaki cargo pants and a Hamilton Liberal Arts logo-embossed sweatshirt from Sean's side and tossed them to Eddie, along with a pair of deck shoes. "Go put these on. We roll in ten minutes."

****

Being without a car was a constant problem for Gary. How was he going to get from the far side of Hamilton Liberal Arts College to the south side of Belford? Brenda had texted him back that they— "they?"—would wait and save him some pizza, but if he tried to walk, he'd be at least another hour getting there. And it was cold out. The only solution was to call a cab and hope he had enough money in his debit account to cover it.

Fifteen minutes later the cab let him out in front of Tony's. Gary gave the driver his credit card, held his breath as the guy ran it, and breathed a sigh of relief when the driver handed him his receipt without comment.

Gary hurried inside. Off in the same corner where they'd all eaten the last time, he spotted Brenda, happily chatting with Dr. Paxton. Sean and Annabeth waved him over and he was surprised to also see Eddie nestled between Brenda and Caryn, his hood pulled up over his head.

"We saved you some meat-lover's special," Brenda said, patting the chair next to her.

Gary hung his jean jacket on the back of the chair and shoved his backpack underneath the table. His stomach growled loudly as he opened the lid of the pizza. He pulled out one of the three slices left and took a big bite, moaning with pleasure as he savored the lukewarm flavors. Brenda shoved her half-empty glass of tea over to him and he took a swig between bites. Finally he came up for air and smiled at his mom. "Thanks for not giving up on me."

"Never," Brenda said with a wink. "But we've got kind of a situation here. This young man"—she indicated Eddie—"has a well-known face."

Dr. Paxton nodded in agreement. "When Sean texted and asked me to meet him here, I had no idea my son had been harboring a fugitive."

"Dad," Sean said, "you make it sound like Eddie's committed a crime. He's the victim."

"Did you have a chance to check him out, Dr. Paxton?" Gary asked between bites of pizza. "I mean, Eddie's kinda had a rough couple of weeks."

"I gave him a cursory once-over," Dr. Paxton replied. "This young man's been fairly resourceful. He's not malnourished or suffering any long-term effects of his time in hiding."

"But the reason he was hiding is scary," Caryn said.

Gary lifted an eyebrow at Caryn. "Scary how?"

Caryn readjusted the knitted scarf around her neck. "I sorta heard from…"

"Caryn had a conversation with her dead uncle who was talking to Eddie's mom," Annabeth said, clapping her hands in excitement. "All in your dorm room this afternoon!"

"Lucy," Gary informed them. Eddie's eyes widened in surprise as Caryn glanced at him with a quizzical expression. "Yeah, I've talked to her. For some reason she thinks it's up to me to look after her boy."

"She might be right," Caryn said with a nod. "I mean, from what I heard…"

"Wait," Dr. Paxton said, raising his hand like a traffic cop. "Will someone please explain what's going on here?"

"Caryn's a psychic, Dad," Sean said. "And Gary—you know he sees ghosts, right?"

Gary watched as the color sort of drained out of the doctor's face. It was always like this when someone found out what he could do. But somehow Gary thought Dr. Paxton already knew, either from Sean, or from being his pediatrician when he was a kid, or from hearing it from Brenda, who worked as his receptionist.

"Brenda," Dr. Paxton said, "I remember back when Gary was a child and you were sure his imaginary friends were, well, imaginary. I thought he'd outgrown that."

Brenda looked chagrinned. "His so-called imaginary friends turned out to be ghosts. There are people who can really do what that lady in the TV show did. Gary talks to them and helps them cross over."

Dr. Paxton sat in stunned silence. He shook his head, took a big slurp of water and opened his mouth to speak, but nothing came out. So he finished off the water.

"That's why I was trying so hard to get him to join Ghost Stalkers," Sean told his father. "He's a natural. I finally talked Gary into going with us to the Pelson farmhouse, which is how we found Carson here."

Gary looked up from his food. "You didn't so much talk me into it as roped me into it."

"So the question remains, what do we do about Eddie now?" Brenda asked everyone at the table.

Gary wiped his hands on some napkins, tossed the last piece of crust back into the pizza box, and glanced around the table. Sean was holding hands with Annabeth, who was giggling as usual, and neither of them were focused on Eddie at the moment. Eddie was slumped down in his chair as if he were trying to make himself invisible, and eyeing the door like he was going to make a run for it any minute. Caryn kept glancing between Brenda and Dr. Paxton, probably waiting for them to weigh in. Suddenly Gary felt that chill in the air and he noticed Caryn's eyes widen, too, so she must have felt something. Eddie's mom materialized behind her son.

Lucy put her hands on Eddie's shoulders and the kid reacted by shivering and glancing nervously around him. "Gary, you have to convince your mother to look after my son for a few days," Lucy said.

"What? Why?" Gary asked her.

"Why what?" Dr. Paxton asked.

Gary and Caryn exchanged glances. He knew she was also aware there was a ghost present, even though she couldn't see or communicate with her. "Lucy suggested we let Eddie stay with Brenda for a few days. Just till we figure out what to do next."

Brenda thought about that. "I still have to work, but I guess it's better than leaving him in a college dorm with nothing to do."

"I had plenty to do!" Eddie exclaimed. "I did Gary's calculus homework."

Gary rounded on the kid. "You did what?"

Eddie shrugged. "I told you I could help you out. I dug through your desk and found your work. It was all wrong, man. So I redid it. You'll get an A+."

Everyone at the table looked wide-eyed at Eddie. "Claims he's a genius," Gary told them. "But listen, kid, stay out of my stuff from now on."

Brenda smiled. "You know, Gary, that's exactly how I imagined you'd talk to a younger brother, if you'd had one."

Caryn gasped, then clapped her hands over her mouth. When Annabeth mouthed What? she shook her head, grabbed her class of tea and took a big gulp.

"Mom, it's more than just the kid being bored," Gary said. "He's not safe at his house."

Brenda's brow furrowed. "Oh." She looked carefully from Gary to Eddie, and Annabeth and Caryn nodded in agreement. "Well, this is serious." When no one said anything else, she put on her coat, reached for her handbag and stood up to leave. "So it's settled then? I'll take Eddie home with me. Gary, we'll see you in a few days at opening night." With that, she patted Eddie's shoulder, indicating he should come along. Annabeth, Dr. Paxton, and Sean followed them out.

"Caryn, got a minute?" Gary asked.

"Well, Annabeth's my ride," she said, glancing at the door.

"Sorry I never got back to you today."

Caryn had one eye on the door and the other on Gary. She stopped, listening to her muses, Gary figured, and then shook her head. "I was digging through the newspaper archives. Some stuff about Lucy. Nothing that couldn't wait." She reached for the door.

Gary held it open for her and they walked out together. "Before you go, can you at least tell me what happened to Lucy? She won't talk about it."

Caryn wrapped her scarf around her neck and threw her bag over her shoulder. "Car accident. She was on her way to file for a divorce. That sorry husband of hers wasn't just abusive to Eddie but to her, too."

Gary shuddered. Poor kid, he thought. Even though his own bio dad had all but disowned him, Gary was at least glad he hadn't had to live with that kind of hell. And now he was beginning to understand Lucy Carson's urgent need to make sure Eddie was safe before she crossed over.

"Will I see you this week?" Gary asked Caryn. Wait. Why did I ask her that? He swallowed hard and hurried to add, "I mean, opening night of *Pride and Prejudice*?"

Caryn actually smiled at him. "Wouldn't miss it."

She hopped into Annabeth's car, leaving Gary to

wonder what he'd just gotten himself into. Another bad review? He hoped not.

Chapter 13

I'd done the initial research on the article I wanted to write for the newspaper yesterday, but I went into the office this afternoon to polish it up and get it ready to go in the Monday morning edition.

Eddie's story was crazy important, not only for him but for other children who were in similar home situations. After reading about Lucy Carson Seville's car accident and tuning in to my radar, I couldn't just sit on the information I got from the Universe. I desperately wanted to do something to help Eddie, without helping him into a foster home, of course. I may have gotten most of Lucy's story from paranormal sources, but I also had to incorporate real-life research.

I texted Del to get his okay to do the story, and once that was cleared, I went to work. Anybody can write a story from online research, so I decided I needed some quotes from experts. I got on the phone and tried to contact the head of HLAC's Sociology Department for statistics about domestic violence. Since it was Sunday I got voice mail, but her assistant called me back within the hour and agreed to give me a quote. Next I spoke to a graduate student from the School of Educational Psychology that staff reporter Sydney Marshall had used on a previous story about school behavior issues. The graduate student said a child's poor academic performance can sometimes be a direct result of living in an abusive environment. I didn't know how Eddie had been doing at school, but it made sense he was miserable because of his mom's death.

The next part was a little trickier. I mean, let's face it, Eddie was listed as a missing child, and my friends and I not only knew where he was, we were actively hiding him. After thinking about it a long time, and even picking up the phone and then hanging up a couple of times, I finally put in a call to Detective Albers at the Belford Police Department, the same detective who detained all of us the night of the campus snowball fight. I'd have to be careful what I asked, though, because I didn't want to let on that I knew Eddie's whereabouts.

"Detective," I said when he answered his office phone, "this is Caryn Alderson from the Hamilton Campus Herald. We met in the police station the night of—"

"Yes, I remember," he replied. "What can I do for you?"

Well, he's rude. I could even see in my mind how he was about to snap a pencil in half while talking to me. "I'm working on a story for the paper. I was wondering if you might share any experiences you may have had with domestic violence cases, and especially child abuse as a result."

There was a long silence on his end. "What for?"

"I've been thinking about Eddie Carson, that boy who, uh, went missing from Belford Middle School last month." It was all I could do to keep from choking on the "missing" part.

"What makes you think he was a victim of abuse?"

The detective sounded suspicious.

Even before we found him, it seemed obvious to me that the kid hadn't been abducted but was more likely a runaway. And kids don't run away from happy homes. Frankly I couldn't believe the detective hadn't already figured it out. "I don't think, Detective, I know. I'm psychic, remember?"

I heard him snort on the other end. "Oh yeah, right. Psychic."

"So perhaps you'd be willing to share your general impressions of how domestic violence affects the kids in the family."

I was relieved when he agreed to briefly discuss some hypothetical situations. I jotted down quotes, thanked him for his time, and finished work on the article.

****

Despite the chaotic weekend, Gary and Sean followed their usual routine on Monday morning, which was fine with Gary, because he wanted some normalcy to put the events of the past few days behind him. They went to the dorm cafeteria where Sean piled his plate high with eggs and sausage while Gary chose black coffee and a sweet roll.

"Don't look at me like that," Gary said. "Who knows when or if I'll get lunch?"

"All the more reason to eat real food." Sean tilted his head in the direction of an empty booth on the wall farthest from the drafty entryway, and plopped his tray down. Gary picked up a copy of the campus newspaper on his way to join Sean.

"Busy week?" Sean asked him.

Gary's shoulders slumped. "Exams in English and

calculus, dress rehearsal, then opening night next Saturday. Plus work every afternoon. I won't resurface till Thanksgiving."

"Yeah, I've got an Econ paper due this week." Sean took the newspaper from Gary to peruse the front page. They ate in silence as he flipped through it before stopping on the Features page. "Hey, dude, look at this. Your girlfriend's got a half-page story here, byline and all." Sean folded the paper and pointed out the section to Gary.

"Girlfriend?" Gary felt his face burn. What was Sean thinking? Yeah, he and Caryn had come to a truce, but she wasn't his girlfriend. He took the paper from Sean and looked at the title: Domestic Violence is Child Abuse, by Caryn Alderson. He read the story with growing appreciation for the hard work she'd done in such a short amount of time, even quoting that cranky police detective from Belford and some professors in the field. She finished with statistics on abuse and telltale signs to look for.

Sean lowered his voice and leaned in close so as not to be overheard. "Does she mention Eddie?"

"Sort of," Gary said as he pointed to a paragraph. "She mentions him as a local high-profile missing child case, and then speculates on why he went missing."

They finished reading the story in silence. "Is this gonna sic the cops on Eddie? 'Cause she makes it sound like she knows for a fact he's been victimized," Sean said.

"We both know she does." Gary looked around the cafeteria to see who might be reading the story, since it was buried in the middle of the second section. He couldn't tell, because although several students were reading the paper, they could just as easily have been looking at the sports page. "But she sticks to her facts pretty well, leaving the conclusions up to her readers." He folded up the newspaper and shoved the last of the sweet roll in his mouth while reaching for his coffee.

"Where ya headed?" Sean asked.

Gary pushed his backpack over one shoulder and said, "Oral Interp class, but I'm gonna take a detour to the newspaper office on the way."

"Say hi to Not-Your-Girlfriend," Sean said as Gary turned to walk away.

Gary decided to ignore his roommate's snide remark. He glanced at the time and realized his class started in ten minutes, but decided to risk being late. He could probably just text Caryn, but he told himself Eddie's safety was at stake.

As he walked across campus, he pulled his jacket hoodie over his head and kept his head low so as not to encounter anybody he didn't want to talk to—living or dead. He hadn't seen Lucy for a couple of days, which was a relief, but Gary knew she wasn't the only ghost hanging around campus. He hoped Lucy had taken his advice and crossed over, especially since Eddie was safe at Brenda's house for the time being.

"Nice story in the paper," a voice in front of him said.

Gary stopped walking and, against his better judgment, looked up. "Lucy," he groaned.

"Tell your psychic friend that I appreciate her calling attention to Eddie's situation."

"I'll send her your regards," Gary said as he plowed right by—or through—her.

The campus carillon was striking nine a.m. when

he arrived in front of the building that housed the newspaper office, and Gary silently berated himself for coming here instead of going to Oral Interp. Besides, someone might overhear his and Caryn's conversation in that office, and then Eddie would be outed for sure. He turned to leave, reminding himself there were only a few weeks left before final exams in December, and his scholarship still hung in the balance. He couldn't afford to miss class.

"Gary?"

Gary turned back around to see Annabeth coming out of the building, her bag over her shoulder and camera slung around her neck.

"Oh, hi. I was going to talk to Caryn, but…" He glanced nervously at the clock on the tower.

"She's gone to class, but I'll walk with you."

It was a frosty November morning and Annabeth pulled her scarf a little tighter around her neck. "I guess you read Caryn's story."

"Yeah, and it's got me worried. At this rate, Eddie's not gonna stay hidden much longer."

"But did you really read it, Gary?" Annabeth asked him as they hurried across campus. "It barely mentioned Eddie, but it did call attention to a serious problem that lots of families keep quiet about."

Gary thought about that. "Yeah, I guess so. By the way, the kid's mom—you know, ghost Lucy—said to tell Caryn she approved."

Annabeth's eyes widened. "I'll be sure to give her the message." They stopped in front of a classroom building. "This is me. And don't worry, 'cause I think Caryn's story's gonna make an impact." She waved goodbye.

Gary watched Annabeth go. As long as he was already late and with Eddie on his mind, he pulled out his phone and sent Brenda a text, but kept it generic.

—*How's the kid?*—

Brenda replied a minute later, just as Gary was entering his classroom and enduring Dr. Danson's look of disapproval for being late. He glanced down at the text anyway.

—*He's okay. I'm at work and our guest is on my home computer doing math. Way over my head kind of stuff. Talk later.*—

****

"You know what they say," Foster Benning told his actors as he motioned them to gather around on the stage. "Bad dress rehearsal, great opening night."

"Then we should be freakin' awesome," Gary said with a groan.

The dress rehearsal the previous evening had been a near fiasco. Tricia aka Elizabeth Bennet still didn't know all her lines and she kept tugging at the ill-fitting corset she was forced to wear as part of her Regency-era costume. Kevin Michaels arrived late, breathless from a soccer tournament on the south side of Indianapolis, didn't even bother with makeup, and proceeded to get sweat and grime all over his vest and cravat. In the third act, when Darcy's proposal to Elizabeth should have been sincere, Kevin accidentally repeated his Act One arrogant proposal, causing Foster to call a halt to the scene and start over. Delia Ferguson as Jane Bennet was at least on time and prepared, but when they started the Country Line Dance, she tripped over the edge of her skirt and twisted her ankle. Now she was hobbling around, and underneath her skirt and stockings was an ace bandage. Gary kept tugging at his waistcoat, since it was cut too short for someone his height. Luckily his also too-short pants could be tucked into his riding boots. Even the lighting and sound went haywire, with blackouts mid-scene, the curtain closing before the end of Act One, and on and on.

"Since Jane Austen has such a huge following, we've got a packed house tonight," Foster told his cast members. "Let's not disappoint them. Places everybody. Break a leg! And Delia, I don't mean that literally."

Gary pulled back the curtain a couple of inches and sneaked a peek. Foster was right, almost every seat was taken. He did a quick glance around the audience and saw Brenda front row center, like she always was at every one of his plays. And next to her was a kid wearing sunglasses and a baseball cap pulled low over his brow. Eddie. Hopefully no one would recognize him and he would keep a low profile till the lights went down. In the middle of the auditorium and a little to his left he spotted Sean, Annabeth, and—was that Caryn? He blinked. Yes, it was her, note pad at the ready. Gary felt a surge of nerves when he thought of what she might write about his performance, or was that just opening night butterflies? No, it couldn't be. After all these weeks of rehearsal, Gary felt confident about his own part. Unfortunately he couldn't say the same for his cast mates.

And then just before the house lights dimmed, he caught sight of someone walking in and taking a seat in the back row. A tall, slender blond guy who looked like an older version of himself. Ned Harrington? What the…?

No time to think about that now. As Mr. Bingley, Gary wasn't in the first scene, but he needed to get into character beforehand, so he forced all thoughts of Ned to the back of his mind. He went to the wings and paced back and forth, repeating lines and blocking, while he awaited the opening of the scene at the Meryton Assembly where Mr. Bingley singles out Jane Bennet.

The play came off a lot better than Gary had expected. Kevin as Darcy only went up on one line, albeit an important one in his first proposal to Elizabeth Bennet. However, he recovered well and Gary hoped the audience didn't notice. Or more importantly, he hoped Caryn didn't notice. Delia managed to cover her bandaged ankle with her skirt, and she powered through the dancing scenes with barely a visible limp. At the end of the play when Gary's character was happily reunited with Delia aka Jane, and Darcy and Elizabeth proclaimed their love for one another, Gary could feel the audience's approval as they gave the cast a standing ovation. Hey, it wasn't Shakespeare, but Gary hadn't felt this good about a performance since last summer's Shakespeare in the Park.

As the curtain closed and the house lights came up, Gary hopped off the edge of the stage and looked around for his mom. Before he could locate her, though, he felt a tap on his shoulder. It was Caryn standing behind him. Annabeth and Sean were next to her, Sean's arms around Annabeth, her head resting on Sean's shoulder.

"Not bad," Caryn said.

"High praise coming from you," Gary replied.

Annabeth elbowed Caryn in the ribs. "Come on, girlfriend, admit it. The play was good."

Caryn smiled as her cheeks reddened. "Yeah, okay."

"More than okay," Brenda said, stepping up to her son and wrapping an arm around his waist. "I thoroughly enjoyed it."

Gary gave his mom a hug, but quickly let go when she recoiled. He knew he was sweaty from being under the stage lights, and his face makeup was starting to run down his neck. He loosened the tight cravat, unbuttoned the linen shirt, and slipped out of his waistcoat, which he carefully placed on a nearby front-row seat. "Thanks, Mom. It's good to see you here." Gary looked over her shoulder and craned his neck around her. "Um, where's...?" He didn't dare say Eddie's name out loud, but he didn't see the kid anywhere.

"Men's room. And I told him to keep his cap on and not to talk to anyone, just in case."

Annabeth and Caryn exchanged glances, and Caryn said, "Brenda? You brought...our friend?"

Brenda nodded. "I felt guilty leaving him home alone after he'd been by himself everyday while I worked. And you won't believe it, but he's actually read *Pride and Prejudice* and did a running commentary all evening on how the play differed from the novel."

"Of course he did," Gary said.

"Mind if I join you?"

Gary turned around to see Ned standing there, hanging back from the group a little, but looking eager to step in. Gary groaned inwardly, but then he noticed Brenda blanch. No way was he letting this guy make his mom feel uncomfortable. He started to step between them, but Caryn reached out and put a calming hand on his arm.

"Let your parents talk," Caryn whispered.

"Ned?" Brenda said in a raspy voice. "Ned Harrington? What are you doing here?"

Ned took a step closer. "I came to see my...to see our...to see Gary in the play." He cast a quick glance at his son. "No ulterior motives, I promise."

This was awkward in the extreme. Gary's parents in the same room for the first time since, well, probably since they were teenagers. The two of them stood mere inches apart, staring at one another, Ned towering over Brenda's petite frame. Brenda looked like she was about to burst into tears, and Ned looked...Gary didn't know what that look was. Regret? Gary glanced at his friends, hoping he'd get a hint of what to do about this situation from their expressions. Nothing.

"Hey, what's going on here?" Eddie was back from the men's room, still wearing the sunglasses and baseball cap, but speaking way too loud if he was trying to fly under the radar.

Gary tossed the kid a warning look while Brenda and his friends shifted uncomfortably. Caryn stepped back to survey the scene. Gary recognized the familiar tilted-head stance she always took while listening to her spirit guide.

"Who's this?" Ned asked, indicating Eddie.

No one answered. Then Caryn said, "Excuse me. Story deadline," and ran up the aisle.

****

Okay, so that may not have been the coolest move I ever made. But between something I already knew psychically, my surprise at seeing Ned, and then Eddie, I knew I had to get out of there before I blurted out something I shouldn't. I needed to talk to Gary, but looking over my shoulder I could see he was preoccupied with the awkward situation with his birth parents. I felt bad for him, I really did, but I had to get out of there.

Since I came with Annabeth and Sean, I was forced to walk across campus on my own. My phone pinged with a text from Annabeth.

—*What happened? And don't tell me it's the play review deadline. That's for Monday.*—

I didn't know what to say.

—*Sorry I was rude*—was the best I could do. Okay, it wasn't an answer, but right now, I couldn't tell her or anyone else what I knew. I needed to sit with it awhile, and maybe talk to Uncle Omar. I veered off in the direction of the dorm, checked my handbag to make sure I had both my notes on tonight's performance and my room key, pulled my hat down over my ears and ducked my head against the cold November wind.

****

Gary couldn't take it anymore, this awkward silence between Brenda and Ned. Brenda had tears brimming in her eyes, Ned looked like his collar was choking him, and Eddie was standing back, arms crossed, a puzzled expression on his face as he watched them both.

"Why did Caryn run off like that?" Sean asked Annabeth.

She shrugged and showed him Caryn's text.

Sean tossed a meaningful glance at Gary and his parents. "I say we head to the Student Union for some coffee," he said, steering Annabeth toward the exit.

"Thanks for coming, guys," Gary said. He faced

his mom, deliberately turning his back on Ned. "I need to scrub off the makeup and get changed. I'll meet you there."

Ned didn't budge. "Brenda, would it be all right if I called you sometime? To talk about Gary, I mean."

Gary watched his mom as her eyes widened, but to his surprise, she nodded her head, took Eddie by the arm and hustled him out.

Ned watched her go before turning to his son. "Who's the kid?" he asked again.

"Houseguest," Gary mumbled.

Ned shifted his stance. "Gary, I just wanted to say I enjoyed your performance, and…"

Gary wasn't interested in anything his bio dad had to say. "Thanks for coming, Ned." He turned on his heel, jumped up on the stage, and never looked back.

He reached for the doorknob to enter the men's dressing room when he felt that familiar tingle on the back of his neck. Sure enough, there was Lucy. He sighed. "You still here? I thought you crossed over."

"Soon," she replied. "Just as soon as one last piece of the puzzle falls into place."

Gary blew out a puff of air. "And what might that be?"

"Well, of course it's about Eddie," she said with a playful grin.

It was amazing how solid she looked, and how upbeat she seemed from the last time he'd seen her. Still, Lucy was dead and she needed to move on. "Look, my mom's looking after your boy for the moment. Don't worry about him."

The smile faded from her lips. "I can't help but worry, especially with Clyde…"

"What about him?"

Lucy didn't answer. Just as she was fading out she said, "You need to talk to Caryn."

"About...?" Gary asked. But she was gone. Dead or alive, women were confusing. He rolled his eyes and stepped into the dressing room.

Chapter 14

I never need caller ID, since I always know who's calling before the phone rings. So when I picked up the phone and said, "Hey, Mom," I didn't know why she was surprised.

"Caryn," she said. "How did you..." She stopped and chuckled. "I wanted to talk about the holidays. Thanksgiving first, of course."

"I'm done with classes tomorrow afternoon, so I'll catch a ride home with Annabeth and be there to help you shop for groceries, or cook, or set the table, or whatever you need me to do."

"Caryn, you have many talents, but cooking isn't one of them. I'll take care of all that. It's just going to be you, me, and George anyway, so nothing fancy. What I do need is for you to come into the store and do some readings. I've got people calling constantly, insisting I book them a spot."

"Okay, sure," I said. "Now get to what you really wanted to talk about. And I know it's not turkey and dressing or psychic readings."

There was a pause on Mom's end, long enough for me to think ahead to our usual Christmas celebration. We always start the morning with flavored coffee and her delicious made-from-scratch sweet rolls, and then Mom, George, and I open our gifts. After phone calls from Dad and Michael in Houston and George's son in

Hawaii, we set out for a late afternoon meal at whatever Chinese restaurant we can find open. But for some reason the vision for this year was really fuzzy.

"Caryn, how would you like to spend Christmas in Houston with your dad and Michael?"

Didn't see that coming. But then I never do when it's about my own life. "I haven't heard from them, Mom. Did they invite me?"

"I texted Guy and he's excited about it. So what do you think?"

"Yeah, that would be great, but what will you be doing?"

"George has a pharmaceutical conference in Hawaii the week between Christmas and New Year's."

Oh, okay. Now I could see clearly what she hadn't been able to put into words. I knew why she was hesitating, but it was so exciting for her and I didn't want her to worry about me. "Oh, Mom, what a great opportunity! A proper honeymoon for you and George, since you never really had one, a chance to spend Christmas in paradise, and of course George can see his son...get married, right?"

"I can't put anything past you, Caryn."

"Go for it, Mom. I'll have a wonderful visit with Dad and Michael. Hey, it's warm in Houston in December, too, or at least warmer than here. We'll both get a break from the cold."

I could hear Mom exhaling with relief. Like I'd try to spoil this for her with a guilt trip. "I'll see you in a few days, Mom. And go ahead and book those readings at the store. Might as well make some money while I'm home."

"One client has been particularly persistent, Caryn.

Said his name's Ned, and that you know how to reach him."

I didn't know if I was surprised by that or not. I pretty much knew what he wanted to talk about—Gary—but one thing Ned didn't know was the other piece of information I was sitting on. "Okay, Mom, I'll call him."

We hung up and I faced a dilemma. I knew what I had to tell Ned was important, but I didn't know how to say it. Gulp.

****

Gary only had two days of classes before Thanksgiving break, but those two days were scheduled down to the last minute. And Monday afternoon, after his last class of the day and before work, he had his all-important audition for Macbeth. Gary was determined to get the coveted part. After taking on a secondary role in a play he never would have done if there had been any other choices, he felt this was his opportunity to shine.

Caryn Alderson wrote a surprisingly positive review of *Pride and Prejudice*. She called it "a pleasant diversion" and praised Foster Benning's directorial choices. Caryn mentioned Delia with a few kind words about her performance as Jane Bennet and then expressed her disappointment in Kevin Michaels as Darcy, since literally and artistically he didn't measure up. And she totally slammed Tricia Palmer's mumbling and forgettable Elizabeth Bennet. But after that scathing newspaper review of his audition last month, Gary breathed a sigh of relief when Caryn gave high praise to his portrayal of Bingley, saying his supporting character stole every scene he was in. Gary carefully clipped the review from his copy of The Herald to save for the scrapbook Brenda kept of his play reviews over the years.

Students he didn't even know congratulated him when they saw him on campus or at the bookstore. Gary was justifiably proud of his performance, fueling his soaring confidence about getting Macbeth.

At the rehearsal studio that afternoon, Gary scouted out the room filled with Shakespearean actor-wannabes. His only real competition for the lead was Foster Benning, but Foster was short and stocky, and didn't have the commanding physical presence Macbeth needed. At least that was how Gary saw it.

The audition scene was Act Five Scene Five, where Macbeth learns of his wife's death. Each of the actors trying out for the lead read the lines, with Dr. Danson reading Seyton's short intro line from his seat while jotting notes on a legal pad. First up was Foster, and Gary had to admit his reading was good, but he was stuck to the book like glue, never once looking up. The next actor to audition for the part was Kevin Michaels. And not surprisingly, he sucked. Gary tried hard not to smirk.

Then Tricia Palmer hopped up onto the stage.

"Miss Palmer," Dr. Danson said, "we're auditioning for Macbeth right now. Lady Macbeth auditions are tomorrow."

Tricia waved off his comment, pulled a ponytail holder off her wrist, and tied her hair back in a tight bun. "I'm auditioning for Macbeth. If Glen Close could play Hamlet, a woman can play Macbeth."

Loud groans issued from all the other actors, but Dr. Danson sighed and said, "Then get on with it."

Tricia pulled out her script and read the scene. Gary thought she was okay, probably good enough to get Lady Macbeth if she'd bother to actually learn the lines. But he hoped that Dr. Danson was looking to cast this play traditionally—with a man in the part.

"And last up, we have Gary Riddell." Dr. Danson looked at him skeptically. "Are you ready, Mr. Riddell?"

"Yes, sir," Gary said. He walked regally onto the stage, sans script, and delivered his lines already memorized.

Dr. Danson read Seyton's line, "The Queen, my lord, is dead." He then waved to Gary to begin.

MACBETH:
> "She should have died hereafter;
> There would have been time for such a word.
> To-morrow, and to-morrow, and to-morrow,
> Creeps in this petty pace from day to day
> To the last syllable of recorded time,
> And all our yesterdays have lighted fools
> The way to dusty death. Out, out, brief candle!
> Life's but a walking shadow, a poor player
> That struts and frets his hour upon the stage
> And then is heard no more; it is a tale
> Told by an idiot, full of sound and fury
> Signifying nothing."

When he finished, the room went silent. Gary had a moment of panic. Did I forget a part? Not put enough emotion into it? Then slowly everyone in the room—fellow actors, stage crew, tech people, and even Dr. Danson—applauded. Gary dipped his head in acknowledgment and knew the part was his.

****

I put off making that phone call as long as I could, but after my last class on Tuesday, I couldn't stall any longer. I definitely needed some privacy, though, because of the sensitive nature of the conversation. I was too far from the dorm, and I was pretty sure the Student Union bookstore and coffee shop would be crowded with kids who were still on campus before leaving for the long holiday weekend. The only place I could think of was the library, and it was nearby. Lucky for me it was pretty empty in there. I was able to find a vacant study room, checked my phone's call log for Ned Harrington's number, and dialed. I almost hoped it would go straight to voice mail. Naturally he picked up.

"Harrington," he said, sounding a little out of breath.

I concentrated a little and saw him out jogging. He answers his phone while on his run? I just don't get these corporate people. I waited till his breathing slowed before jumping in. "Hi, Ned, it's Caryn Alderson. My mom tells me you've been trying to book an appointment with me. At her store." Silence on his end, making me figure I either caught him off-guard or he had no idea who I was, so I added, "In Indianapolis?"

"Oh, yeah, right," he said.

"I could see you tomorrow if that works," I said.

There was a long pause on his end. So long, in fact, that I pulled back my phone and stared at the screen to see if we'd lost our connection.

"I guess that would work," he finally said. "Of course, as always—"

"You want to keep our meeting private," I finished for him. "Got it. Would morning or afternoon work for you?"

"I've got some clients, so what about after work. Six o'clock?"

"See you then, Ned." I disconnected and then blew out a puff of air. I had no idea how I was going to pull this off.

"Don't worry, kiddo," Uncle Omar said loud and clear. "I've got your back."

I turned completely around, expecting to see him lurking somewhere in the book stacks or a study carrel, wearing his army fatigues and that ever-present grin on his face, but he'd chosen not to materialize this time. I put my phone back to my ear for the benefit of any onlookers and said, "Okay, thanks," as I exited the study room.

Naturally the phone chose that minute to actually ring, causing the few students who were there studying to give me dirty looks. And Erica Stone, the seventeen-year-old prodigy, pointed at the Please silence your cell phones sign.

I turned my back on Erica. "Annabeth? Hi," I whispered into the phone.

"Caryn? Are you there? I can barely hear you."

"I'm in the library." I started walking for the exit, hoping to minimize the disruption. I stepped out into the crisp November air and took a deep, cleansing breath. "Okay, I can talk now."

"Why were you in the library?" she asked. "I thought you were done with classes."

"Yeah, I…Never mind. What's up?"

"I'm in our room," Annabeth said, "packing. I thought you'd be here since you said you wanted a ride home."

"On my way."

****

"Need a ride home, dude?" Sean asked Gary.

Gary surveyed the mess in their dorm room—okay, his side of the room. He hadn't done laundry in a couple of weeks. He eyed the ever-growing pile of dirty clothes at the foot of his bed, and hoped Brenda wouldn't mind when he landed on their doorstep with all his laundry. Then he remembered that his mom was still taking care of Eddie, which meant double the smelly socks, stained jeans, and rumpled T-shirts. Maybe he'd do his own wash this time.

Gary pointed to his pile of clothes. "Do you have room for all this? Because Mom can come pick me up when she gets off work."

"No need," Sean said. He picked up his small duffel bag sitting at the foot of his bed and tossed it over one shoulder. "I'm ready when you are."

Gary pulled his own duffel bag out of the back of his closet and crammed in dirty clothes and towels, and then stuffed in the muddy tennis shoes from the night of the snowball fight that he hoped would come clean. The bag filled up fast, leaving him wondering if he had room for the few changes of clean clothes he had left.

"Put the rest in your backpack," Sean said, like he could read Gary's mind. "Your mom will make short work of that mess."

But instead of packing, Gary ran his fingers through his hair and sat down on the edge of his bed. "I can't ask her to do that," Gary said. "She's still got Eddie there."

Sean frowned. "Yeah, that's a conundrum." Setting aside his own neatly-packed bag, he took Gary's backpack off the chair where it always landed when Gary walked through the door, and emptied it of textbooks, loose papers, blue books, and scripts. Sean handed the now empty bag to Gary. "Your mom's a candidate for sainthood with that kid."

"I know. Once we get through Thanksgiving we gotta figure something out." Gary stood up and dug through the dresser drawer to gather what clean underwear and socks he had left. He removed his last clean pair of jeans, a hooded sweatshirt and a sweater from the closet, and rolled them into balls small enough to stuff into a backpack.

"What are your plans?" Sean asked. "For Thanksgiving, I mean."

Gary shrugged. "Mom always just cooks for the two of us, although sometimes we go to the grandparents' for dessert. Except I don't know how we'd explain Eddie." He tried zipping the backpack, but it was overstuffed.

Sean nodded. "I'll talk to my dad when I get home. See if he's got any ideas. And Annabeth's dad might be able to help, too." With both hands he pushed down on Gary's backpack so Gary could get it zipped, then picked up his own duffel bag. "Let's hit it, dude."

****

"Traffic's terrible," Annabeth said as she honked her horn at a driver who failed to notice the light had turned green.

I glanced out the window and then looked over at Annabeth's odometer. In an hour's time we'd only made it a few miles from Belford on our way southbound to Indianapolis. Between rush hour traffic and people leaving town for an early start on the

Thanksgiving weekend, it was slow going. Twenty miles an hour slow. At this rate we'd be lucky to be home by supper. As if on cue, my stomach growled and I remembered the granola bar and hot chocolate that had passed for lunch today. Visions of my mom's veggie chili danced in my head.

"Got plans tomorrow?" Annabeth asked as she eased her car into the intersection. "Caryn? Helloo…?"

I'd been kind of in a zone, staring out at the stop and go traffic, when I realized Annabeth was talking to me. "Oh, sorry. You mentioned supper and I'm starved. What about tomorrow?"

"Well, nothing really. Just making chit-chat." She punched some buttons on her steering wheel and the radio came blasting on. "Eek!" She quickly adjusted the volume down, and then flipped over to the smooth jazz station.

"Mom called," I told her, "and I've got some clients to see at the store."

"Well, don't work too late, because I'm picking you up at six a.m. Thursday morning."

I widened my eyes at her. "We're doing that again?"

The first year I met Annabeth, she dragged me out of bed at what felt like the middle of the night on Thanksgiving, along with her friends from church Sydney Marshall and Mel Something-or-other, and we went to downtown Indianapolis to help with the huge Thanksgiving dinner a charity sponsors every year. Several thousand hungry people show up, so they need lots of volunteers to help cook, serve, and clean up. It felt really good doing something so important for those in need, so Annabeth and I have continued the tradition every year since.

"Of course we're doing it. Why wouldn't we?" she asked.

I shook my head. "No, I'm going. I just kinda spaced it, what with this situation with Gary, and Eddie, and his mom, and..." I clamped my mouth shut before I said too much. Client confidentiality and all.

"...and?" Annabeth prompted before stifling a giggle. "Did some flash of psychic insight hit you?"

I rolled my eyes. "I'll be ready Thursday morning at six," I told her, and hoped she'd let it drop.

One more glance out the window told me traffic wasn't going to let up, so I leaned back against the headrest and closed my eyes, the soft jazz helping me to relax. I wasn't going to sleep or anything, just hoping for a vision or some answer to this mess I'd gotten into the middle of. Maybe I was trying too hard, though, because nothing came.

****

"Mom? You home?" Gary dragged his duffel bag through the front door of their condo. He glanced around the living room, happy to be home after three months of dorm living.

He remembered the day the two of them had moved in after years of being dependent on his grandparents. Grandma and Granddad Riddell worked long hours and struggled to keep the bill collectors at bay, so when Gary came along, another mouth to feed was a complication they hadn't needed. They told his fifteen-year-old mother in no uncertain terms that she had to pull her own weight, so Brenda juggled schoolwork and part time jobs while the two of them were crammed into her childhood bedroom. By the time she was nineteen, though, Brenda had been working full time as Dr. Paxton's receptionist for nearly a year, so she could afford to move the two of them out of her folks' house and into a small apartment. A few more years of pinching pennies, and Brenda had saved up enough money for a down payment on a home of their own. The condo wasn't very big, but they each had their own bedroom and bath, the kitchen was adequate even though it was a little outdated, and there was a study off the main living room where Gary had done homework.

Gary called out again, but no one answered. Brenda was probably still at work. He started up the stairs to his bedroom, where he heard the beep beep of a video game emanating from the other side of the closed door. He opened it to find Eddie sitting cross-legged on Gary's bed, punching the keypad faster than Gary had ever been able to. The TV in Gary's room was small and about ten years old, a relic from Brenda's childhood bedroom, but it was fine for the small game collection Gary had amassed. Eddie was totally focused on the screen and didn't even look up when Gary dropped his overstuffed bags on the floor with a thud. With still no reaction, Gary tapped Eddie on the shoulder.

Eddie jumped, dropped the remote, and then scowled. "Don't sneak up on a guy like that."

"Sorry." Gary didn't like it either when someone came up behind him when he was running lines or concentrating on schoolwork, so he understood where the kid was coming from. He unzipped the duffel bag filled with dirty laundry and tossed it into the hamper in his closet.

"Don't you have anything better than"—Eddie picked up the plastic cases and read each one before tossing it aside—"Super Mario, Batman, and this 2007 Grand Theft Auto? They're old-school, and so easy I finished them in minutes."

Gary narrowed his eyes at Eddie. "First of all, who gave you permission to get into my stuff? And secondly, I didn't have much time for video games. I was either studying or rehearsing."

Eddie scowled back as he ticked numbers off his fingers. "First of all, your mom, second, I forgot about your Shakespeare stuff, and—" He peeked out of the corner of his eye at Gary. "And I'm starved. When do we eat?"

"When Mom gets home, I guess. And speaking of home…" Gary started to say This isn't yours, but he stopped himself. Even though Eddie was a pain in the butt, the kid had had a rough life. "Have you made any attempt to contact your dad?"

Eddie crossed his arms and glared at Gary. "For the millionth time, Clyde Seville isn't my father."

"Yeah, well, he's the only parent you've got. And last I checked, he was still looking for you."

Eddie clenched his teeth. "Sucks to be him. I'm never going back there."

Gary sat down on the edge of his bed. "You're thirteen, Eddie. Your choices are Clyde or foster care." Gary watched as Eddie's face went from pale to red with anger.

"Neither!" Eddie reached under the bed and pulled out his backpack, snatched up the worn-out hooded sweatshirt from the hook on the back of Gary's bedroom door, and stomped out of the room, slamming the door behind him.

"Hey, where ya going?" Gary called out, but knew it was futile when he heard the front door slam shut as well. Gary sighed. He knew this situation couldn't go on much longer. Hiding a runaway kid was wrong and possibly illegal. He was glad he was home to help his mom figure out what to do.

"Eddie's right, you know. Clyde's a lousy excuse for a father."

Gary felt the tingle on the back of his neck and turned around to see Lucy. It occurred to him that Eddie looked just like her when he got angry, because Lucy's arms were crossed like her son, she had a scowl on her semi-translucent face, and she was soundlessly tapping her foot.

Gary shoved all the game cartridges aside and flopped down on his bed. "So you got any suggestions?"

"Find Eddie's birth father," Lucy said.

Gary sat straight up. "His...what?" He ran his fingers through his hair and closed his eyes, trying to think this through. "Why didn't you tell me this before?" He reopened his eyes.

But Lucy was gone.

Between his Macbeth audition the day before, classes that were getting intense because of looming final exams, his job at the bookstore, and the constant encounters with this particularly pesky ghost, Gary was drained. He stretched out on his bed planning to just rest, but he must have dozed off, because the next thing he knew he heard the garage door open, meaning Brenda was home. He bounded down the stairs and into the kitchen.

"Gary," Brenda said with a warm smile. She hugged him with one arm as she set two plastic bags filled with groceries on the kitchen counter with the other. "I was hoping you'd be here." She tilted her head toward her car in the garage and then hung her coat on the hook by the door.

Gary retrieved the other three shopping bags from her trunk and set them on the counter beside the others. "Mom, can we talk?"

"Always." Brenda dug into the bags and began putting the frozen and refrigerated items away first. She handed Gary the bag with the nonperishables. "Does it have to be now, or can we eat dinner first?"

Gary shook his head as he put away cereal, crackers, cookies, and canned goods. "I'm hungry, but I need to tell you this while Eddie's out of the house."

Brenda stopped unpacking groceries mid-bag. She seemed panic-stricken as her eyes darted around the kitchen and into the living room. "What do you mean out of the house? Where did he go?"

Gary stopped to think. "Out?" It had never occurred to him that Eddie shouldn't be out roaming around on his own. Yeah, he was a really smart kid and pretty self-sufficient, but he was still a kid. Not to mention a runaway whose face was plastered all over the media. "I-I guess I don't know. We got into a squabble about something stupid, and he stormed out."

Brenda glanced nervously at the clock. "When did all this happen?"

Gary shrugged. "I don't know. Couple of hours?" He watched as Brenda clenched her jaw and reached for the coat she'd just hung up. "Wait, Mom, I need to tell you this."

Brenda turned and gave Gary her full attention. "Make it quick because I've got to go look for Eddie."

Gary felt a twinge of jealousy that his mom seemed more concerned about this kid whom she barely knew than him, but he shook it off because he was sitting on information that could be a game-changer. Maybe it would fix things for all of them. "Lucy was here."

Brenda seemed puzzled as she buttoned up her coat. "Lucy?"

"You know, Eddie's mom. Dead mom." Brenda nodded, so Gary continued. "Lucy says the kid's birth father is out there somewhere."

Brenda appeared as surprised at this news as Gary had been. "Did she happen to tell you who he is, or where to find him?"

Gary shook his head. "But I'm sure she'll be back. In the meantime, maybe I could call Caryn. She might get a psychic hit on the kid's dad."

"Great. Do that. But I can't leave him out there by himself in the cold." Brenda picked up her handbag, dug for her car keys, and turned to Gary as she was about to leave. "It's the least I can do for his poor, dead mother."

Gary didn't have as much sympathy for Lucy as Brenda did, mostly because she was driving him crazy, but then he felt a chill and heard her whisper something in his ear. He leaned into the garage and called out, "Mom, Lucy says Eddie used to always go to the library if he was upset or trying to hide out."

She waved, started the car, and backed out.

Gary finished putting away the groceries, his stomach growling as he wondered what among these delectable items Brenda had been planning to cook.

Salmon? Maybe grilled with some of the fresh asparagus he'd just tossed in the fridge's veggie crisper? Or possibly the lasagna, judging by the package of noodles and sauce left sitting out on the counter. Maybe I should call out for pizza? He pulled the well-worn takeout menu out of the junk drawer, perused its contents, but decided against it. He didn't have the money to pay for it and besides, he didn't want to insult his mom, who prided herself on her cooking. But a quick glance at the digital clock on the stove told him dinner would be late.

To distract himself, he sent a text to Caryn.

—Can we meet tomorrow? Interesting news from Lucy.—

Another loud rumble from his stomach forced him to pull a bag of microwave popcorn from the cupboard and set it to pop. He removed the hot contents from the oven, opened it slowly, and was pouring salt straight into the bag when his phone pinged with a response.

—9am Peterson's Coffee Emporium, Rosslyn Village, down the street from Mom's store.—

Gary wasn't even aware that Caryn's mom had a store, but he figured he could catch a bus and be down in Indianapolis by 9:00. He texted a quick OK and was shoving popcorn in his mouth when the garage door cranked open. Eddie walked in with Brenda right behind him.

Gary shot a dirty look at the kid who had caused his mother so much concern. "I see you found him."

"Sitting on the curb outside the library, like Lucy said," Brenda replied. "It closed and they told him he had to leave."

Eddie seemed stunned as he glanced between

Brenda and Gary. "You mean my mom?"

Exasperated, Gary crossed his arms and leaned his back against the kitchen counter. "You already knew I could talk to her. Her ghost anyway. If it wasn't for your mom popping in unannounced, Brenda wouldn't have known where to look for you." He shoved a big handful of popcorn in his mouth to keep from saying something about Eddie's manners.

Eddie sighed, lowered his overstuffed backpack off his shoulder, and for once, seemed contrite. "Sorry I scared you, Brenda. But this guy"—he jerked his thumb at Gary—"just pushes my buttons."

"All right, all right," Gary grumbled. "Enough. Why the library?"

Eddie grinned as he opened his backpack. "I had overdue library books. And look what I got!" He pulled out copies of the Steve Jobs biography, the latest Hunger Games sequel, and a couple of Kurt Vonnegut novels.

"I would have thought you'd read all of Vonnegut's stuff," Gary said, turning over a copy of *Slaughterhouse Five*.

Eddie shrugged and repacked the books into his bag. "Yeah, but that's my favorite."

Brenda took Eddie by the shoulders and looked him in the eye. "Eddie, did anyone see you? Anyone you know? Like a school friend?"

"No, but…"

"But…?" she asked.

Eddie stepped back, the color draining from his face. "There was an old woman in those apartments across the street, staring out of the window when I went outside," he whispered.

Gary couldn't believe Eddie hadn't thought about all the ramifications of being out in public. "Let's hope she didn't recognize you." He glanced at his mom who had that expression on her face, the one she'd always gotten whenever Gary had scared the daylights out of her.

"You guys get out of my kitchen. I'll call you when dinner's ready." She pulled a large pot out of the cabinet, filled it with water, and put it on the stove to boil.

Eddie didn't say a word as he scurried out.

"Mom, should we…?"

"What? Call the police and tell them we've been harboring a runaway?" She turned her back, busying herself with pans, ingredients and casserole dishes. "I'm not eager to spend Thanksgiving in jail."

"Look, Mom, even if that lady recognized Eddie and called the police, which she probably didn't, they still wouldn't know where he is. We've got time to sort this out."

Brenda sighed and tossed a handful of noodles into the boiling water.

Gary watched her for a minute, feeling bad that he had brought all this trouble home. He gave his mom a hug, holding on tight. "I'm meeting Caryn for coffee in the morning. Maybe she can make something out of what I got from Lucy."

****

I was up and dressed Wednesday morning by 8:30, surprising myself as well as Mom when I met her in the kitchen. She lifted an eyebrow as she poured hot tea into her travel mug. "Caryn! What are you doing up at this hour? I thought you'd sleep in on your first day of vacation."

"I wanted to catch a ride to the store with you."

"Great!" Mom's face lit up as she screwed on the lid. "I could use some help with inventory."

I shifted my weight back and forth, a dead giveaway I was feeling guilty about something. "Well, sure, I could help out later, but…"

"But that's not why you want a ride," Mom finished. She glanced at my attire and lifted an eyebrow. I wasn't wearing my usual faded jeans and plaid shirt that I reserved for digging around in the dusty stockroom. Instead I had on a pair of pink skinny jeans, a white T-shirt paired with a gray asymmetrical cardigan, and faux leather boots. "Psychic reading?"

I shrugged. "Yeah. Later."

"Tell Sis about your date," Uncle Omar whispered in my right ear.

I waved him away, but I saw Mom watching me with a curious expression, so I said, "Fly."

"In November?"

"Okay, I'm meeting Gary Riddell for coffee at Peterson's."

Mom stopped to think, a puzzled expression on her face. "The guy from school? The one you went on the ghost hunt with?"

I nodded. "He's got something to tell me, and frankly I've got something I need to tell him, too."

Mom grinned as she stuffed her travel mug in an outside pocket of her handbag. "Do you like this boy?"

I rolled my eyes and whined like I did when I was fifteen. "Mooomm…"

"Well, it's been almost a year since you and Quince broke up. Maybe it's time you started dating again."

"You sound like Annabeth. And believe me, I'm not in the market for a boyfriend."

"If you say so," Mom said. "But if you have time after your date, uh, coffee, you can always bring him back to the store for a while." She gave me an exaggerated wink as she pulled her car keys out of her bag on the way to the garage. "And you don't even drink coffee."

We were silent on the drive over to her store, Mom concentrating on her driving and probably thinking of all the inventory she needed to replenish before the holiday shopping season, and me thinking about Gary. Not thinking about him thinking about him, but just considering some things. Like last summer when I was still hurting from Quince's rejection and definitely hadn't been interested when Annabeth tried to set me up with him. And like how I had loathed him when he called me Carolyn that day on campus after I'd seen him talking to some ghost. And then I wrote that scathing review of his *Pride and Prejudice* audition, mostly out of spite. And how we pooled our respective talents to find Eddie Carson.

And now I was meeting him because we had to finish what we started, and get Eddie back where he belonged. I was pretty sure we'd need help from both the living and the dead to accomplish that.

Peterson's Coffee Emporium is a chain of coffee houses where a person can order a quick coffee to go, or sit down at a table and drink it leisurely. They are all over Indianapolis, and popular with both kids and adults. Mom was right about one thing, though. I don't drink coffee because the caffeine always sends my sixth sense into overdrive. I've always preferred soothing herbal tea. Fortunately at Peterson's, they have as good a selection of teas as they do coffee.

Mom dropped me off at Peterson's and then went to work. The coffee shop was pretty quiet because the morning rush was over, so I sat down at my favorite table by the window overlooking the main street in Rosslyn Village's trendy shopping district to wait for Gary. After a while I checked my phone for both time and messages and groaned when I saw that it was nine fifteen and no texts. I ordered some mint tea, took it back to the table and wondered if I'd been stood up.

But then Gary sailed through the door out of breath, wearing a thick navy blue pea coat with no hat or gloves. He blew on his hands as he scouted out the room until he spotted me. He lifted his head in greeting and hurried over.

"Sorry I'm late, but the earliest bus available didn't pick up till eight forty-five."

I motioned to a chair. "No problem." Gary hesitated as his eyes drifted toward the counter. "Go get your coffee first," I told him. We had a lot to discuss, and the guy was a caffeine junkie who wouldn't be able to focus without his fix.

Gary returned, hung his coat on the back of his chair, and sat down across from me to address his latte. "So," he said after a few swallows, finally glancing up at me. "Lucy popped in yesterday."

I winced. "Still hasn't crossed over?"

Gary took a few more sips before answering. "No, she's not going anywhere till her boy's taken care of. She's pretty adamant that he can't go back to Clyde."

"I agree." I was trying to let Gary tell me if he had

any information I didn't already know, but I was bouncing nervously in my seat, about to burst with what I knew. We both sipped our drinks in silence. Finally I couldn't stand it anymore. "Eddie's father is…"

While at the same time Gary said, "Eddie has a father…"

We both stopped, stunned.

I pushed my cup aside and leaned my arms on the table. "What do you know?"

Gary fortified himself with a large swallow of coffee and shook his head. "You go first."

"Okay, so I know who—and where—Eddie's bio dad is."

Gary's eyes widened. "How…?" But he stopped short. "Oh, right. Well, I just found out last night that Eddie even has a father. So who is he?"

I gulped. I had no idea how I was going to break this to him. But while I was mulling over my options, Uncle Omar popped in. He fully materialized, dressed in his military olive green T-shirt and camouflage pants, and took a seat in the chair next to Gary. I ducked my head and stifled a giggle.

"What?" Gary asked.

"Uncle Omar decided to join us." I let my eyes drift toward the chair. My uncle leaned back on two legs and Gary's eyes nearly bugged out of his head when the chair seemingly moved on its own.

Gary took some loud gulps of hot coffee, then winced and fanned his burning tongue. "I've seen lots of ghosts, but that"—he pointed to the chair—"is weird."

"I'm not a ghost." Uncle Omar set the chair back down, much to Gary's relief. "Caryn, keep what you know to yourself. Let it play out in real time." And then my uncle vanished.

Ohmigod, I did not expect that. Now I had to stall. "My uncle says to remind you he isn't a ghost, but he had to leave."

Gary glanced at the now-empty chair out of the corner of his eye. "Then why was he here? In my experience, they always have an agenda."

"Um, well…" I stopped to think. How was I supposed to deflect Gary's questions? "Well, you know tomorrow's Thanksgiving, and stuff's going down…"

Gary rolled his eyes. "What is going down?"

"You've said enough," Uncle Omar warned me.

I waved him away like I'd done earlier, but Gary wasn't going to buy that I was trying to swat a fly any more than Mom had. I shook my head. "Sorry, but my uncle's saying for me to leave it alone, let events unfold like they're supposed to."

Gary sighed and slumped down in his seat. "Great. So you and"—he pointed upward like he thought my uncle was floating on the ceiling or something—"your spirit guide are keeping secrets."

I felt bad for him. Yes, he was involved in all this, but I had to follow both my instincts and Uncle Omar's advice. Then I had an idea, maybe a way to distract Gary. "Say, would you like to see my mom's store? It's a new age bookstore, so you might like it. Anyway I promised her I'd help with inventory."

"Nice dodge." Gary gave me a half-smile, nodded and pulled on his coat, and then—drumroll—helped me on with mine.

Common sense and Uncle Omar forced me to leave out some important information, but we still found things to talk about. We walked down the block from Peterson's to Bethany's New Age, chatting about school, the weather, and plans for Thanksgiving. Gary even seemed impressed with my plans to join Annabeth again this year to help serve the charity dinner.

Gary paused in front of Mom's store, studied the exterior, and gave it an approving nod. I had to admit that meeting Gary this morning was fun, and I hadn't had a good time like that in months. It was a relief to spend time with someone who didn't judge me. I could see Mom's knowing smile as we walked in.

****

I saw some psychic clients mid-afternoon, since Mom planned to close the store early Wednesday evening. Business was slow most of the day, probably because most of her regulars were home getting ready for Thanksgiving dinner. Of course we were both hoping they would come back with their pocketbooks wide open on Black Friday.

I told her I had one last client coming at six. "You can go if you want, Mom. I'll lock up."

"Then how will you get home?" Mom shook her head as she untied her green work apron with the big, round Bethany's New Age logo on the front, and hung it on the coat hook near the register. "No, I'm not leaving you alone here with some random client. I'll be in the office working on the books." She turned on her heel and headed toward the back of the store, effectively closing the subject. I sighed, but she did have a point about the transportation thing.

The old-fashioned bell atop the antique entryway door jingled. I turned to see…Gary? I blinked a couple of times from across the room before realizing it was

Ned Harrington strolling in. His blond hair and deep blue eyes had me fooled for a moment. He was wearing an expensive-looking gray wool overcoat over his business suit, and a tie with muted colors peeked out from under the collar.

I walked over and extended my hand. "Hi, Ned. You're right on time."

Ned's eyes shifted nervously around the store as he offered his own hand to shake.

"Don't worry, we're alone. Mom closed the store early." I didn't think it was a good idea to mention that she was still here. No need to spook the guy.

"Speaking of spooks…"

My eyes widened in surprise. I put my hand over my mouth to pretend-cough. "Uncle Omar. What are you doing here?"

"Just looking out for your best interests, Niece."

I groaned. "I don't need any help."

"Don't need help with what?" Ned asked.

It unnerves people when I talk to my spirit guide out loud, but even though I was pretty sure I had this particular psychic reading under control, it was always good to know I had backup. With a smile that I hoped would put him at ease, I turned to Ned. "Why don't we talk out here instead of the back room?" I pointed to the comfy reading area near the book section. Ordinarily I didn't use this space for readings, but Ned and I were the only ones here (except for Mom in the back office, which Ned didn't need to know about, and of course Uncle Omar, which he also didn't know about), so we couldn't be overheard. At least not by Mom.

Ned gave a hesitant nod and followed me. I sat in the armchair and pointed to the sofa. Before sitting down on the farthest edge from me, he did a quick glance over his shoulder to make sure we couldn't be observed through the store windows. But that was the beauty of this cozy reading area that Mom so tastefully designed, because it was pretty well secluded from street view.

I leaned back against the cushions in an attempt to get comfortable, but it didn't really work because I felt as nervous as Ned looked. "So what did you want to talk about?" Maybe we needed to ease into it.

"Aw, come on, Caryn, get to it," Uncle Omar said a little too loudly in my right ear.

I tried to appear nonchalant while I rubbed my ear.

"Well, then, I'll be forced to bring in reinforcements," Uncle Omar said. He gave a courtly bow, extended his arm like he was welcoming the star of the play onto the stage, and Ned's grandmother Olivia materialized. I wrinkled my nose at the cigarette smell that accompanied her and coughed for real.

"Are you okay?" Ned asked.

I waved away the nonexistent smoke, which miraculously disappeared. "Your grandmother is here."

Ned sort of gasped as he loosened his tie, but he didn't say anything to disrupt my concentration.

I listened to Olivia and then passed on her message. "She says you've come a long way in your relationship with Gary, but you still have work to do."

Ned was too nervous to stay seated. He stood up, unbuttoned his overcoat, and started pacing back and forth in front of the book stacks. "Well, of course I do. What I need is advice on how to proceed with Gary. And his mother."

"Tell him he isn't going to make headway by

261

lurking in shadows," Uncle Omar said.

"Give me a chance," I snapped back, which made Ned glance at me funny. I sighed. "Just so you know, I'm not talking to myself. I have a spirit guide with a wicked sense of humor and no patience. He suggests you make your intentions known to both Gary and Brenda."

Ned collapsed onto the sofa. "How? Every time I get near Gary he growls at me or just runs off. And Brenda…" His voice trailed off as he lowered his head into his hands, his eyes misting over.

"Caryn, dear, you must tell him about his son's abilities."

I nodded because I knew what Olivia meant. "What do you know about Gary?" I asked Ned.

The expression on his face was like he'd replied duh. "That he's my son."

"And…?"

He bit his lip for a moment and took a deep breath. "I know he's angry at me, and very protective of his mother. And he's one helluva Shakespearean actor."

"All true," I said. "But did you know he can talk to ghosts?"

"What?" Ned jumped to his feet. "Where did you get an idea like that? Listen, if you're just making stuff up—"

"No, not at all." I motioned for him to take his seat again. Once he appeared somewhat calmed down, I continued. "Gary's been able to see and talk to earthbound spirits since he was a little kid."

Ned didn't seem convinced. "What are you saying? He's like you?"

I shook my head. "I'm psychic, and believe me I

have no idea how that works. I'm also a medium, meaning I can talk to spirits who have crossed over, like your grandmother and my Uncle Omar, who are both here by the way." I stifled a grin when Ned's eyes darted all around looking for anything paranormal. "However, I can't see ghosts who are stuck here like Gary does. But he's not psychic or a medium. I guess you could say our skills offset each other."

Ned took several deep breaths, swallowed hard, and ran his fingers through his hair in that same gesture Gary used so often. "Well, even if I buy any of this hocus-pocus, what's it got to do with my relationship with my fam…with my son and his mother?"

This was the hard part. I drummed my fingers on the arm of the chair and shifted in my seat. How do I say this? "Well, see, Gary's recently been visited by the ghost of a woman named Lucy, and she's refusing to cross over until her son Eddie is safe."

Ned lifted an eyebrow. "Relevance?"

Okay, that made me feel like I was being cross-examined in court. I squirmed a little while I thought this through. I'd hoped Ned would recognize the name Lucy, but he didn't seem to make the connection. And the look he was giving me meant he probably thought I was scamming him, so I closed my eyes, fully opened my energy and let the movie run in my head. Suddenly I was slammed in the gut with how the scenario played out. My eyes popped open.

"What do you see?" Ned asked.

"Tomorrow's Thanksgiving, right?" Ned didn't respond because it was a pretty lame observation on my part. "What I mean is, I'm seeing you going to your son's house—Brenda's house—late afternoon."

Olivia beamed at me and then stepped back into the ether.

"Why would I do that?" Ned asked.

What I wanted to say was, *Because you need to talk to Gary and see for yourself that he can communicate with ghosts.* Instead I said, "I can't explain it now, but I promise it will all make sense."

Ned stood up, buttoned his coat, and handed me a hundred dollar bill, causing me to gasp in surprise. "I'll think about it, but it sounds like a waste of time." And without another word he left, the doorbell jingling loudly. It occurred to me that he and Gary had something else in common—a quick temper.

I exhaled and I hadn't even realized I'd been holding my breath. "Do you think he'll show, or did I screw up, Uncle Omar?"

Slowly my uncle materialized on the sofa where Ned had just been sitting moments before. "No, you did the right thing. Lawyers have to have proof."

I felt a little guilty about not coming clean about what I was pretty sure was going to happen. "So now I've stalled both Gary and his dad." The rest of the vision replayed in my head on hyper-drive. I shivered. "If it plays out like what I just saw, you'd better make sure she is there."

Uncle Omar grinned, winked, and faded away.

Chapter 15

Annabeth pulled her car up into the driveway of our house to let me out. She glanced over at me before checking out her look in the rearview mirror. "Girlfriend, you look as tired as I feel."

"Getting up at six a.m. on Thanksgiving Day will do that to you." Taking my cue from her, I pulled down the passenger side visor and looked at my reflection. "Ugh. I need a shower." I pulled a piece of turkey out of my hair. "And a shampoo."

Annabeth started laughing and used her cell phone to snap a photo of the two of us. I leaned in and mugged for the camera. "Not as good as my thirty-five millimeter, but it'll do for social media." She tapped some keys on the phone and sent the picture on its way.

"Please put in there the reason we look like this," I said. "It was all for a good cause."

Annabeth nodded and tapped in some text. "I'm captioning it 'Just back from the Morris Sutton Thanksgiving Dinner. Served thousands.'"

Even though Annabeth and I have helped out with this charity dinner for the last three years, I'm still amazed at how exhausted I feel afterwards. Yet despite being tired, I was exhilarated. We not only dished up lots of plates of food, we helped pack carryout boxes for delivery to people who couldn't come to us.

"Go get your shower," Annabeth said, putting her

phone away. "I'll pick you up at four."

I groaned and leaned back against the seat. "You mean we're really going?"

She nodded. "Yes. Gary invited you for dessert at his mom's, and then Brenda told him to include Sean and me, so we're going. Now go get gorgeous."

I waved goodbye as I closed the car door. I'd already seen this scenario at Brenda's playing out in my head a few times, so I knew what was coming. At least I thought I did. Since spirits and ghosts can be totally unpredictable, who knew what could happen?

****

Brenda seemed to be doing mental math as she stared at her baked goods. "How many people did you invite for dessert? I hope I made enough." She studied the apple, pumpkin and pecan pies laid out on her kitchen counter and ticked off the number of guests on her fingers. "Let's see, you, me, Eddie, Sean, Annabeth, and..." She tossed a sideways glance at Gary, "...Caryn?"

Gary knew what his mom was getting at, so he dodged that minefield. "Yeah, well, you always bake too many pies and they go to waste."

"Get out some plates," Brenda said. "I'm going to go freshen up." She headed toward the stairs to her bedroom.

Gary took seven mismatched plates out of the cupboard.

"They look yummy," a voice behind Gary said.

Gary nearly jumped out of his skin and in his surprise, juggled the plates to keep from dropping them. He knew it was Lucy, so he carefully set the dishes next to the desserts before turning around. "How many times have I—"

"Yes, I know, don't sneak up on you. Next time I'll let out a ghostly wail." She leaned over the counter for a closer look at Brenda's pies. "I missed having Thanksgiving with Eddie," she said with a hint of sorrow in her voice. "But your mother's pumpkin pie looks better than mine ever was."

Gary rolled his eyes. "If you're so miserable here, go to the light!" He watched Lucy step away from the counter, but she didn't appear to be going much farther than that. "Look, Lucy, what do I have to do to get you to cross over?"

"Don't worry, it's all taken care of." And with that, the ghost vanished.

Gary had no idea what she meant. He was beyond tired of that particular ghost, even though he understood her concern for her son. He just wished she'd move on and let the three-dimensional people take care of Eddie. Just then the doorbell rang.

"I'll get it!" Eddie called from the living room.

Gary stepped out of the kitchen in time to see Eddie mute the TV before bounding to the door. "Eddie, that's not a good idea till we know who it is," Gary told him. But it was too late, because Eddie had already flung the door wide open.

"Oh, it's just you," Eddie said. He went back to the sofa, turned the TV volume back up, and resumed watching the football game.

"Never mind our rude houseguest," Gary said with a scowl at Eddie. He opened the door wide to admit Sean, Annabeth, and Caryn. "Can I take your coats?" The three of them slid out of their overcoats. "Eddie? Here. Take these upstairs."

"You're not the boss of me," Eddie shot back.

Gary felt like his head was going to explode. This kid was driving him crazy, and for some reason his mother wouldn't contact the authorities or even Clyde Seville. She just kept making excuses.

"Here, I've got this," Annabeth said with a dirty look shot Eddie's way. She gathered up their coats and headed for the stairs. "I'll just toss them on Brenda's bed."

Brenda and Annabeth came back down the stairs together. Brenda walked into the living room, smiling happily as she encircled Sean and Annabeth with warm hugs, and then embraced Caryn. "Welcome. I'm so glad you were able to join us."

Caryn pulled back a little. "Um, well, thanks…"

"Watching the game here," Eddie growled. He turned up the volume and made a big show of craning his neck around the four of them standing in front of the TV.

"Come on into the kitchen," Brenda said, waving them along.

Gary reached out for Caryn's hand, but stopped himself when he realized what he'd almost done. All he knew was that he'd enjoyed her company yesterday and today Caryn looked really pretty, with her black leggings topped with an oversized black and white sweater, and knee-high boots. Her shoulder-length hair was held away from her face by a small headband, and she was even wearing diamond stud earrings. Gary had never seen Caryn look like anything but a professional journalist, and he found this casual look of hers quite appealing. But Caryn seemed nervous. Her eyes kept scanning the room, covering every corner of the living room and then the dining room as they were passing through it.

Gary took her arm and gently pulled her aside as the others went into the kitchen. "You okay?"

Caryn smiled up at him, a smile Gary thought looked forced. "Sure, yeah, just wondering if..." She glanced around the room again.

"You're wondering if Lucy is here," Gary finished for her. Caryn nodded. "Well, she was, but after complimenting Brenda on her baking skills, she vanished. With any luck, she finally crossed over."

Caryn shook her head. "No, she didn't. I don't know that for a fact, of course, but I don't think her business here is finished yet."

"Gary, Caryn, what kind of pie do you want?" Brenda asked.

Gary could hear silverware clanking as it came out of the kitchen drawer. He put his hand on the small of Caryn's back and ushered her into the kitchen.

Her eyes widened at the sight of Brenda's pies. "Smells delicious. Is that pumpkin?"

"I'm pumpkinned out," Annabeth said, "after serving up hundreds of slices at the Morris Sutton event. I'll take apple."

"Not me," Caryn said. "I want some pumpkin pie." She waved the aromas toward her and inhaled deeply. "Ahh, heaven."

"I want all three, but an especially big slice of pecan," Sean said as he grabbed a plate. "Shall we?"

Brenda started cutting pie slices in each of the three pastries. "Eddie?" Brenda called. "What kind of pie do you want?"

"Whatever," Eddie answered back, but then the

doorbell rang again and he called out, "I'll get it!"

"Eddie!" Brenda shouted. She dropped the knife in the sink, and hurried out with Gary and Caryn on her heels. But it was too late. In the open doorway were Police Detective Albers and Clyde Seville.

"Uh-oh," Eddie said.

****

I was thinking something a lot stronger than uh-oh when I saw who was standing on Brenda's porch. Gary looked surprised, Brenda seemed thunderstruck, but poor Eddie's face reflected pure terror. I didn't blame him. That stepfather of his was one scary dude.

Clyde Seville pushed his way into the condo ahead of the police detective and grabbed Eddie's arm. Eddie's shoulders slumped and his eyes dropped to the ground. "Boy, where ya been?" Clyde gave his surroundings a quick once-over. "You been hiding out here all this time?"

"How did you find me?" Eddie wiggled but was unable to free himself from Clyde's grip.

Clyde got in the boy's face and growled, "That neighborhood watch lady recognized you, and then she saw you," he said with a sneer at Brenda, "and jotted down your license plate."

Detective Albers addressed Brenda as he stepped across the threshold. "Ms. Cravens takes her duties very seriously. Not much that goes on in that neighborhood escapes her notice."

Brenda groaned in misery as she staggered back from the door.

Clyde released Eddie after a disapproving look from Detective Albers and a scowl from Gary, who could be kind of intimidating at six foot five. Eddie rubbed his arm and quickly scurried over to Brenda. She put a protective arm around his shoulder and pulled him back out of Clyde's reach.

"You barge into my home, manhandle this child—" Brenda was trying to sound indignant, but I could tell she was almost as scared as Eddie.

"Ma'am," the detective said, "there are laws in this state against harboring runaways."

"And I can sue your ass off," Clyde mumbled.

Gary stepped in front of Clyde and stared him down. "Don't you dare speak to my mother like that."

Detective Albers raised his voice. "All right, enough. Ms. Riddell, I'm returning this boy to his legal guardian. And I'd advise you to contact an attorney."

"On it. Calling Dad right now." Annabeth whipped out her phone, and pushed a number on speed dial.

I glanced around the room, hoping to see Uncle Omar, but he was nowhere in sight. Probably off having his own turkey dinner, if spirits actually did that sort of thing. Still, knowing how close I'd gotten to this situation, and knowing I'm not psychic about my own life, I was beginning to wonder if maybe I'd invented the whole scenario I'd been replaying in my head. Maybe it was wishful thinking, not psychic insight. Maybe…

But then a car pulled into Brenda's driveway. I peered out the window and saw Ned Harrington's silver Jaguar. Perfect timing. Yes, his presence was needed, but more importantly, I quickly regained confidence in my predictions.

"Hello?" Ned knocked on the open door and stuck his head into the living room.

"You can hang up," I told Annabeth. "Seems

we've got an attorney."

"Ned? What are you doing here?" Brenda's face flushed, her eyes sparkling with tears that threatened to spill down her cheeks. She brushed them away impatiently.

If Brenda was surprised, Gary's expression was…well, it was a cross between anger and relief. He glanced at me, maybe hoping for a clue which I wasn't about to divulge, and then turned to Ned. "Good question. What are you doing here?"

"Well, it was suggested…" Ned glanced at me and thankfully didn't finish that thought. He gazed round the room, nodded to the police detective, and saw Eddie cowering next to Brenda. "I see the runaway has been located."

"We found the kid," Sean said, "Annabeth, Caryn, Gary, and me, on that ghost hunt a couple of weeks ago. He was hiding out at the old Pelson house, pretending to haunt the place."

"Is that true?" Detective Albers asked Eddie.

Eddie lifted his chin in an attempt to appear brave. "Yeah. What of it?"

"He's only been staying here a few days," Brenda said. She may have fibbed a little, since it was longer than that, but none of us were going to correct her.

"And Eddie's obviously much safer here than with him." Gary glared at Clyde.

"Ms. Riddell," the police detective said before turning to Ned, "and Mr. Harrington, this boy's stepfather has been worried about him, wants him back, and I'm legally required to return him." He stepped over to Eddie and got down to his level. "Unless you have something you'd like to tell us. Like why you ran away in the first place."

Eddie just stared at the floor, tears flooding down his cheeks.

Sean jumped in. "My dad's a pediatrician and he checked the kid out. Found bruises."

"Probably got those crawling around that old house," Clyde harrumphed.

Eddie opened his mouth to speak, closed his mouth and swallowed hard. I could see he was shaking. Just as I was about to speak up and tell everyone what I knew, Gary's back stiffened. He ran his fingers through his hair, rubbed the back of his neck, and stared off into the corner of the room.

"Gary," I said, hoping I was right, "is she here?"

Gary nodded and put up his hand to quiet me and everyone else.

"What the hell is going on here?" Clyde demanded as he watched Gary's unusual behavior. "All's I want is my boy, and I want him now!"

"His mother is here," Gary said.

"His mother is dead," the detective said.

"What kind of scam are you trying to pull?" Clyde demanded, his voice getting louder. "Doing some kind of parlor trick by pretending to talk to my dead wife?"

Ah, the parlor trick accusation. Seems like every time someone was skeptical about what people like Gary and me could do, they'd claim it was all smoke and mirrors.

Annabeth turned on Clyde, hands on hips. "Gary can talk to ghosts. If he says Lucy is here, she is." Annabeth was a great friend to have on your side, and furthermore, you didn't ever mess with her belief in the paranormal. Clyde had just crossed both lines.

Ned was staring open-mouthed at Gary, finally seeing for himself what I'd already told him about his son, while Gary was obviously listening to Lucy. Detective Albers seemed frustrated, and Clyde clearly wasn't buying any of it.

I stepped closer to Gary and whispered, "What's Lucy saying?"

Gary slowly turned around to face all of us. His gaze drifted from Brenda, to Ned, to Eddie, and then back to me. "You knew, didn't you?"

I nodded. "I knew. But it's not my story to tell."

"If this is some kind of prank, or hoax—" Clyde growled as he lunged for Eddie, who ducked his grasp and shrank back.

"No, it's not," Gary said. He sank down onto the sofa and ran his fingers through his hair.

I felt for him, because this had to be a huge shock, and under similar circumstances I might also be speechless. Oddly enough, Ned was also running his fingers through his hair in frustration. Like father, like son.

"What did Lucy tell you?" Brenda asked. She sat down on the sofa next to Gary and patted his knee. "Maybe we can clear this up right now, without courts or lawsuits."

"Aw come on, folks, no one's gonna believe some college kid's been talking to a dead woman," Clyde said. "Come on, Officer, I wanna take Eddie and get outta this nut house."

"Just hear him out," I said. I silently asked for Uncle Omar's intervention, and surprise, surprise, Clyde stumbled a little like someone had smacked the side of his head, and then caught himself on the edge of the sofa. I ducked my head and snickered.

"Ned," Gary said, turning to face his father, "she says you knew her. Lucy Carson."

"Lucy Seville," Clyde said, rubbing his head for no apparent reason.

Ned furrowed his brow and was quiet for a long time. Yesterday when I mentioned her name to him it hadn't rung any bells, but I never said her last name. "Lucy Carson. Yes, I do remember her. She was a paralegal in my dad's law firm, and I was fresh out of law school, doing an internship with Judge Sizemore."

"Hey, I've known the judge since I was a kid!" Annabeth said. She turned to Detective Albers. "He's part of my dad's law firm, Walton, Harrington, Harrington, and Sizemore."

"Well, that's how I met Lucy," Ned said. "We had a couple of dates, a few laughs..." He shrugged. "Then she suddenly quit the firm and moved back East to be with her family. Never heard from her again."

Gary nodded at his unseen visitor and said, "But while she was in New Jersey, she gave birth to Eddie. Edward Harrington Carson, named after you, Edward Harrington, Jr." He crossed his arms and gave Ned a stony glare. "The Great Impregnator."

Ned's eyes widened as he glanced at Eddie. His other son. "You're...Lucy and I..."

"Yeah, it looks that way, Pops," Eddie said. He turned to Gary with a grin and offered up a fist-bump. "The Great Impregnator. Good one!"

Gary returned the fist-bump before continuing. "Then about five years ago, Lucy moved back to Indiana, got a new job in Belford, and met this jerk," Gary said, glaring at Clyde, "at the gym. She says he was her personal trainer. She confided in him the whole story about Eddie, and shortly after that, Clyde proposed. It wasn't till later that Lucy realized Clyde was hatching a plot to extort money from the Harringtons."

"Liar!" Clyde shouted.

Gary stood up and got in Clyde's face. "Am I? And who put all those bruises on Lucy when she threatened to expose you? She showed them to me. And then there's the little matter of her brake failure. She thinks you had something to do with that, too."

Clyde didn't back down. "You can't prove a thing!"

"I'm afraid he's right," Detective Albers said. "Her car was totaled. Mr. Seville took possession of it after we were through with our investigation. I'm sure it's long since been sold for parts."

Clyde folded his arms in silent triumph, a sneer creeping across his face. I sighed. Even though I knew, and Gary just heard, that Clyde had possibly tampered with Lucy's brakes, there would never be a way to prove it.

Eddie stifled a sob. Brenda pulled him in, and in fast-forward style I could see the whole scenario flashing across my mind. Clyde hitting Lucy, Clyde smacking Eddie when he tried to intervene, and then Lucy running out of the house while a tearful Eddie ran to hide in his bedroom. I closed my eyes to try to block out the visions. I hoped I'd never see anything like that again.

Gary turned to Eddie. "Lucy says she started to come back for you, but now she's glad she didn't."

Ned turned to Clyde and measured his words.

"Well, Mr. Seville, it seems I am this young man's biological father, a fact that can be easily proven." Ned whipped out his phone and pushed a button. "Happy Thanksgiving, Arthur." He paused to silently mouth to the detective, *Judge Sizemore*. "I have a favor to ask. I need a court order, emergency temporary child custody. The child's name is Edward Carson, and the temporary guardian is, uh, Brenda Riddell."

Detective Albers tapped his toe impatiently as he turned to Brenda. "I guess it's good to have friends in high places."

"Got it. Thanks, Arthur. See you next week." Ned handed his phone to the detective with the electronic emergency court order on the screen. "And now, Mr. Seville, I'll thank you to leave my family alone."

Clyde didn't bother looking at the court order. He turned on his heel and stormed out the door, slamming it behind him.

"Dude. You're a big brother." Sean gave Gary an exaggerated wink. "Hope you have better luck with yours than I've had with mine."

Gary rolled his eyes, but for the first time he was looking at his newly-discovered sibling with curiosity instead of contempt. I even saw a resemblance between Eddie and Gary, especially around their eyes. I walked over to stand next to Annabeth, who was hand-in-hand with Sean. The three of us could barely contain our excitement.

"Folks, I'm truly sorry about this," Detective Albers said. "I never did fully trust that man, but I had no idea..." He shook his head. "For now, Eddie Carson is safe with Ms. Riddell." He turned to Ned. "Mr. Harrington, I suggest a DNA test as soon as it can be arranged. I'll be in contact next week."

When the detective was gone, Brenda released Eddie and crossed the room to where Ned was standing all alone. She reached out and gently touched his arm. "Ned, just now, you said something about your family."

Ned took both of Brenda's hands in his. "You and Gary, and now Eddie. In my mind we're a family, and we've been apart way too long."

Gary stepped over to his mother's side. "Well, Dad," he said, "there's the little problem of your abandonment of Mom and me, no child support, nothing. That's unforgiveable in my book."

"Gary," Brenda said, "your father tried to reach out. It was mostly my pride that kept the two of you apart."

"And I did get you that full ride scholarship at Hamilton Liberal Arts," Ned told him.

My jaw dropped about the same time Gary's did. Now that was one detail my psychic sense hadn't provided me with. "Wow!" was all I could think to say.

"Son," Ned said before checking himself. "Gary, I knew what a talented actor you were, and I just wanted to make up for my lack of financial and emotional support for the past eighteen years."

Gary lifted an eyebrow. "And how would you know anything about my acting?"

"I attended every single play you were ever in, mostly hiding out in the back of the auditorium." Ned cautiously reached for Gary, careful not to overstep his boundaries.

But it was Gary who finally let down his defenses and allowed Ned to draw him into a father-son embrace. Then Brenda joined them and pulled Eddie into it, and suddenly I felt like an interloper. I caught Annabeth's eye and pointed to the door. She nodded and tiptoed up the stairs to retrieve our coats.

Gary pulled back from his family hug and looked off into the corner of the room again. "Lucy's saying something." He listened for a moment. "Goodbye. She said goodbye."

"I've got her!" Uncle Omar exclaimed in my ear, so loud that I winced.

After all this time I could finally see Lucy, and she looked radiant. Eddie has her dark hair and small frame, but I could also see Ned in him. "She's with my uncle on The Other Side. He's taking her with him." I smiled. "Lucy's going to be fine. She wants Eddie to know she couldn't leave till he was reunited with his father…"

"…and got a new mom," Gary finished. Surprisingly, he took my hand and squeezed it.

I watched as Lucy hooked her arm through Uncle Omar's and the two of them strolled off into the ether.

Chapter 16

The next day I was helping Mom and her assistant at the store, which was crammed with Black Friday shoppers, and much to my surprise Gary dropped in. "What brings you here? And how did you get here?" But before he could answer I already knew. "Ned, right?"

He grinned and nodded, beaming. Gone was the scowling, angry Gary, and in his place was a guy with a spring to his step. "Yeah, he dropped me off. I told him I wanted to do some shopping while he and Eddie are getting their blood tests."

Gary told me that Ned had done some online research to get a look at Eddie's birth certificate. Lucy had listed her son's father as Unknown, so Ned was forced to follow through on Detective Albers' suggestion that he prove he was Eddie's birth father. I already knew for a fact he was, and the resemblance between the two of them was obvious to anyone, but legally they needed the confirmation.

Gary chatted with me a little more, but I had to get back to work so I pointed him in the direction of some books I thought he might be interested in. After a while he caught my eye and waved as he headed out the door.

It was a whirlwind of a Thanksgiving holiday. Annabeth and I drove back to school together, and late Sunday night I was sitting at my laptop in our dorm room, with a huge story to write for The Herald. I'd been sitting on this mind-boggling information about Eddie, Lucy, Ned, and Gary for so long that I was eager to finally be able to tell the story. I'd sent a lengthy text to Del, who replied that instead of telling him, I should tell the readers of the school newspaper. I promised Del I'd finish the story in time for the next edition.

By late November there were only three weeks left till the semester ended. How this story was received, and how I did in the rest of my classes, would determine if I had a future in journalism. But hey, no pressure!

****

"Dude. You made the papers again," Sean said as he neatly hung his coat on the back of his chair in the dorm cafeteria.

It was early Monday morning, too early for Gary's tastes, but he was glad his roommate had rousted him out of bed. He didn't want to be late to his classes, and he had a lot to accomplish today. Gary had been pretty sure he'd gotten the lead in Macbeth, but it was still a relief when he saw the online cast list with his name at the top. Today was their first read-through in the rehearsal hall, and then he had to go to the bookstore to talk to Ellis. Gary took a sip from his cup of hot, black java, watched with distaste as Sean tucked into his pancakes, and glanced at the copy of The Hamilton Campus Herald which Sean had spread out on the table.

Gary was looking at the story upside down, but he got the gist of it. "How did she get that story into today's edition so fast?"

Sean grinned and shrugged. "Annabeth said Caryn was up all night writing the big reveal about Eddie, and

Annabeth pulled up some shots of you to go with the story."

It wasn't a bad picture, but it was Gary in his costume from *Pride and Prejudice* and not necessarily the way he wanted to be depicted. "So now I'm going to be the talk of the campus. Again." He glanced around the cafeteria to see which students might be reading the story. Well, lots, as it turned out. On Monday morning at eight a.m. after a long holiday break, the place was full of students eating breakfast and ready to hit the books. Gary glanced at the nearly empty rack near the cash register that held the copies of The Herald. He turned Sean's copy of the paper around so he could read the headline:

Local Actor/Ghost Whisperer
Rescues Missing Teen
by Caryn Alderson

"Seems you and Caryn have come a long way. Listen to this," Sean said as he read aloud from the story. "'Gary Riddell, one of the rising theatrical stars in this year's freshman class, and oh, by the way, the same guy who has that little talent of talking to ghosts, put his skills to use in a very special way...'" Sean looked up and pointed to the rest of the story. "She makes you out to be the hero."

Gary was pretty sure he was blushing. "Well, yeah, but you guys were there, too. Caryn's intuition was a huge part of this."

Sean shrugged. "Maybe she's just being modest, but a lot of the credit goes to the only person who could see and communicate with Eddie's dead mom."

Gary did feel a little like a hero. He'd helped his kid brother find his—their—father and get rid of that monster of a stepparent, sent Lucy on her way, and best of all, he'd seen his mother happier than she'd ever been. All because Ned, a man Gary had previously despised, turned out to be a decent guy.

Thanksgiving night the four of them—Gary, Ned, Brenda and Eddie—had sat up all night in Brenda's living room. They talked, laughed, cried, finished off the pie, and simply got to know each other after all their years apart.

Gary finished reading Caryn's story, shoved the paper aside, and nodded his approval. "Maybe Caryn isn't so bad after all."

"Ya think?" Sean said. "Isn't there a line in Macbeth about somebody protesting too much?"

Gary snorted. "That's from Hamlet, and it's about a woman. But point taken." He felt a tap on his shoulder.

"Hey Gary, nice article about you."

Gary turned around to see Erica Stone smiling seductively, her long dark hair in thick curls falling around the stylish scarf draped over her coat. He politely stood up and because they were close to the same height, was able to look her in the eye. "Thanks."

"Maybe we could get together some time, you know for coffee or something? You could tell me all about the ghosts you see."

Gary looked at Erica, who was gorgeous by the way, but realized he didn't have any interest in her anymore. Her appeal had been her height, her brains, and yes, her aloofness, but right now the only thing on his mind was a short, spunky psychic. "Sorry, but I'm taken."

Where did that come from?

283

****

"Did you get the email?" Annabeth asked me.

I'd only had a couple of hours of sleep, so I was cranky and headachy. She caught me as I was about to dash out of our dorm room and head to my morning classes, which I couldn't miss this close to finals. I sighed and turned back to Annabeth, who was sitting on the edge of her bed pulling on a pair of leather boots.

"I get lots of emails. Which one in particular?"

Annabeth giggled. "From Barry Lansing, of course. About that ghost stalking we did."

"You mean the one that mostly lacked ghosts? Yeah, I got it."

"Well?" Annabeth stood up and slipped her bulging tote bag over her shoulder. "Will you be there tonight? Ms. Pelson's dying to hear what we found out."

I sighed. "I'm not even a member of the club, Annabeth, and I sure don't understand all that EVP stuff. Shouldn't you guys be the ones to explain things to her?"

"You were there, Caryn, and you already knew Eddie was hiding out in that basement. Ms. Pelson's gonna want to hear from you, too."

I blew out a puff of air. "Yeah, okay, I'll go. Student Union at seven, right?" I turned to leave, my hand on the doorknob.

"Say," Annabeth said, a teasing lilt to her voice, "maybe Gary could walk you home afterwards."

Say what? I opened the door and left.

After classes I went to the newspaper office to consult with Del about my story assignments. They were always posted on the bulletin board of course, but if I was being honest, I was hoping to hear if we'd had any reactions to my article.

I tapped lightly on his half-open office door. "You busy?"

Del was wearing his signature jeans and black turtleneck. He waved me in as he was hitting send on something or other.

"I see you put me down for that story on Finals Fashion Week aka wearing pjs to exams."

Del swiveled in his chair, leaned back and nodded. "Yeah. Good job with the story today, by the way. Lots of positive feedback. But I think it's time you got off the Gary Riddell track and onto something else. We don't want you pigeon-holed."

"I simply covered the biggest news story, and it so happens Gary was in the middle of it. Besides, this is a small campus and not much ever happens here."

"Well, as a matter of fact it does," Del said. He turned back around and scrolled through his emails. "I got this one from Serena Farrell from—"

"The Indianapolis Star?" I gasped.

"Yes, and she was impressed with your series on the Ghost Stalkers and the resulting discovery of that missing boy. She wants to talk to you about a possible internship next summer. Now that's newsworthy!"

Ohmigod, my dreams were coming true! I've thought about an internship at the biggest newspaper in Indiana for ages, but I assumed I'd be farther along in school before I got the chance. I felt like hugging someone, but Del was an inappropriate choice, so I settled for a smile and a polite, "Thanks. I'll give her a call." Then I twirled around and bounced across the room to my desk, pulled my phone from my purse, and was about to ring Serena when a text popped up. From Gary.

—*Your story was great. Thanks for not trashing me. :)*—

I smiled, thinking I deserved that gentle ribbing.

—*You going to the Ghost Stalkers meeting tonight?*—

—*Yes. You?*—

—*Annabeth's making me.*—

—*I'll be at the SU Bookstore. Stop in and we can walk up together.*—

I thought about that. Did that make it a date, just to walk up a flight of stairs and take a seat next to someone?

"Niece, don't blow this. He gets you."

Uncle Omar was right. I felt like I could be myself with Gary. Quince never really understood my psychic abilities and certainly never felt comfortable when I used them, but Gary just accepts me for who I am. I gave my spirit guide a thumbs up and sent Gary an Okay. Hey, it's a start.

****

Gary finished his morning classes and was running late getting to the bookstore. As usual. But he needed to talk to Ellis before his shift started. He rushed out of the theatre building, pulled up the collar of his coat and walked briskly across campus. But then he came to a dead stop in the middle of The Commons. The dry brown leaves on the ground made a swishing sound when he walked through them. The empty tree branches, covered with a light frost, seemed to catch the sunlight and wave in the breeze. As he looked around, Gary realized he'd never taken the time to enjoy the majesty of the historic buildings on campus. He was always in too much of a hurry. A lot had changed over Thanksgiving, and he felt an internal calm he'd never known.

"I say, young man, you shouldn't be lollygagging. Have you no place to be?"

There it was, that familiar tingle at the base of his neck. Who says "lollygagging" anymore anyway? "You still here?" Gary asked the ghost. It was the same professor he'd seen around campus all semester, pipe smoke and all.

"I have no intention of leaving," the ghost said in a huff. "You young people need someone to keep an eye on you."

Gary shook his head. "If you'd just cross over, you wouldn't have to worry about us. Now if you'll excuse me, I'm running late." He took off, not bothering to look back.

"That's the problem with this generation," the ghost called after him. "No respect for your elders."

"How was your Thanksgiving, Gary?" Ellis Garrett peeked out from behind the cash register as she was handing a student his credit card slip to sign.

Gary squeezed past her, swiped his badge on the time clock, and tied his apron on. "You mean you didn't read Caryn's story in the paper this morning?"

Ellis chuckled as she handed the customer his purchases and receipt. "Oh, I read it. I just wanted to hear it from you."

Gary looked around the store and noticed that it was fairly empty. The rush would start when most classes had dismissed for the day and students were jonesin' for caffeine. That and needing last-minute supplies for their final exams. He decided to take advantage of the relative quiet. "I wanted to talk to you about something. I've enjoyed working here, but I won't be able to second semester, so I'm giving you my notice."

Ellis lifted an eyebrow. "You got another job? 'Cause they're scarce on a college campus with a ready supply of workers."

Gary shook his head. "No. No job, but I want to thank you for this opportunity. I learned a lot from you, and I really appreciate your sympathetic shoulder that I cried on a lot."

Ellis smiled and blushed a little. "So if you're not taking another job…"

Gary grinned. "Ned—that's my dad—he's already paying my tuition and room and board, but he wants me to focus on my studies and my acting career. So he's giving me an allowance."

Ellis wrapped an arm around Gary's shoulder and squeezed. "That's wonderful, Gary. And I totally understand about the job." Tears welled up in her eyes, so she turned around and busied herself straightening the display on the counter. "Say, tell me about this brother of yours. What's he like?"

Gary thought for a minute. How in the world could anyone explain Eddie? He barely knew the kid, and what he did know was annoying, but he also had to admire his ingenuity and determination, getting himself out of the fix he was in. The two of them had a lot to learn about each other, but they had plenty of time. "He's a genius." Gary saw the dubious expression on Ellis's face. "No, really. IQ over one-fifty. Ned pulled some strings and got him accepted to Willowby Prep starting second semester."

Ellis let out a low whistle. "Now that's a pricey place."

Gary agreed, and at first he'd been a little envious that he hadn't had the same advantage, but then he realized a school that small didn't have much of a drama department. His theatrical opportunities would have been greatly limited. "Yeah, but Eddie needs a lot more than Belford Middle School can offer him. Willowby's gonna put him in eighth grade for a semester so he can acclimate, and then he'll start high school next fall."

"Lucky kid. And lucky you, Gary. I'm happy for you," Ellis said.

For once, I'm happy, too. Gary winked at her and got to work.

****

I stared up at the huge vintage clock over the Student Union's main entryway. Six fifty-five. I was supposed to stop down in the bookstore to collect Gary and then be at that meeting with the Ghost Stalkers in five minutes. But I had a bad case of butterflies and I couldn't bring myself to open the glass doors. My head knew this wasn't a date, but my emotions begged to differ. I swallowed hard, gave myself a little pep talk, and went inside.

I didn't have to go down to the bookstore after all because Gary was waiting for me in the lobby. He toasted me with his carryout coffee cup and walked over to join me. "Ready?" he asked.

"Not really. I mean, I'm not even a member of the Ghost Stalkers Club."

We started up the stairs, side by side. "Me neither,

but Ms. Pelson needs to know what was going on at her house."

We walked into the same second-floor room the Ghost Stalkers used before, the converted former library. But this time the room was staged informally, with a large conference table and about a dozen chairs encircling it. Annabeth waved at me and pointed to a seat next to Sean, so Gary and I joined them.

"Where is everyone?" Gary asked, surveying the room.

I had to wonder the same thing, because at the moment it was just the four of us and it was a few minutes after seven.

As if in answer to his question, the door opened and in walked Scott Tildren, Barry Lansing, and Clara Pelson. Poor Ms. Pelson looked nervous, like she was about to hear the bad news that her house was hopelessly haunted and she'd never be able to open it as a bed and breakfast.

Scott stopped and shook hands with Gary before helping Clara into her chair. "Read about you in the paper," Scott said. He turned to me and added, "Nice investigative work."

I blushed. "Thanks."

Barry set his laptop on the table, yanked his chair out causing a scraping sound, and booted up the computer, rolling his finger around the mouse pad until he found what he was looking for. His demeanor indicated he was peeved, and he didn't even bother with any niceties.

His expression steely, Barry turned to me and Gary. "What I don't get," he growled, "is how you knew Eddie Carson was hiding in that house, how you got him out of there without anyone knowing, why you didn't bother sharing that with anyone, and why you misled everyone into thinking there were ghosts in that farmhouse." He seemed to recover himself after his mini-tirade and offered a half-smile to Ms. Pelson that didn't quite make it to his eyes. Everyone could see he was furious because someone else had stolen the limelight and usurped his role as lead Ghost Stalker.

I glared right back at him. "I was the only one who knew Eddie was there, so back off, Barry."

Gary turned to Clara and explained in a much kinder tone, "There was a real ghost in the house. Is a ghost in your house." Ignoring Barry, Gary craned his neck around Ms. Pelson to speak to Scott. "Didn't your EVP equipment pick up anything?"

Barry muttered something under his breath as he pulled up camera footage of what appeared to be a white puff of something floating down the stairs. He turned the laptop around so everyone could see.

Oh wow! The ghost had actually been photographed. "Cool!" I said.

"The lady in white that people have seen for decades is still there," Gary told Clara. "She's a sweet old lady, spinster former school teacher, and not interested in crossing over, not as long as there are children who need looking after. She was keeping an eye on Eddie."

Clara smiled and clapped her hands together in excitement. "So the farmhouse really is haunted?"

Huh?

Gary seemed as surprised at Clara's enthusiasm as I was, but he nodded. "And she's harmless. My brother caused all the noises and the vandalism."

"Wonderful!" Clara exclaimed. "Now when I get my farmhouse restored I can advertise that my newly established B&B is officially haunted. It'll be great publicity."

The six of us exchanged amused glances. "It will be very successful," I predicted, "and the resident ghost will make frequent appearances."

The meeting adjourned and Barry, still grumbling about having his thunder stolen, stormed out, his laptop under his arm.

Scott helped Clara out of her chair and then shook hands with Gary. "I hear congratulations are in order."

Gary's jaw tensed. I wouldn't blame him if he didn't want to get into the details about his family stuff. "For…?"

"Didn't you get the lead in Macbeth?"

His jaw relaxed. "Yes. I hope you'll come to a performance in January."

"Wouldn't miss it," Scott said. He offered his arm to Ms. Pelson and waved goodbye.

Gary, Annabeth, Sean, and I all walked out together, just as the custodian came in to sweep the room. We stopped in the hallway.

"How's Eddie?" Annabeth asked Gary.

"Okay, I guess. He's still sad about his mom."

I shook my head. "She was driving a 2001 Saturn with over two hundred thousand miles on it, so it's possible her brakes failed on their own because the car was so old. Still sad, though."

Gary raised an eyebrow. "How did you…? Oh."

"Right," I said.

"Say, anybody want to go get a coffee?" Gary glanced at the three of us, but then settled his gaze on me. "Or tea?"

Annabeth hooked her arm through Sean's and let a mischievous smile creep onto her face. "Sean and I have to go..." She mumbled some ending to that sentence, but I knew she was just making an excuse so Gary and I could be together.

"Caryn?" Gary asked.

I caught Annabeth's eye and her expression said, "Go for it." "Sure," I told him.

Gary took my hand, causing a tingle I hadn't felt since Quince, and led me down the stairs to the lobby.

"All's well that ends well," I heard Uncle Omar say in my right ear.

"Quoting Shakespeare now?" I asked him. Unfortunately I said that out loud and my date, uh, Gary looked at me funny.

"I didn't say anything." Gary squeezed my hand before releasing it.

I smiled and pointed toward my right ear. "Uncle Omar. He always has to have the last word."

We got to the bookstore just as it was closing, so Gary ordered a to-go coffee for himself and hot mint tea for me. We took our drinks and went outside, because it was a beautiful late fall evening with a full moon. The night air was crisp and there was no wind to chill us. Since we were both dressed warmly and were sipping hot beverages, it was a pleasant stroll across the deserted campus.

"What are you doing for Christmas?" Gary asked me.

I laughed and almost choked on my tea. "Uh, we just had Thanksgiving, and we've still got final exams to get through."

Gary put an arm around my shoulder, a gesture I never would have allowed a few weeks ago. Now it felt natural. "I know. Just asking."

"I'm going to Houston. Mom and George are going on a belated honeymoon to Hawaii, and attending the wedding of George's son while they're there. So I'm hopping a plane Christmas Eve morning to spend the holiday with my dad. Dads." I cast a sideways glance at Gary to see how he took that. He didn't flinch. Awesome! "Dad said he got the three of us tickets to The Nutcracker downtown that night."

Gary nodded and we walked along in silence. Not an uncomfortable silence, just a peaceful, companionable quiet.

"I'd ask you what you're doing, but I already know," I said.

Now that got a reaction. Gary tossed his empty cup into a nearby bin and turned to face me. "Even I don't know what's planned for Christmas."

"Want me to tell you, or do you want to wait?"

Gary wrapped his arms around me and pulled me in close. He was obviously thinking about it. Finally he asked, "Is it good or bad?"

"Good."

He gave me a hug. "Okay, just the highlights."

My ability to see other people's futures is truly a gift, but sometimes I think it would be better if I just let them find out the old-fashioned way—by living life. Sort of the way I have to find out stuff about my own life. Still, I could see the whole scenario playing out super-fast in my head, and it took all my willpower not to blurt it out, blow by blow. For the record, here's how it's going to go:

Ned's going over to Brenda's house Christmas Eve, supposedly to help hang stockings. He reaches into his pocket but genius Eddie figures out his true intentions and calls him on it.

Ned's going to say something like, "Yeah, okay, you got me. I was going to slip something into Brenda's stocking when she wasn't looking." Since Eddie's already figured it out and Gary's dying of curiosity, Ned will pull a jewelry store box out of his pocket, get down on one knee and pop the question.

Brenda won't answer right away, mostly because she's overcome with emotions. Good ones. "Yes, I'll marry you," she will finally choke out at barely a whisper.

Ned will place a huge solitaire emerald-cut diamond on her left hand. Then he'll pull her with him under the plastic mistletoe hanging in the doorway and kiss her.

Eddie will say something like, "Ewww, gross!" but Gary won't say anything. He'll be taking the whole thing in. Pretty soon he'll wonder aloud what both sets of grandparents will have to say about Edward Harrington Jr. marrying the daughter of blue-collar workers. Neither Brenda nor Ned have an answer for that, but I'm hoping that both the Harringtons and the Riddells will be happy for them, once they get over the shock. I know Olivia will be thrilled from the Other Side.

And best of all, Ned and Brenda will get married on Valentine's Day. Kind of a cliché, but also kind of romantic. I hope I get to go, because the glow I'm seeing on her face in my head can't be half as great as the real thing.

I pulled back a little so I could look Gary in the face. "So the Reader's Digest version is that Ned's got a very expensive Christmas present for your mom. She's gonna love it."

I think maybe Gary knew what I meant, but our thoughts weren't on parents at that moment. We were both way too distracted by that romantic full moon overhead and the fact that we were there together. I mean really together. Gary pulled me in and lifted my chin. Starting out slow and soft, he built up to a long, passionate kiss.

I sighed and kissed him back. Quince who?

A word from the author...

I am a former high school English teacher and author of *CONFESSIONS OF A TEENAGE PSYCHIC* (The Wild Rose Press Inc., 2010), which was a 2011 Epic Ebook Contest finalist. My YA novel *GENIUS SUMMER* was released in November, 2014 and was awarded The Literary Seal of Approval in 2015. Contemporary romance *CERTAINLY SENSIBLE* was released by The Wild Rose Press Inc. in December, 2015, and received The Literary Classics Seal of Approval in 2016. And CERTAINLY SENSIBLE was a 2016 Literary Classics Gold Medal winner.

Thank you for purchasing
this publication of The Wild Rose Press, Inc.

If you enjoyed the story, we would appreciate your
letting others know by leaving a review.

For other wonderful stories,
please visit our on-line bookstore at
www.thewildrosepress.com.

For questions or more information
contact us at
info@thewildrosepress.com.

The Wild Rose Press, Inc.
www.thewildrosepress.com

Stay current with The Wild Rose Press, Inc.

Like us on Facebook

https://www.facebook.com/TheWildRosePress

And Follow us on Twitter
https://twitter.com/WildRosePress